I0618066

JONATHAN CHATEAU

Faith Against the Angels

Book Two of The Travis Rail Series

HALF WING PRESS

First published by Half Wing Press 2020

Copyright © 2020 by Jonathan Chateau

All rights reserved. No part of this publication may be reproduced, stored or transmitted in any form or by any means, electronic, mechanical, photocopying, recording, scanning, or otherwise without written permission from the publisher. It is illegal to copy this book, post it to a website, or distribute it by any other means without permission.

This novel is entirely a work of fiction. The names, characters and incidents portrayed in it are the work of the author's imagination. Any resemblance to actual persons, living or dead, events or localities is entirely coincidental.

Jonathan Chateau asserts the moral right to be identified as the author of this work.

Jonathan Chateau has no responsibility for the persistence or accuracy of URLs for external or third-party Internet Websites referred to in this publication and does not guarantee that any content on such Websites is, or will remain, accurate or appropriate.

Designations used by companies to distinguish their products are often claimed as trademarks. All brand names and product names used in this book and on its cover are trade names, service marks, trademarks and registered trademarks of their respective owners. The publishers and the book are not associated with any product or vendor mentioned in this book. None of the companies referenced within the book have endorsed the book.

Black cross graphic by Ramchand

Angel graphic by Mourad Mokrane

Author Photography by David Lally

For more about the author, visit www.JChateau.com

First edition

ISBN: 978-0-9988504-7-4

Cover art by Jonathan Chateau
Cover art by TS95 Studios
Editing by Serena Fisher
Editing by Diann Merit

This book was professionally typeset on Reedsy.
Find out more at reedsy.com

To Mom, for all of your support.
To my wonderful sister, Jessica, for her input and contributions.
To Grant and Serena, for being unfailing in helping me shape this into the best book possible.

"You only live once, but if you do it right, once is enough."

– Mae West

"The wicked plots against the just, and gnashes at him with his teeth."

– Psalm 37:12

"No matter how ugly the world gets or how stupid it shows me it is, I always have faith."

– Gerard Way

Contents

Chapter 1 – Phosphate and Angels

They never saw him coming.

Instead of being huddled around a table, playing cards, smoking cigarettes and pounding cheap beer, this particular handful of Rift agents should've been more alert.

In their minds, they had no reason to worry.

No one had ever dared raid the Rift in their own territory. The last people who even came close to stealing from the Rift were Rift agents themselves, Lomak and his defectors. But they were all wiped out in a deal gone bad six months ago.

Given the remote nature of their hideout, it was all too easy to get lost in self-entertainment and shooting the shit. Only the Rift knew about this place: a rotting warehouse with a cracked exterior, hidden away within the campus of a vacant phosphate processing facility. It was one of many plants located within what is collectively known as Bone Valley, an area stretching across several Central Florida counties responsible for the production of fertilizer.

Florida is known for oranges and phosphate.

But these Rift agents were not here for mining or OJ production.

They were here to keep a fallen angel imprisoned until further notice from their boss, Marcus Gladius. They were to keep watch, holding the seraph for an indefinite period until Marcus sent word that it was time to move.

The Rift were always on the move, and that's how they kept a low profile.

At least that's how Marcus liked to run things. He didn't revel in spending lavish amounts of money on an expensive office space in Downtown Miami like Vanessa had. He kept things frugal where necessary, off the radar and without drawing much attention. In his eyes, the centuries had worn on the Raven sisters. Vanessa and Viola had grown overconfident and impatient in their decision-making.

Changes had to be made.

Tough choices.

Marcus made those choices.

Vanessa was dead—no longer around to flaunt her chaotic will. A similar, less final fate fell upon Viola—a decision made by both Marcus and the Council. The sister CEOs of this organization had now been stripped of their power. One at the hands of Travis Rail, and the other Marcus's.

In the six months since the sisters' fall from power, Marcus swayed the other Council members towards a more tempered and focused approach.

The angels he caught were going to play a big part in his plan.

They already were.

Particularly this male angel, who was the strongest of those Marcus had captured. Sure, the seraph was securely chained against a wall, but these restraints were only a back-up measure. What really kept the colossal seraph entranced and in a perpetually weakened state was put in place by black sorcery wielded by the witches and warlocks of the Rift Council—now being maintained by a thin-framed balding witch.

Perching atop a large stack of crates, the balding witch sits in an almost feline posture. One arm is wrapped around her knees. The other arm extended. Fingers splayed. Each digit aglow with unnatural blue light. With skin as pale as a sun-bleached seashell, the blue light of her enchanted fingers ripples across her face, highlighting it unnaturally.

The angel's head hangs low, his body occasionally writhing under the twisting swirls of charmed light that twirl out from the witch's hand. He's a beast, built like he was made to wrestle bears. His physique flawless. Not an ounce of fat, not a blemish, a freckle or scar, save for the massive red handprint covering almost his entire face as if someone had held it like a basketball.

"Hey! Baldy!" one of the agents shouts to the witch, making her jump and nearly break her concentration.

"What?" she answers with a hiss, attention and magic still focused on her prisoner.

"You ever wonder what it'd be like . . . to *fuck* an angel?"

"No," she snaps as she suppresses any urge to glance back at the imbecile egging her on.

"Yeah, right. Even you freaks must get horny," the jerk says as the other agents laugh between swigs of beer. "You can't tell me you're not even the least bit curious."

She bites her tongue, eyes focused on the writhing angel.

The jerk goes on, "I mean, I heard they can do humans. That said, don't you want to know what it's like to get fucked by one?"

Though she's mentally at her tipping point, she doesn't respond. She was stuck here with these low-level pieces of shit that she had to share the shift with. Had she not already been tasked with keeping this winged behemoth in the Rift Council's trance, she would have opened a gate to the dark place and sent these losers there.

"Look, I only ask," the jerk chuckles to himself, almost unable to contain his laughter, "because if you're ever curious . . ." he spreads his arms open. "I'm right here."

All the agents break out in laughter, exchange high-fives, and toast one another.

She holds back, not wanting to upset Marcus. He was good to her. Promised to promote her soon. To allow her to learn more magic from some of the most supreme witches in the Rift. Witches who studied under Vanessa and Viola.

"What?" the jerk asks. "You're not interested?"

I'm interested in doing a lot worse to you, she thinks. *While I can't send you to the dark place, per se, I can . . .*

"What's your name?" she asks the jerk. She hadn't bothered to get to know the names of these grunts because they don't matter. They are hired help. The dregs of the Rift.

"My name?" he asks, raising an eyebrow in surprise. "I'm Tony."

3

"Well Tony, I'm Shiya." Without taking her focus off the angel once, she goes on, "As you can see, I'm a little busy keeping the big guy here under wraps. However, I do have a free hand," she says with a wicked smile, "And I *would* like to know what it feels like to have an angel . . . in that hand."

"In your hand?"

"Yep." Shiya giggles with a hint of promise in her tone. "You know what I'm talking about." Shiya keeps one hand aimed at the unconscious angel. With her other, she beckons him to come over. "Come here. Let me see how you feel in my hand. That will give me an idea of how you will feel inside me."

The other guards take interest now, lowering their cards, chuckling amongst themselves. They urge him to get off his ass and go to her. Which he does, with glee, bounding towards her like he's God's gift to women. "On the way, *She-Ra*."

"Shiya!"

"She-Ra, Shi-ya. Whatever," the jerk says with a scoff.

Attention still locked on the angel, she tells him, "Spread your legs."

Tony flinches, then looks back at the group, who wave him on.

Sensing his hesitation, Shiya asks, "You need their permission or something?"

Tony shakes off her comment with a shrug. Says "Shit," but it sounds more like "sheeeeeet." He puffs out his chest. "Not hardly."

"Then come closer and spread your legs."

It's all fun and games screwing with these shit-bags, she thinks, *but don't lose focus on this angel. He comes to and we're all dust.*

Tony takes a step. "What are you planning on doing down—"

Shiya slides her hand down across the front of his pants. Does so with a firm but assertive manner. Tony is taken aback. Then surprise turns to excitement.

"I like the way you feel," Shiya says.

"Do you now?" he asks with a heavy breath.

"Yes. You feel . . . heavenly."

"Heavenly, huh? Well come to think of it," Tony quips as he casts a glance

4

towards the captive angel, "who needs an angel, when you got a devil like me?"

"You're right." As she runs her hand up and down his groin, her palm glows, a blue fog emanating from it.

The glib smile melts from Tony's face as uneasiness creeps up his body.

"You know," Shiya continues, "it'd be a shame if you were to go and lose your balls."

Tony jerks back.

Shiya breaks out in laughter.

"The fuck?" Tony pats himself down while the men at the table crack up. "What did you do?" He pulls at his pants to find that he's completely bare of any semblance of genitalia. The pitch of his voice raises an octave. "What the fuck did you do!"

"Somewhere in hell," Shiya answers, "a dick is floating around without its master."

"You crazy bitch! I'm gonna send you to hell!" Tony jerks out his pistol—

The room thunders as the side door flies inward off its hinges. The sound is deafening.

Tony whirls around towards the commotion and is greeted by a red light that dances on his chest. *Pop-pop-pop.* He jiggles with each round and then explodes into dust.

The Rift agents jump out of their seats and flip up the table, turning it into a makeshift barrier.

The blue light connecting Shiya's spell to the angel flickers and fades. She breaks away and cowers behind a stack of small wooden crates. One of them lies on its side, slightly open. She slips inside and watches. A sliver of light cuts vertically down her face as she presses her eyeballs against the crack.

"What the fuck was that?" one of the agents shouts as he and the others ready their weapons. Then he calls out, "Yo! Who's there?"

No response.

Silence is followed by a hail of ordnance. Bullets ring out as they strike metal, splinter wood, and chip concrete. One of the agents is hit. He turns to dust.

The remaining men exchange confused looks.

Who the hell is shooting at them?

The agents check on the angel, whose head hangs low, still weakened by whatever noxious magic Shiya had bewitched him with. Then the thugs look to each other. One of them signals the group that they should split up in three . . .

Two.

One.

They file out from behind the table and make for opposite sides of the room. Guns whipping about, scanning for movement. Weapons fused to their bodies. Not taking any chances with whoever this is that got the jump on them. Unfortunately, they're only met with an unnerving quiet and the acrid smell of gun smoke and singed flesh.

One of the thugs hugs the west wall like a roach, shoulder pressed close to the siding, his trigger finger ready to lay waste. His heart drums against his chest. Palms sweating. He tries to steady his breath as he creeps closer to the entrance—closer to where their assailant entered—but there is no trace of him. Or her.

"I don't know who you are," one of the agents shouts as he makes his way through the building, "but you're going to regret the day you ever set foot in here." He cranes his neck towards the catwalk above, scanning the rusting walkways for the interloper.

But he sees no sign of anyone up there.

"No one fucks with the Rift and lives to tell about it," the agent yells. "Do you hear me?"

Something rattles behind him, the tinny sound of metal clacking against the concrete floor. The agent spins on his heels and succumbing to the panic, loses any sense of trigger control. Opens fire, spraying wildly. An empty soup can bounces about as the bullets shred it to pieces.

The thug takes a few hesitant steps forward to investigate, eyes surveying the distant wall. A slight sound catches his attention, causing him to turn in time to catch sight of the butt of a rifle just before it connects with the side of his head.

A hooded figure looms over him. There's a bizarre twinkle in his left eye.

"Who are you?" the agent pleads, his voice cracking a little.

The man doesn't respond. Brings up his gun and turns the thug to dust. The shot rings throughout the expanse of the room.

Shiya flinches from inside the crate. Her teeth chatter. She hugs herself, shrinking into a ball, making herself as small a target as she can.

Several screams echo through the room. Shiya listens to the pleas as more of the pigs she reviled mere minutes ago are reduced to ash. She feels the electric tremble of fear ripple through her body, transferring to her hands, and she tucks them under her armpits, not wanting to acknowledge how frightened she is. Without a proper weapon, or even the training to use one, she couldn't be more vulnerable. Sure, she could use some dark magic against the shooter, but such spells required concentration and training, skills she is still mastering as a mid-level witch.

Holding a weakened angel hostage in a semi-permanent stupor was one thing.

Taking on an armed attacker while dealing with a massive panic attack was another.

The final agent slinks along the back wall now, almost tiptoeing towards the source of that last gunshot.

"Ronnie?" the agent calls out in a whisper. "Ronnie?"

As he makes his way to the western wall, he finds a pistol, a radio and a pile of black dust spread across the floor of the warehouse.

"Oh shit, Ronnie." The agent fumbles for his cell phone. He needs to call for backup, something he should have done moments ago, but in the panic and chaos, failed to think of. He starts to press the contact—

A two-by-four connects with the agent's wrist.

His phone goes airborne.

The next strike hits him in the face, sending him bouncing against the wall and dropping to the floor. His gun is yanked free from his shoulder and the end of the two-by-four presses against his windpipe. He struggles to breathe. The veins along his neck and head swell. Breathing becomes impossible. He's staring right at the gunman but can't make out his face. His features are obscured by his hooded sweatshirt. Only the peculiar twinkle in the man's eye is visible.

"Tell the witch to come out," the man commands.

The agent can barely breathe, let alone talk.

The gunman steps back, releasing the wooden stud from the thug's neck and allowing a surge of welcome oxygen to fill his lungs.

"I said to tell the witch to come out!" The gunman tosses the two-by-four aside and brings up his carbine.

The agent fumbles to get her name out, "Sh-Sh-Shiya. Hey, Shiya, come out here . . . please." No response. "Shiya! I kind of need you out here right now!"

Still nothing.

The muzzle of the carbine explodes. The agent screams as the side of his leg bursts open, bloodying his pants. Hands futilely clutch the bullet hole that steadily seeps blood. "Shiya!" His tone is desperately haggard as he pleads, "Jesus, Shiya, please get out here!"

There's a shuffling sound, followed by a very timid Shiya making her way out into the open.

The gunman notices her now, his face still obscured by his hoodie.

"Ok, bud," the agent says. "There she is! Now please just let me go—"

Several bursts from the carbine and the thug slumps to the ground, then turns to dust.

Shiya jumps; a yelp escapes her.

"Done." The gunman trains his carbine on her now. Between the beams of sunlight that leak in from the bullet holes and the gaping maw from where the side door once stood, Shiya looks like something dug fresh from the Earth. In this new light, her pasty skin appears almost translucent. The webbing of her blue and pale pink veins is now disturbingly visible.

The gunman gestures towards the angel, who is still very much in a daze, oblivious to the tumult that erupted around him.

"Wake him up," the gunman instructs Shiya.

She freezes.

"I won't ask again."

"Are you . . ." Shiya swallows. A lump of dread sticks in her throat. "Are you going to kill me?"

The gunman says nothing.

"Well . . . are you?"

"Yes."

Shiya feels her body go cold.

This is not what I signed up for! she thinks, as her palms and forehead leak sweat. *I was promised freedom. Purpose. A change from my bullshit childhood. A future that would put my "gifts" to use. Not this. Not an execution by a complete stranger who came out of nowhere.*

"Please," she begs. "I'll do what you want. Just let me go. Please. I haven't seen your face."

The gunman says nothing for a beat, then assures her, "Ok. I'll let you go."

But these words ring hollow for Shiya. There's an unease in his tone that makes her skin itch.

"Now . . ." He shakes the gun as if to suggest for her to *get to it. "Wake him up."*

Shiya approaches the angel, brings her hands up, fingers splayed open, lighting up with that blue flame emanating from each digit.

He's going to kill you.

The hibernation spell breaks. The angel slowly brings his head up, eyelids fluttering. The hazy light pouring in from outside reflects off the gemlike onyx of his eyes. They are void of color and beauty. Just pools of black.

"Unlock him," the gunman says.

"So, are you . . . with the Rift?"

"No."

He's going to kill you, Shiya. "Then who are you working for?"

"Not the Rift."

Shiya searches the gunman's expression but can't see his face beyond the shroud of his clothing. The only visible thing on his face is the twinkling of his left eye. Like a distant star. It's so odd.

"I said unlock him!"

Shiya jumps again. She pulls out a key, hands shaking as though caffeine were running through her veins. It takes a few uncoordinated moments to work the series of locks free, but once she does, the angel shakes off the chains as if they were nothing more than a nuisance.

"Ok. I did what you asked." Shiya turns back to the gunman. Her heart goes berserk, bouncing erratically inside her chest as if it were trying to find a way out of her body. "Can I go?"

"Yes." The word escapes the man's lips, but his body doesn't move. The carbine is still pointed in her direction.

"Look. I won't say anything to the Rift," Shiya says putting up two hands as she backs away.

"I know."

It's now or never, Shiya. Marcus isn't here to rescue you. His promises don't mean shit now.

Shiya looks to the angel, who is completely free of his restraints. He glares at her silently.

Then, she makes her move.

Her hands burst into blue flames.

She opens a portal to the dark place in hopes of sending the gunman into it, but the gunman is a split second quicker than she and squeezes off several rounds, sending her stumbling backwards. Before she turns into black dust like the others, her last image is of an angel zooming towards her and knocking her into the dark place.

The gunman lowers the carbine and then turns to the angel. "Hi, Balco."

A beat. Then the angel asks, "You know my name?"

"Of course, I do."

"And who are you?"

"My name is Simon Lajudas," he tells him. "And you're going to help me get back my wife."

The portal promptly shuts.

Chapter 2 – The Date

Travis launches out of bed, awakened by the relentless ringing of his cell phone. Panting and covered in sweat, he tears the sheets off his body and snatches the phone.

It's Duncan.

Or at least the man *claiming* to be Duncan.

"Travis?" Duncan's voice sounds distant.

"Yeah . . ."

"It's Duncan."

"Ok."

"Is now still a good time?"

"Um, well . . ." Travis wipes the sweat off his face using the sheet. "That depends."

"On?"

"On if you're actually going to meet me or not."

"Where are you?"

"Where am I? I'm *here*."

"Where's here?"

"Chattanooga!" Travis snaps as he bundles up the sheet and chucks it across the room. "You told me to meet you here six months ago!"

Silence from Duncan's end.

"Six months!" Travis jumps to his feet and peeks out the window. "You made it sound like you were on the way."

"I *am* on the way."

"Are you walking here?"

"No, Travis." Duncan sighs. "I have had to deal with other matters for the Covenant."

"I mean, did your phone break in the process?"

"I told you, I have been busy attending to other—"

"Just shut up!" Travis presses a hand to his head, suppressing the sensation that it may explode at any moment due to Duncan's detached tone. "I don't care what you've been doing. I don't care if you were rebuilding the ark or solving world hunger. You're six months late, dude. You're lucky I waited for you."

"As opposed to retiring and ghosting on us? Yes, I am *lucky* and *so* grateful you waited."

"Don't fucking turn this on me—"

"Please don't curse at—"

"Retirement implies relaxation." Travis goes on, talking right over him. "And I'm far from relaxed!"

You don't know what I am running from, Travis thinks. *That mess in Miami. The wharf. The shootout. No telling if the Rift got there before the cops did, and what got 'cleaned up,' and what didn't. If the cops have leads, if they don't. Did Simon go back? Did he not?*

Travis didn't want to think about it.

Part of him just wanted to hide from the world. Hide from the Rift, the Covenant, the cops.

Everyone.

But part of him wanted to see things through. Put an end to the Rift. They operated beneath the surface like an infection. A viral outbreak on society without a cure.

Maybe I'm the cure.

"Look, I'm sorry to have made you wait," Duncan says. "Trust me; it was not under my control."

"You suck at communication."

Duncan lets out a frustrated sigh as if trying to compose his next words carefully, not sure of the right thing to say. "Unfortunately, I have had to tread lightly these days. Your phone may be bugged. Your room. You might not even be Travis for all I know."

"And you might not be Duncan."

Indeed, this still could be a trap. Perhaps the Rift kept him waiting so they could assemble and ambush him. On the other hand, Travis wonders if maybe he could use this to his advantage, proactively going after the Rift instead of waiting for them to pursue him. Perhaps he could get to Viola and shut her down too, just like he did her sister.

I'd love to eradicate these assholes for good.

But then again, maybe this is Duncan? To Travis, it sure does sound like him.

Or maybe the Rift are just that good?

They do deal in witchcraft after all.

Duncan's tardiness gives Travis an unsettled feeling. Perhaps he is overreacting, but still, the last time Duncan ran late, his gut was sliced open and his innards were spilling out.

"Again, I apologize for the considerable wait." Duncan clears his throat. Then offers, "Pastor Graham is very ill. Much of the delay can be attributed to the time I've spent attending to him when I can."

Travis says nothing. His anger and frustration override any inkling of compassion.

"Anyway, I should be in Chattanooga tomorrow morning," Duncan says.

"Where are you coming from?"

"I'd rather not say. The less you know, the better."

"Remind me how it worked out the last time you left me in the dark." Travis slides open the shades, allowing the warmth of the sun to fill the musky hotel room.

"Yes, I know, and I'm sorry again about that."

Time for a little test. "Do you remember what you said to me after the Rift got the jump on me?"

There's a pause. Duncan sighs.

Does he remember, Travis wonders.

"Yes," Duncan replies. "I told you to trust me and that I would explain everything later."

13

"Later is now." Travis informs him. "There's a Dunkin' Donuts just off I-75. Meet me at 8 a.m. sharp. Don't be late. No excuses." Travis hangs up. Pauses. His mind reeling. The call could've been tracing him, sending the Rift right to him.

Time to pick a new hotel.

He dresses quickly, picks up his Beretta, checks that it's loaded, and slides it into its chest holster. He throws on a leather jacket and catches his reflection in the mirror.

Specifically, he notes the corner of a tattoo peeking out from just beyond the cuff of his jacket.

Since I've got time to kill, maybe it's time to update my resume.

Chapter 3 – New Ink

The gypsy life is something that Travis is used to. Moving around. Different hotels, different beds, different states. His passport has almost as many stamps as he has tattoos.

But Tennessee can still be home, he thinks. *Someplace in the mountains. Peace, tranquility and just being left alone. Now that is my idea of Heaven.*

For now, he pulls up at his next temporary refuge: an armpit of a motel near the interstate. It's also within eyeshot of the Dunkin' Donuts where he'll be meeting Duncan in the morning. The proximity to the meeting spot could be risky, given that the Rift could be staying here too, but due to anger or impatience – or both – it's a chance Travis is willing to take.

Inside the motel office, Travis is greeted by a shaggy-faced employee who looks like he's had too many losing fights with alcohol. He reeks of sour beer and bad choices. A limp toothpick hangs out of one corner of his mouth. His tired appearance reflects the overall ambiance of the rundown hotel itself. Travis can afford a nicer place, but he's going to sleep like shit no matter where he stays if he's got Duncan, or Duncan's imposter, on his mind all night.

Perhaps sleep isn't the best thing for him right now, especially given that Travis's dreams as of late have been too realistic for him to really feel rested the next day. This was as good a time as any to get some errands done: restock from the local gun store, grab food, and get some new ink.

Travis settles up with the attendant and asks the guy where the nearest tattoo shop is.

"Dark Ink Tattoos," he answers with a distinct twang in his voice. "'Bout five miles north on Hickory Valley Road." The attendant pulls back the sleeve on his right arm, exposing a tattoo of two busty mermaids, multicolored, with extravagant detail. "Ask for Fazio. He does amazing work. His shit don't fade."

Travis nods. "Fazio, huh?"

The attendant shrugs absently, hands Travis his room keycard. "Yeah, he's from Italy or Morocco or somethin'."

Italy or Morocco? Travis had visited both and never came across a name like that. This guy was probably guessing. Then again, to Travis, the attendant didn't appear to be the most worldly. Probably didn't leave this motel unless he needed to get more alcohol.

Travis thanks the man and is off. He catches lunch, namely the face-melting burrito. It delivers. Then he restocks at the local gun store and talks all things ordnance and self-defense. He ends up losing track of time, deep in conversation with people who are not out to give him supernatural guidance or kill him.

Dark Ink closes at seven.

It was a quarter till.

He wants to get that tattoo done while he still can. The gun store owner assures him he'll make it there in no time. It's not like he is driving through Miami. It is Chattanooga, a far cry from the hectic pace of South Florida.

It takes all of fifteen minutes of driving through lush green hills and quiet country roads to reach Dark Ink. It's a small shop at the back end of a parking lot riddled with potholes and loose pebbles that crunch under his tires. The building is shrouded by thick trees and is barely illuminated by the milky haze of a streetlight.

The shop didn't appear busy. Almost unoccupied. A lone red Jeep is parked close to the building.

Travis enters the shop and is greeted by the sight of a rail-thin man with elaborate ink trailing up his neck. His hair is black as tar, cut short. A thin mustache outlines his upper lip. In his ears hang two six-gauge skull plugs. My Chemical Romance blares their emo hit "I'm Not Okay" in the background as he hunches over, elbows propped on the counter. He stares intently at his laptop while bobbing his head to music, in sync with the manic riffs of the band's guitarist, Ray Toro.

Along with the blasting rock music, the ecstatic moans of a woman echo from the laptop's speakers.

"Hi," Travis says.

The man sees him, goes white as the woman's groans pierce the room. "Hi . . ." He quickly shuts the laptop, slides it under the counter, and mutes the music with a small remote. "I didn't even hear the door chime."

"Neither did I between the music and the moans."

The man gulps. "Sorry, but I'm about to close for the night."

"I know," Travis smirks. "Fazio, right?"

The man raises an eyebrow. Cautiously, "Yeah . . .?"

"You came highly recommended. Older guy . . . had a tattoo of two mermaids. Said you'd be the man to see about getting some new ink done. He works at the motel next to Dunkin' Donuts."

Fazio relaxes, his shoulders sinking downward. "Oh . . ." He laughs to himself. "Liam?"

"Sure?" Travis shrugs. "Didn't get his name, but I got yours."

"Cool. Could you come back tomorrow?"

"Probably not," Travis says. "I'm willing to pay the after-hours rate."

"The after-hours rate?"

Travis plops down a wad of cash.

"Wow." Fazio asks with a scoff, "Were you planning on going to the strip club?"

"If you don't take my money, then I guess they will."

"Well . . ." Fazio drums his fingers on the glass counter. Then checks his watch and sighs. "What were you looking to get done?"

Travis introduces himself. Then goes on to describe the spectacles, the Eyes of God. But only in enough detail so that Fazio has an idea of what Travis is wanting.

"If you don't mind," Travis suggests, "maybe we could pull up a few pics on that laptop of yours and I could show you exactly what I'd like."

Fazio shoots him a look. Brings the laptop back out.

"Don't worry," Travis reassures him. "I won't tell anyone that you watch porn."

"It was a movie."

"Aren't they all?" Travis smiles flatly. "Look. I don't care if you were watching a musical about feral unicorns, as long as you do good work."

Fazio cocks his head to the side. "Trust me. I know what I'm doing."

"Perfect."

Fazio instructs him to grab a seat and get comfortable in the chair, a chair that could easily double as a massage chair. It has a head rest that stares down at the floor. Travis removes his jacket and shirt and leans forward, planting his face against the cushion.

While Fazio is setting up, Travis checks his cell phone. No further calls from Duncan.

Unfortunately, nothing from Amanda either.

Wonder if I'll ever hear from her?

Fazio preps and situates himself next to Travis.

"So, if you don't mind me asking, where are you from? I mean . . ." Travis turns in his seat, "Liam, right?"

"Yeah."

"He mentioned you're from Italy or Morocco."

"Argentina actually."

"How long have you been doing ink?" Travis asks, thinking that perhaps this is a question he should've asked before the tattoo started.

"If you ask my wife," Fazio replies, "too long. She told me I should sell the business and move back to Argentina. We have a lot of family there. She wants the quiet life."

"Chattanooga seems pretty quiet."

"Still not rural enough for her."

The needle hits Travis's skin. That first bite is always such a bitch.

"So why don't you do it?" Travis asks, ignoring the pain.

"Do what?"

"Sell the business and move."

"Because I love what I do."

"You mean watch porn and do ink?" Travis asks with a laugh. "Sorry . . . had to."

Fazio pauses for a second. Leans back in his chair. Resigns himself to a response of, "Yeah, exactly."

Both men share a laugh.

The jingle of the door chimes steals Fazio's attention. He curses under his breath for not locking the door. Three men enter, all dressed in the same manner: dark clothes, rich blue denims, and *sunglasses*. Two of them wear dark ball caps. One of them is completely bald, save for a few tiny gray hairs that trace where his hairline once was.

"Hey, guys," Fazio greets them tepidly with a tone polite but apprehensive enough for Travis to notice. "I've just started with this client, running a little behind obviously. But we actually just closed."

The bald man points at the plastic hours sign. "Said *OPEN* when we walked in."

"Yeah, uh, I forgot to flip it over."

"Hey, no problem," the bald man responds and points to one of his friends. "We'll get that for you." His friend flips the sign over and proceeds to lock the door.

"What are you doing?" Fazio asks.

Travis pushes up from his chair, looks over his shoulder at the men. They're dressed in dark attire and have the grimy swagger of the Rift. He glances at his jacket, where his holster rests. Too far to reach without being obvious. Assuming they're armed, they'll put a bullet in his back before he can get to his Beretta.

"So, whose lovely Plymouth Barracuda is that out there?" the bald man asks as the other two study the selection of flash artwork on the wall. One of them feigns interest, flipping through a catalog of tattoos.

Fazio looks to Travis, who answers, "Mine. There a problem?"

Travis starts to get up from his chair, but the bald man is lighting quick. Whips out a gun. Fazio's face cycles through several shades of white, and he instinctively puts his hands up.

"Yes. We *do* have a problem." The bald man shakes the gun in Travis's direction. "That car ain't yours."

Travis nods towards his pocket. "Got the keys right here—"

"Get your hands up! We're not here for the car," the bald man barks. "*That car led us to your dumb ass.*"

Damn, Travis thinks, *they tracked the car. I should've known better than to steal from a thief. I got to get my head straight. I've been too rattled to use my own common sense. Idiot!*

"Whoops!" The bald man chuckles as if reading Travis's thoughts. "Didn't think about that, huh?"

I did. I've just let my nerves and my brain get the best of me. "Ok, so, if you don't want the car," Travis asks, "what do you want? Me?"

"You?" The bald man laughs once more. "Hell no. We want the money."

"What money?"

"The money you stole from Lomak," the bald man explains.

Travis replays Miami in his mind.

The bullets.

Lomak.

Simon's face getting split nearly in half.

The men he killed, whether members of the Rift or part of Simon's gang.

The briefcase of money.

The bricks of cash he gave away—

"Don't act like you don't know what I'm talking about!"

"And how do you know I have it?" Travis asks. "How do you know that Simon didn't take it back? Were you there? I mean, all of Lomak's guys died."

"No," the bald man corrects him as he waves a finger. "Not all of them."

The other men halt their feigned perusal of the store.

"When we never heard from Lomak," the bald man continues, "we headed for the wharf. We got there a little too late. We *were* the backup."

"*You guys* were the backup?" Travis laughs.

The bald man rushes Travis, punches him in the face, knocking him off the chair. "You left quite the mess there, Travis!" He presses a revolver against Travis's head, spittle flying as he speaks, "And you oughta thank me for phoning the Rift and their cleanup crew, as I'm sure they got there before the cops did and made those bodies you left behind disappear!"

Through gritted teeth, Travis growls, "I didn't kill *all* of those men."

"I don't care. I ain't a cop. But maybe I should turn your ass in."

"Do it. I'll incriminate you, too."

"You can try, asshole. But me and my boys here will be on the beaches of Cozumel sipping on Coronas long before the police get wind of our whereabouts. Now, I don't care how much money you took, but we want it." He nods outside without looking back. "And we'll take the car, too."

Travis laughs to himself. "I gave it all away."

"You what?"

Travis repeats himself, his tone unwavering, "I donated it."

"You *donated* it?"

Travis nods.

"Hey, guys, uh, I hate to interrupt," Fazio interjects, "but I got a wife that's waiting for me—"

"Shut the fuck up!" the bald man yells. "No one's going anywhere—"

Travis drives his heel into the bald man's shin. He howls and buckles. The gun goes off, the bullet splinters the floor near Travis's head.

One of the other men leaps over the counter as Travis gets to his feet. He pulls out a gun, but Travis grabs a chair and charges into the guy. Using the chair as a battering ram, he pins the thug's spine painfully against the counter.

The third guy trains his gun on Travis.

Fazio yelps as he is maneuvered into a headlock by the bald guy, who presses his gun against the young man's temple.

Travis freezes.

"I will fucking blow this dude's brains out!" The bald man presses the gun so hard Fazio winces, practically closing his eyes. "You want that on your conscience? Or do you even care?"

Travis says nothing, not wanting to give the bald man an edge.

The second thug rubs his lower back, grimacing. He also trains his gun on Travis.

"Why am I wasting my time? You don't care about others. You're a lone wolf, right? Mr. Famous Transporter. Got the Rift all fucking scared of you." The bald man shakes a hand in the air, pretending to be scared as he says, "Oooohhhh. Look at me. Got me shivering too." He laughs it off. "Give me a fucking break. Here's a better idea." He shoves Fazio towards Travis, and asks the artist, "What's your name?"

Fazio stammers. Barely able to speak. "F-F-Fazio."

The man chuckles. "Ok, Fah-Fah-Fah-Fazio. Mr. Rail here came to see you for a tattoo, right?"

Fazio acknowledges this, as two large sweat stains appear under his armpits. His face is speckled with beads of perspiration.

"Perfect! Then let's give the man what he wants." The man points at the chair. To Travis, "Sit your happy ass right here. Lie on your stomach."

Reluctantly, Travis does as told, moving a little too slowly for the bald man's taste, so the second guy forces him into the chair, shoving his face down into the headrest.

The bald man points at Fazio with his gun. "Get your needle."

Fazio pauses. Not sure if what he heard—

"Get it!"

Fazio obliges, flips it on, and it buzzes to life.

The bald man nods to the second guy, who steadies Travis from behind. He pulls back on Travis's hair, and Travis lets out a grunt.

The third guy moves in front of Travis, keeping the gun pointed in his direction.

"Now, let's have some fun." The bald man points with his gun at Travis's eye. "So, Fah-Fah-Fazio . . . Have you ever . . . tattooed an eyeball?"

Fazio recoils, his face contorting. *Why didn't we leave for Argentina,* he thinks. *Maybe my wife is onto something? If I could get out of here, I'd give up the porn and the shop in a heartbeat. We're only in our twenties for Christ's sake—*

"Hey!" the bald man barks. "I asked you a question, Fozzy!"

"Fazio. And no, I haven't."

"Well it's time to level up," the bald man says as he shakes the gun at him.

"Now go on with it. Get to work. And don't worry if you fuck up. He's got two of them."

"Don't make him do this," Travis hisses through clenched teeth.

"Then give me the money," the bald man repeats, his breath reeking of whatever foulness he had for lunch.

"I already told you," Travis growls. "I gave it away."

"Bullshit." The bald man looks to Fazio, "His optical canvas is yours, Picasso. Get creative!"

Fazio remains frozen—

"Move it, asshole," the bald man demands, "or you're not clocking out tonight!"

Fazio makes a noise, an internal whimper of unwillingness, but he doesn't have a choice. He levels the needle with Travis's eyeball, which is now being held open by the third guy. Fazio feels his stomach churn at the thought of using his instruments of creativity to mar someone.

"Do it!" the bald man's shout make Fazio jump in his shoes. With a quaking hand he closes in.

Here we go, Fazio thinks. *I wish I had closed earlier.*

Travis's glossy brown eye shines under the fluorescent light. There is a fresh sheen of sweat all over his face.

"Last chance to keep your twenty-twenty vision, Travis," the bald man threatens. "Where is the money?"

Travis mentally prepares himself for the experience.

Is that funky angelic healing ability going to kick in? How about the slowing of time? Was all that just a load of crap that Zach fed me?

And where is Zach, anyway?

Perhaps Zach was as much a figment of his imagination as anything else. Maybe he actually died in his 2014 Mustang, on the side of the road in a ditch. Maybe the Rift got to him after all—

"Where. Is. The money?"

No, this was not the afterlife.

Travis felt it in his bones. He did not imagine Zach.

He is genuinely stuck in a bad situation and not sure how to get out of it.

23

He quickly reviews his life and realizes after all he's gone through, it's about to end with him tortured and killed in a tattoo shop by three ex-Rift stooges.

"Fuck it." The bald man shoves Fazio. "Get on with it!"

Fazio's hand trembles as he closes in on Travis's eye. This is going to suck for both of them.

Travis mumbles something.

"What?" the bald man asks.

Travis continues muttering.

"I can't hear you."

Travis's speech is inaudible.

"What are you saying?" the bald man asks. "What—What are you doing?"

Travis stops abruptly. "I'm praying."

"Praying?" The bald man laughs. "For what—"

The front door explodes, glass goes everywhere. Everyone looks up in time to catch a large man pushing his way through the falling doors. His face is obscured by a faded gray hoodie. He opens his arms as if to give everyone a hug and two gray wings sprout from his back, unfurling like feathered hands.

Oh, wow, Travis thinks as he lifts his head. *Is that . . .*

Zach?

Did Zach hear my prayer?

Is that how this whole half-wing thing works? Can I pray and speed-dial an angel?

No. That doesn't seem right.

And something in Travis's gut tells him, this is not Zach who just entered. It's someone else.

Chapter 4 – A Hooded Visitor

The hooded angel steps forward, arms collapsing to his sides. The soft light from the bulbs above spills across his face, but the shroud of his hood obscures everything except his mouth.

"Who the hell are you?" the bald man demands.

The angel remains motionless, limbs and wings rigid.

"Whatever!" The bald man fires, and the angel shifts his body to one side so fast, he almost appears transparent. The man takes a moment to wrap his brain around what he just saw. He then shoots again. Still the angel is unharmed, swaying left and right, his feet never once leaving the floor.

The other agents exchange bewildered looks, then unload their clips.

The room roars with gunfire, but the angel continues his glimmering dance, shifting side-to-side, untouched by a single bullet.

"Jesus Christ!" one of the men shouts. "Are you guys seeing this? He just—"

"Shut the fuck up and call Marcus!" the bald man yells without taking his eyes and gun off the angel, who marches slowly towards them. "We got a stray fairy!"

One of the men reaches for his cell phone, and that's when Travis leaps out of the chair, steals the needle from Fazio, and jams it into the thug's neck. He gurgles, clutching his throat, as Travis brings him to the ground.

Before Travis can move onto the next thug, something strikes him in the back of the head. He sees stars and drops to the ground, landing on his knees and his palms. Pain reverberates through his skull like a sound wave.

There's not even a moment of respite before Travis is kicked in the face and sent crashing onto his back. Spots swirl across his vision in a cloud of pain.

"Who are you calling a fairy?" the angel asks as he zooms towards them. With a flick of the waist, his wings whip out and smack the thugs in the face.

Their sunglasses split.

There is a shared moment of shock.

Then the angel stiffens his wings, and like two feathered spears, they pierce the men's chests. Angelic quills drenched in blood and flesh explode from their backs, followed by their bursting into black dust.

The bald man is next. His jaw drops. A baffled and frightening expression flickers on his face, wondering what to do next—

The angel is upon him, ensnaring him in a cocoon of dark feathers. There's a whimper and then the crisp pop of bones being snapped and crunched.

As if performing a macabre magic trick, the angel opens his wings to reveal that the bald man has been transformed into a charcoal cloud that dances through the air, then dissipates like a fine mist.

Travis looks to Fazio, who is curled up in the corner, shivering.

The angel whirls around. His massive wings fold neatly and disappear behind his back.

"Zach?" Travis asks, though his gut screams that this angel is not the deliverer of prayers.

The angel scoffs. Begins a slow and measured march towards them.

Fazio kicks out his legs, pushing himself closer to the wall, as deep into the corner as possible. "Please!" he cries. "Please don't hurt me! I have nothing to do with any of this. I don't even know what the fuck is going on!"

The angel stops short. Gazes down at the frightened young man. "Do you believe in Heaven?" the angel asks, his voice raspy, gritty, as if it hurts to talk.

Fazio freezes. His mouth is open, but his mind is unsure how to respond to this angel of death.

"Well? Do you?" the angel asks again.

Fazio hesitates, then warily offers, "I guess."

"You . . . *guess?*"

"I—I—I don't . . ." Fazio struggles. "I don't know."

The angel closes the gap between them, his footfalls on the tile reverberating like the steps of a giant.

Travis eyes his gun.

The angel's left wing shoots up, pins Travis against the wall. A jagged feather bores into Travis's shoulder, earning a pained grunt from him.

"Where are you from?" the angel inquires of Fazio.

Fazio opens and closes his mouth, a fish on dry land. Speechless. His gaze falls to the floor, fear overpowering abilities like talking, breathing, concentrating.

The angel repeats himself; however this time, his tone is terse, more direct: "*Where. Are. You. From?*"

Words falter. Then Fazio whispers, "Argentina."

"You miss it?"

Thankfully a question Fazio can answer without requiring speech. He nods.

"Is that *your* Heaven?"

Fazio processes this, then nods again, this time more fervently.

"Then you should go back," the angel says. "I'd go home if I could."

Cautiously, "Is Heaven your home?"

The angel abruptly rises, retracts his wings. He clenches his fists, lips twisting into a snarl as he answers, "I don't know."

He releases Travis, who slides down from the wall and lands hard on his tailbone. He grimaces and places a hand on his bleeding shoulder.

With a dismissive wave of the hand, the angel growls, "Go! Go to your Heaven. Never tell anyone about this." The angel leans forward, the light cutting across the bottom half of his face, accenting the hard lines of his chin. "Or I'll find you."

Fazio pushes off the floor, sliding his back up the wall. Eyes glued to the angel. He goes for his car keys and runs out the front door.

The angel doesn't watch him leave; instead he approaches Travis, who rests his head against the wall and cups his profusely bleeding shoulder.

"Am I next?" Travis asks.

The angel takes a step closer. He cocks his head to the side, sizing up Travis.

Then he kneels in front of him, grabs Travis by the jaw. "You know . . ." He glares at Travis as if looking into the eyes of a stray dog that wandered into the wrong household. "I just don't understand why God would choose someone so pathetic, reckless and stupid as you." The angel releases him and backs away. "You're nothing but an untrained mutt. And you're not ready."

"Ready?" Travis clutches his shoulder as a new surge of pain hits him. "Ready for what?"

The angel heads for the door.

"I asked you a question! Ready for what?"

"Maybe one day, you'll find out." The angel starts to leave.

"Hey!"

The angel freezes.

"What's the deal with you angels, anyway?" Travis gets to his feet, a painful maneuver, but he manages nonetheless. "You're walking conundrums. Nothing but riddles."

"The only riddle around here . . ." he glances over his shoulder. "Is *you*."

"Who are you?" Travis asks. "Clearly you're not Zach."

"No, I'm not." The angel steps out into the parking lot, wings emerging. He flies off into the night.

Travis pulls his hand away from the gash in his shoulder. It's covered in blood. He winces as he touches the wound but finds that it is already healing.

Thank God for this half-angel stuff. However it works.

Travis makes for the door. He's going to have to get out of this town very soon. He doesn't want to stick around *if* the cops show up. They'll be asking a lot of questions, none of which he feels like answering.

I'm sure the shootout at the wharf and the fight at Vanessa's office have given the cops enough to look into. I don't need to be tied to anything else.

He scans the store for cameras. Surprisingly he finds none.

Thank God.

He tries calling Duncan, but there's no answer. He assesses the chaotic state of the store. The place looks like it got hit with a bomb. He takes one of Fazio's business cards.

Mental note: Fund Fazio's trip out of the country.

Outside, Travis stares at the Barracuda. Cursed muscle car led those thugs here. Would there be more? Hard to say. Maybe he could try to find the tracking device? There's only so many places it could be.

But would that even be worth it?

If the Rift could track the car as well, then they probably already knew Travis was here. Although if he was talking to a Rift agent and not Duncan, Travis might have already drawn them right to him.

First, I'll deal with Duncan.

Then go car shopping.

Travis climbs into the car.

Tomorrow is a new day.

The muscle car purrs to life.

Tomorrow I'll find out if Duncan is really Duncan.

Chapter 5 – The Hangar

A lanky man in a gray jumpsuit fires up a cigarette. The night is humid, but the fresh air is preferable to the stuffiness of the hangar he's been tasked to guard. It also beats having to tolerate the sebaceous body odor of the angels. They tend to put off a certain distinct smell. To him, they stunk of birdseed and feathers.

Chained to the walls of the interior of the hangar are four angels: Ardiel, Dumahl, Edos and Zolash. Much like Balco, they are held in an enchanted trance by a witch, this one sporting a single lock of silver hair.

The lanky man brings the cigarette to his lips, puffs and stares up at a milky, white moon—

Something big sails past it.

The lanky man gawks at the moon with a little more intensity. *Damn if these Florida backwoods don't produce some funky critters*, he thinks. *No wonder they call this state the Australia of the US. Crazy ass birds and shit!*

Something passes in front of the glow of the moon again.

Ok.

Fuck this.

The lanky man takes one last powerful drag of the cigarette, flicks it aside and reaches for the heavy metal door to the hangar—

He goes airborne. The stars above whirl about, carving streaks of white in the air as he's thrown backward. When he crashes onto the ground, the lower part of his spine pops. He grits his teeth, the pain echoing up the vertebrae. He rolls onto his stomach, pushes himself off the ground and goes for his gun.

"Don't!" A man wearing a hoodie stands before him. His appearance is sudden, as if he teleported there from some other dimension.

The lanky man pulls out his gun anyway—something swipes through the air, cuts the gun in half. He watches in horror as the gun is bisected. Eyes shift between what's left of the weapon and the stranger in front of him whose face is obscured by the night. "What . . . the . . . fuck?"

"Tell me," the hooded man says, his flat tone stolid and unemotional, "how many men are inside?"

"Who . . . who are you?"

"How many men are inside?"

There's a flash of silver in response.

The lanky man's hand is cut off at the wrist.

Before he can scream, the hooded man is upon him, stuffing a gun into his mouth, muffling his pained cry.

The hooded man's tone changes as he asks with a little more immediacy, "How. Many. Men?"

Inside the hangar, the Rift agents lounge on weathered couches. Some play with their phones. Others entertain themselves with video games.

The witch with the silver lock of hair keeps a hand splayed open at the row of angels. Heads down, backs against the wall, they sit on their butts, legs kicked out in front of them. Their wings are folded tightly behind their backs, secured with duct tape.

One of the men looks up from his phone and over at the witch. He stares at her for a beat before asking, "You ever get a cramp doing that?"

"Doing what?"

He flexes his hand in response, opening and closing it. "I mean, holding your hand like that and all." He slides his phone into his pocket and cracks open a beer. "I mean, I'm getting a charley horse just from watching you."

"We train for this."

"So do we," he answers as he chugs the beer, belches, and then crushes the can. "We train our livers to get used to long shifts."

The men share a laugh.

"Maybe instead of getting drunk," the witch says, "you bums should do a lap around the building. Make sure we're secure."

One of the agents, a Latin man with dark black hair styled with a thick dose of pomade and teardrop tattoos under each eyelid, sets down his Xbox controller and tosses the agent another beer. "Crisis averted." He laughs. "We're all secure now."

The witch makes a face, yet maintains her focus on the angels. She can't let these dickheads distract her too much; otherwise these winged soldiers will cut them down and flee.

Without taking his eyes off the video game, the tattooed agent tells her, "You need to fucking chill, *chica*. No one's gonna find us here."

"You that sure?"

"Yeah, *mija!*"

"So, would you tell that to Marcus if something were to happen?" the witch asks.

The angels stir as though awakening from a nap. The witch narrows her gaze and blasts them with another dose of dark energy, throwing them back into their magical catalepsy.

"Yeah, I will, but nothing is gonna happen." The tattooed agent sets the game controller aside, throws his hands in the air as he turns to her. "We're in the middle of nowhere. No one knows that we exist. Ok? Besides, who wants a bunch of reject angels anyway?"

"If the Rift wants them, someone else will too." The witch puts her free hand to her temple, as if trying to suppress a headache. "All of you shitbags should thank your lucky stars for such an easy assignment. You could be slogging through a third world country right now, holed up in some mosquito infested shit box, babysitting crumbling antiques. But here you've got air conditioning, running water, and a god-damn Xbox. I'd say count your blessings that you work for Marcus and not one of the Council members."

"Don't get us wrong. We're appreciative." He holds up a can of beer and crushes it with one hand. "That's why we're gratefully taking it easy. Now, quit stressing, *mija*, and keep your mojo fixed on them angels. We got enough guns to take on a small country *and* we're in the fucking boonies. Ain't nothing going to happen out here—"

The tattooed agent's cell phone goes off. He fumbles to get it out of his pocket, spilling his own beer and knocking his controller to the ground. As he glances at the caller id, he goes white. Under his breath, "Shit!"

The witch grins. "That Marcus?"

The tattooed agent flicks her off. He turns his back to everyone and answers the call, "Ramone here."

The others look on with growing concern.

The witch smirks.

"No, sir. There's been nothing to report," Ramone assures Marcus. "All quiet." Another pause. Then, "I'm sorry to hear that, sir." A beat. "Will do." He ends the call abruptly, announcing to everyone, "Bad news." He points at the witch. "This fucking *pendeja* jinxed us!"

"Me?" she asks. "I jinxed *you* guys?"

"Yeah! You! Things been pretty good here, until you opened your voodoo mouth and cursed our shit." To the others, "Anyway, some deranged *maricon* knocked over the phosphate plant and lit the place up. Killed everyone; then released the big boy." Ramone gestures toward the angels. "You know . . . their fucking leader."

"What about Shiya?" the witch asks.

"Who?"

"Shiya . . . the one tasked with watching over their angel?"

"Fuck if I know." Ramone shrugs. "Homeboy probably turned her ass into potpourri. He's a big motherfucker. I wouldn't wanna spar with him."

"So, who did it?" one of the agents asks. "Any idea? Any leads?"

"Nada. Marcus doesn't know yet. Hey . . ." Ramone pauses, eyes scanning the room. "Hang on a sec . . . Anyone seen Paulie? He's taking a hell of a long smoke break—"

The hanger door rattles as if hit with a battering ram.

Everyone in the room jumps to their feet.

"The hell is that?" Ramone spins on his heels, gaze locked on the massive door. It rattles violently. Sounds as if someone is knocking on it with a sledgehammer. It buckles inward with each hit.

"Yo!" Ramone gestures to the other men without taking his attention off the trembling door. "Yo, yo, yo! We got eyes out there?"

"No, man," an agent responds. "Paulie was supposed to order us some new exterior cameras, remember? But his dumb ass forgot; that's why he's been on outside duty."

The pounding on the door grows incessant, almost to the point of deafening.

"Well, clearly he's not on duty anymore. Something got to him." Ramone points at the door. "Now light that shit up!"

As the door shakes violently, the agents scurry to get their weapons—clearly not ready for an event like this. Half drunk, they fumble their weapons, load up and take aim.

As they open fire, the aluminum skin of the door flowers outward with each round.

The witch screams. Ears bombarded with the cannonade. The blue light from her hand flickers, her focus wanes, and the angels writhe as though struggling against a nightmare plaguing their minds.

When the gunfire ceases, the door stands decorated with hundreds of holes. The air is acrid, laced with a metallic stench.

Ramone signals to one of the agents to advance. The agent nods and takes measured steps towards the door, hands wrapped tightly around his rifle. Specks of sweat on his forehead sparkle under the coarse spotlights above. He takes a deep breath, leans against the front door and peers outside using one of the bullet holes as a peephole.

The witch catches herself, her magic faltering. She hardens her gaze, and refocuses her energy on incapacitating the angels, who stiffen and are jarred back into their daze.

"All clear. There's nothing out there!" the agent shouts. He looks over his shoulder at the others. "And yeah, I don't see Paulie either—"

The hangar door groans loud enough to wake the dead. This is followed up by several thumping sounds as something thin and fast penetrates the skin of the door.

The agent takes a timid step back. "Guys?"

"Get back!" Ramon shouts. He motions for the others to reload their weapons. "C'mon! C'mon!"

And with one final groan, the hangar door is yanked off its track. Peeled away like the lid of a sardine can.

There's a blink of gray as a zigzag of wind rips through the man.

He stands motionless for a second, then slides apart; chunks of his body slough off like an avalanche of gore.

He bursts into black dust.

Chaos erupts.

The remaining agents unleash round after frantic round in the direction of the gray ghost, unloading their clips until their ammo is spent.

Nothing is there.

Nothing is at the receiving end, save for plumes of dust and shredded wood and metal.

They desperately reload—

A whirlwind of light, a torrent of wild energy, arc swaths of silver in the air.

The men never stood a chance, suffering the same fate as their fellow agent: bodies diced to pieces; arms, limbs and torsos separating at unnatural angles.

Before their appendages hit the ground, they're reduced to black dust.

The witch shrieks. She breaks away from the angels and heads for the nearest door to a makeshift office, slamming the door behind her.

In the center of the floating clouds of black dust, Balco's body swirls to a stop. His wings collapse softly at his sides as he kneels to the ground.

Simon enters the hangar. His hood covers most of his face, but as he studies the room, a flicker of light unnaturally reflects off his left eye.

Balco rises, spies the trapped angels. Turns to Simon.

"Go free them," Simon tells him. "I'll handle the witch."

Balco approaches the angels, and with one swift yank he tears away their chains. The four of them stand up slowly. Eyes darken like the depths of space itself. They acknowledge each other with a stony glare. Faces lack emotion. Long lost statues greet one another.

Simon kicks open the door to the office to find the witch on her cell phone, frantically trying to describe what just happened—

She turns to him, eyes wide, the phone glued to her ear.

Simon rushes her, knocks the phone out of her hand and she screams. The phone lands with a clatter. He steps on it, crushing it like a vile rodent.

"Who are you?" she asks, her voice trembling.

"Nobody to you."

"Well . . ." she inhales deeply, as if trying to suppress her fear, "you're a *dead* Mr. Nobody!"

Simon doesn't react. Not a single inch of his body twitches. He seems to stare right through her.

"Do you hear me, asshole?" Her voice rises with to a screech. "You are fucking . . . dead!" Her hands come up, glowing that uncanny blue, but before she can get off whatever magic she was planning, Simon grabs hold of her fingers, twisting them until they snap at the knuckles. She shrieks and lifts onto her tiptoes, attempting to counter the agony shooting up her arm.

Mouth agape, tears in her eyes, she stammers, "W—what do you want?"

"I want to know where you guys keep everything."

"I don't know what you're talking about—"

Simon cranks on her hand; more bones break. She squeals as he locks up her arm and forces her to her knees.

"Yes, you do," he tells her. "Everything you roaches stole from the Covenant and from wherever else."

"Wait a minute . . ." Powering through the pain, she forces out a wicked, yet uneasy cackle. "You must be the famous Travis Rail. Come here to finish us off?"

"Far from it." Simon kneels close to her, close enough that she can see where his eyeball should be—where a platinum ball with a gem inset at the iris rests instead. "He owes me an eye." He jars her arm, and she lets out a grunt. Through gritted teeth, he asks, "Now where do you keep everything?"

She spits in his face. "Piss off!"

"Tell me . . ." Simon wipes away the wad of saliva, pulls out a knife, and brings it close enough to tickle her eyelashes. "Do you know a magic spell to regenerate an eyeball? If so, I'd love to see it."

The witch squirms in response. The tip of the blade hovers uncomfortably close. She squeezes her eyelids shut.

Simon shakes his head, gesturing *tsk-tsk-tsk*. "Guess you value the Rift more than your eyes."

She wriggles wildly under him. "Fuck you!"

"Ok then . . ." The blade caresses her—

"Alright! Alright!" She opens her eyes. "I'll tell you."

Simon throws open the office door. To the four angels he declares, "That hag is all yours."

The angels file into the office.

"You have reunited us," Balco says, his voice so deep it makes the floor vibrate.

"I did. And now the real work begins." Simon surveys the room. It's a mess of dust, bullet holes, and debris. "We have to move quick. She got a call off. The Rift is spooked and will double-down their security and possibly relocate their stashes."

As the angels exact their revenge on the witch, her pained cries are loud enough to be heard for miles. Unfortunately for her, the Rift generally tends to pick very remote places for storing their property to protect their anonymity. Fortunately for Simon, this also makes stealing from them that much easier.

Simon glances up at a camera, careful not to let his face show from under the cover of his hoodie. "They're watching us now."

"Does that concern you?" Balco asks.

"Not necessarily. If they relocate their goods, we'll be fine. I've got an insider working for me," Simon informs him. "Along with all of you. Now corral the others and let's move."

Chapter 6 – Ways of the Wicked and Crooked

The Tennessee horizon is a work of art. Splashes of soft blues and yellows cascade along cirrus clouds that stretch across an endless river of mountains. Travis marvels at the serenity and charm of the mornings here. Florida is flat for the most part, so seeing some sort of terrain feature other than palm trees and rail-thin pines is a welcome change.

Travis sits parked in the Barracuda at a convenience store next to the Dunkin' Donuts. He sips on coffee from a Styrofoam cup as he watches the movement in and out of the donut shop.

No sign of Duncan yet.

He'd cased the area late last night following the scuffle at the tattoo shop. He catches a glimpse of himself in the rearview mirror. The bags under his eyes say it all.

You look like shit.

The car smells stuffy.

I smell like shit.

He hasn't showered. Nerves on edge after that altercation with the hooded angel and the Rift. He might as well have just slept in his car. He touches the wound on his shoulder, now just a pink line that has closed itself up. This whole healing thing still creeps him out.

Questions roll through his mind:

Who was that angel?

How did he find me?

Then again, he was an angel. Who knows what else they can do?

Well . . . Zach would know.

Maybe Duncan, too?

Where is Duncan anyway?

Travis downs the last swig of the brown liquid and makes a face. *This coffee makes mud jealous.* He crushes the cup and checks his cell phone.

Nothing from Duncan.

Travis drums his fingers on the steering wheel. Mind wandering. 8:00 a.m. This would be the second time that Duncan has been late. He scans the parking lot, the convenience store, and then the exterior of Dunkin' Donuts.

No signs of any Rift-heads.

All appears normal.

Travis's cell phone buzzes. It's Duncan. "Yeah?"

"Morning, Travis."

"You're late. I told you 8:00 a.m. sharp."

"I know. I'm sorry. But I'm just a little behind—"

"Where are you?"

A maroon Chevy Malibu pulls up in front of the Dunkin' Donuts. A man who looks exactly like Duncan hops out, cell phone pressed against his ear. "I just got here." He heads inside the donut shop. "Where are you?"

Travis hesitates. "You come alone?"

"Of course I did." Duncan lets out a little chuckle. "No doubt you're spying on me from afar."

Travis decides to throw out an F-bomb just to test the water. "You better not be fucking lying to me." He watches Duncan take a seat inside.

"My tardiness does not warrant your expletives," Duncan says as he shakes his free hand in the air.

"I watched you die, Duncan." Travis stares at the man inside. Watches Duncan's floppy brown hair spill over his glasses. Watches him casually wipe the hair back from his face and fidget in his seat.

Duncan, if this isn't you, I'm leaving, Travis thinks. *There are way too many people around that could get hurt if a fight breaks out, and God knows, I don't want any innocent blood on my hands.*

39

"Would you come in and join me for coffee already?" Duncan asks.

Travis drums his fingers again on the steering wheel. Takes a deep breath. He says a little prayer to himself as he glances at the heavens.

Watch my back, Big Man.

"Travis?"

"I'm coming." Travis kicks open the car door and slips out. "But if anything goes down or gets crazy, you're going to be the first one I shoot."

Last resort, God. Please let that be last resort.

"Being dead once was enough for me," Duncan answers with an awkward chuckle.

Images of Duncan's final moments flash in Travis's mind. "Right . . ." He hangs up and heads inside.

Duncan catches sight of him beaming with joy. "Travis!"

Travis makes his way over to Duncan's table. Seeing Duncan in the flesh again proves harder to process than he expected.

Duncan moves in for a hug, but Travis takes a step back. Stops him short with, "Whoa."

Duncan makes a face, somewhere between embarrassed and uneasy, then extends a hand. Travis glares at it like it's a foreign object.

"Right," Duncan says with a heavy sigh. He gestures for him to grab a seat. "Sit. Please."

Travis does.

Duncan does a little clap as he attempts to carry on, "Well, I have to admit. It *is* great to see you again." He reaches across the table and gives Travis an unwelcome pat on the shoulder.

Travis glances down at where Duncan touched him, then locks eyes with him.

"Dare I ask, is the excitement mutual?" Duncan shrinks back in his seat.

"You're kidding, right? The last time I saw you—oh, *six months ago*—you were holding your intestines in your hand. You left me in the dark . . . about the package, the Covenant . . . the Rift." He plants both hands palms down on the table and leans forward. "Now here you are, smiling like you just won the lottery, and I'm supposed to be excited to see you?"

Duncan folds his hands under his chin and rests his head on them. He clears his throat, and then asks, "Do you want a large or small?"

Travis glares at Duncan. The random question jarring him for a beat. "What?"

"Coffee . . . What size coffee do you want?"

When Travis takes a little too long to respond, Duncan lowers his head and makes an *are you ok?* face.

No, I'm not ok, Travis thinks. *Everyone around me dies or disappears. I've got this crazy healing factor. Time likes to slow down on its own—randomly. I'm supposedly a half angel. I'm sure Miami PD would love to have a chat with me. Oh, and I helped take down a cult that has been out to kill me since I was . . . uhhh . . . not even born yet. Meantime, you've kept me in the dark for half a year, and now you want to be best friends?*

Duncan presses, "So do you want a small or—"

"Large."

"Creamer?"

"Black."

"I'm not sure if they have Kona or Sumatra blend—"

"Jesus, Duncan. Is this an interview?" Travis pushes back into his seat. "Just get me a cup of coffee."

Duncan takes a deep breath. "You know I don't like when you swear or take the Lord's name in vain."

Travis glances away. "Right now, I don't care what you like."

Duncan nods. Goes and orders coffee.

Travis replays Duncan's death in his mind: guts spilling out, pink, red and wet everywhere. Color drained from his skin and his eyes.

Yet here he is, smiling, vibrant and peppy like he just got back from a six-month cruise.

Duncan slides back into the booth and goes to hand Travis his coffee, but he doesn't take it, instead opting to stare at Duncan to the point of making things uncomfortable.

"You're . . . welcome?" Duncan suggests with a chuckle.

Travis grabs the cup and pops off the lid. A ghostly coil of steam rises upwards. The smell of this coffee is worlds away from that ditch water they served at the gas station. "You died back there . . . in that neighborhood . . . what's left of it."

"Well . . . yes . . . almost."

"Almost?" Travis leans forward. "*Almost?*" Travis catches himself raising his voice. "You looked like you fought a tiger and lost. Like *really* lost."

Duncan nods his head in agreement as he sips tepidly from his coffee. Under his breath, "Wow, that's hot."

"Hey!" Travis pounds his fist on the table. The customers around them stir, shooting them dirty looks. "Sorry," he says aloud, then to Duncan, he speaks softer, yet just as firmly. "How many languages do you need me to say this in, Duncan? I watched you die. Then the neighborhood went up like Hiroshima."

"That's a hundred percent correct."

"So then, enlighten me." Travis takes a sip from his coffee, and with eyes never leaving Duncan, he leans forward again. "What happened?"

Duncan pulls down his shirt collar, revealing a thread of three gold rosary beads, the same ones worn by both Lomak and Vanessa. "I think the number of beads you possess contributes to how fast you heal, but it's just a theory. In hindsight, I should've kept more of these from the Rift, but then again, it's black magic so I really didn't want to overexpose myself in case there were . . . side effects."

"Side effects?"

"Perhaps utilizing such witchcraft corrupts your soul." Duncan shrugs. "Hard to say, though I have had crazy nightmares since I started wearing them."

"Let me get this straight . . ." Travis closes his eyes for a moment. "You, *Mr. Holy Roller*, used magic from the occult, from the Rift, to stay alive? Isn't that an oxymoron?"

"God can use the ways of the wicked and crooked to make things straight again."

"It's too early for a sermon."

"Is it?"

"Yes, it really is." Travis pinches the bridge of his nose. Fighting back the exhaustion of last night's encounter, of not having slept, and now Duncan's antics. "And the explosion?"

"The house was rigged with explosives."

"Well, I kind of figured." Travis takes another sip of the coffee. He returns the lid to retain the heat. "But my question is, who did that?"

"Me."

Travis nearly spits out his coffee. "What?"

"I set the house to blow in case things went south, which they did."

"So, you knew you might be followed?"

Duncan nods *yes.*

"And you didn't warn me?"

"I had to know if I could trust you. That's why I kept you in the dark about a lot of things."

Travis props both elbows on the table, interlaces his fingers. "By a lot of things, you mean the Rift?"

"There was a mole in the Covenant. I had to protect the interests of the organization. I didn't know who that mole was."

"So, you figured that if I was part of the Rift, by not telling me about the Rift, you'd somehow be better insulated from the Covenant's concerns making their way back to them?"

Duncan nods. "Yes, but the mole doesn't have to only work for the Rift. They may not work for the Rift at all."

"Well turns out that mole wasn't me." Travis takes another swig of the coffee. "Technically I wasn't part of the Covenant anyway."

"True. But there was another reason I didn't say anything."

Travis raises an eyebrow.

"Because Pastor Graham told me not to."

Travis shrugs, not sure what that means to him.

"He said that you were to be tested."

"Tested?" Travis asks.

"Yes." Duncan glances down at his coffee and then back to Travis. "He said that you would need to find yourself and your destiny, but that if I were

43

to tell you about the Rift ahead of time, you would've never taken the job."

Travis lets out a laugh. "In hindsight, I guess he's not wrong there."

"Then do you regret going through what you did?"

"You ever regret joining the Covenant?" Travis asks, turning the table on Duncan.

"Never. I was called to do this."

Travis nods his head up and down, a sarcastic affirmation. "Yeah . . ." He pushes his coffee aside. "So why didn't you call?"

Duncan evades Travis's glare.

"Don't look away. Answer me. Why didn't you contact me?" Travis asks. "I mean you walked away from a C-section and a mushroom cloud."

"Walked away is putting it lightly."

Travis talks right over him, "You weren't on that call when I delivered the news to your sister."

Duncan swallows.

"It sucked. You made her cry. She thinks you're dead." Travis clenches his fist. "Six months. And you haven't bothered to tell her you're alive."

"I didn't want to jeopardize her safety."

"Don't lie to me. I'm not above slapping a grown man!"

An old woman at a nearby table glances over her shoulder at Travis and scoffs. She gathers up her belongings and her coffee and leaves. Travis eyes her as she goes. Proceeds with the conversation using a little more discretion by lowering his voice, "Why didn't you tell her, Duncan? Is it because you don't trust her either? You think she defected to the Rift?"

Duncan fiddles with the lip of the coffee cup. The flimsy white lid curls upwards with each flick of his thumb.

"That's it, isn't it? You put your precious cause and Pastor Graham's BS above everything and everyone else. Do you know what we went through? Between Lomak and Vanessa, Amanda almost died twice!" Travis's eyes bore holes into Duncan; watching that cheery façade of his crack under the weight of the conversation. "That's sad that you don't even know your own sister."

"And you do?"

"Maybe she and I didn't grow up together, but I know a good person when I meet one, and she's a thousand times more trustworthy than you. You lied. I bet this supposed next job isn't even going to pay a million bucks like you swore the Covenant could pay me." Travis laughs to himself. "Correct me if I am wrong, but isn't lying breaking one of the ten commandments?"

"You have every right to be upset at me. I have withheld information from you and now this rebuttal is how you get back at me."

"I don't want to get back at you." Travis leans forward, his shoulders rising, seemingly swelling up to crash down onto Duncan like a landslide of pent-up anger. "I want to punch your lights out."

Duncan gapes.

"You put me through hell. Exposed me to the Rift. Then I find out that I'm somehow touched by God!"

Duncan shifts in his seat, glancing uncomfortably from side to side, embarrassed as unease spreads to other customers in the store.

"I also have an unnatural ability to heal myself, to somehow slow down time, and now I'm stalked by angels!"

"Stalked by angels?"

Ignoring him, Travis goes on, "Yeah, you had your weak-ass reasons for what you did. And aside from what you put me through, whatever this fucking test is that you put me through—"

Duncan closes his eyes for a beat. "Please stop with the expletives."

"Shut up!" Travis smacks the table. The coffee cups do a little hop. People gawk. Duncan shrinks in his seat. Travis lowers his voice again. "Just shut up for once and don't tell me what to do. You called *me*, remember?"

"Yes, and I honestly thought you'd be happy to see me."

"I wish I had run into the Rift instead." Travis gulps the coffee. Crushes the cup in his hand. "At least they're consistent about who they are." He rises to his feet.

"Alright, alright! Look . . . I'm not proud of what I did, to you or Amanda, but I did what I had to do. I know you can at least understand that. Sometimes it's best if someone doesn't know everything. This is how God works too, you know? He doesn't tell us everything; only what we need to know. That is what faith is all about. Trusting that the details of our lives will work themselves out."

"You're nothing but a liar. And you still won't be up front with me. You'd make a great politician." Travis pitches the cup into the trash. "Thanks for the coffee."

"Travis, wait!" Duncan bolts up. "There's a lot that I need to tell you, but in due time. I don't know how you will take the news."

"Try me."

Duncan sighs. "Not yet. But I need you to trust me."

"Nah. I'm done trusting you."

"But I still need your help. I have another job for you."

"Then go find someone else." Duncan opens his mouth to respond, but Travis holds up a hand. "I know. I know. There *is* no one else. Can't say I'm surprised about that considering how you treat the people around you."

Without looking back, Travis storms towards the door, knowing that's the best thing he could do right now considering how bad he'd like to beat the crap out Duncan for what he did. For what he put Amanda through. And is *still* putting her through.

"Travis!"

Travis spins around. Keys in hand.

"Please don't tell Amanda you spoke to me."

"Don't worry," Travis says as he heads for his car, "she doesn't want to talk to me anyway."

Without giving him a second look, Travis jumps into the Barracuda and races off, tires skidding. A rush of white smoke surrounds Duncan, leaving him coughing in the distance.

Chapter 7 – Missing Her

Simon is in a waiting room. He lifts his head up from his hands. Several doctors hover over him like white giants. The wash of the sterile fluorescent lights above them make them appear more heavenly than they are. But the news they deliver is far from divine.

"Do something!" Simon shouts. Tears brim in his eyes.

The doctors observe Simon wordlessly as if conducting an experiment on the reactions to grief and what it does to the human expression.

"Don't just stand there with your thumbs up your asses! Do something!"

Simon jumps to his feet, and the mute physicians take a unified step back.

"I've done so much for you, for this hospital, for your . . . *research*." Simon grabs one of the doctors, shakes him. "I have practically gone broke funding your worthless tests and treatments. And for what? So you can just let my wife die? What was the point of giving back—" he makes quotes with his hands, "—to the community? I could've kept all that money, gotten a medical degree and saved her my goddamn self!"

Simon pushes the doctor away, cuts through the wall of useless beings and storms into the hospital room.

Cynthia lies in bed, a skeletal, sunken shadow of her former self.

Her hair is gone.

Eyes hazy and recessed.

She looks like she's already dead.

Simon stares at her in horror.

Where's the rose red in her cheeks? Where did her river of brunette hair go? That soft smile, the sparkle in her eyes when she looked at him, the music of her laugh.

All of it . . . gone.

He is staring down at a corpse, not the love of his life, but a morbid promise of tomorrow.

Cynthia.

His everything.

Simon's world. She is fading away.

Today a skeletal shadow.

Tomorrow, the cold black print on a newspaper obituary. A two-line blurb on the local news. A passing hyperlink buried in the depths of the internet:

Cancer Philanthropist's Wife Dies Ironically of Cancer.

The very thing she urged him to parade against ended up being the very thing that killed her.

Simon could've invested more money in his online marketing company. It was poised for continued growth. The economy was on the upswing and he was at the forefront, which afforded him to – at Cynthia's encouragement – give back, pay it forward, or whatever the charitable catch phrase of the day is.

So, he did.

Campaigned for cancer awareness and cancer research.

A half-million people die each year from cancer.

And yet with all of Simon and Cynthia's social awareness marketing efforts, donations, and black-tie dinners, here she is:

Beaten down.

Sick from chemo.

Shriveling in her bed like some forgotten pet left out in the cold to perish.

But she isn't alone.

Simon takes her hand, kneels by her bedside.

That's not to say that the medical staff of other hospitals, other organizations, and other research facilities haven't done their part to save lives. To rid other patients of this dreaded disease.

But those other people don't matter to Simon.

Only Cynthia matters.

"I'm here." He kisses the soft skin on her knuckles. A hint of decay wafts into his nose. She used to smell of citrus and sunshine. Now she reeks of death. "I'm so sorry I couldn't do more to save you, babe."

"You did." Cynthia can barely move. Takes her a century to reach over and stroke his face, "All you could."

"It wasn't enough." Simon lays his head on her shoulder. "But I'm going to change that. I'm going to make it right." He caresses her face, holds her head in his hands like it's the cup that Jesus drank from. "I'm coming to get you."

"Please, don't." The words are almost inaudible.

"What? *Don't?*" Simon recoils, offended. "What do you mean? Don't you miss me?"

"Yes. Of course I do. But . . ." Her voice trails off.

"But what?"

There are tears in her eyes—tears of blood. "You don't know everything."

Simon breaks away, takes a step back. "What's wrong with your eyes?"

"You don't know everything." The blood is borderline brown.

"I know that I did the right thing. Gave back to the community. Invested in others. I campaigned for more than just myself for once. Hell, I even lied to a thief about not having a cause to cure cancer . . . and here I—*we*—tried to cure cancer!" Simon seethes. "You took a selfish guy like me and made him into a selfless man."

"Then you did it out of your own heart."

"And look what that got me!" Simon wraps his fingers around the guard rails of the bed, his knuckles whitening as he tightens his grip. "All that money. All those stupid formal dinners. All that time parading around like we were saving lives, actually doing something altruistic and honorable, and here you are. Nice and dead."

She looks away. "I'm sorry that it cost you so much."

"It's not about the money. I'd spend every last dime all over again. It's the fact that it was pointless!"

"It wasn't pointless." Cynthia's eyes pool with an atramentous liquid, as if she's crying motor oil. "Your efforts, financial and physical, helped so many others. It was not all in vain—"

"I don't care about anyone else; don't you get it?" Simon hammers his fist on the rail, and it collapses under his strength. "I did it for you! I donated because you wanted it, and for fucking what? You're gone. If I would've known you were going to get sick and die, I would've spent all that money and time and energy on us. Talk about a bucket list—more like a *bathtub* list—we could've enjoyed every waking minute in each other's arms." He runs his hand along her cheek and sits at her side again. "Aruba. Tokyo. Greece. Hell . . . I would've gladly hiked Siberia with you and now . . . now I have nothing."

"You have your life."

"So what?" Simon shrugs. "I don't have *you*." He smooths her hair and wipes the bloodied streaks from her face. "Nothing else in this world matters."

She shakes her head *no* as she says, "Don't come for me."

Simon's brow furrows, eyes narrowing as he tries to make sense of what she's talking about. "So, you don't want to see me?"

"I miss you more than you know," Cynthia whispers, "but God has a place and a plan for all of us, and your place isn't to tinker with it. By His grace, I deliver you this warning."

"God?" Simon throws his hands up in the air. "God! Where is God now? He let you die in spite of all the good we did." He smacks the bed rail. "That's why I'm not waiting on God. I don't need Him. My plan is better. My plan will bring us together."

More blood rains down her cheeks and she insists with words heavy and deliberate, "Don't. Come. For. Me."

"What about free will?" He points at himself. "He lets me choose the path of my own volition, right? Isn't that how God works?"

"You don't know how God works. No one does. We're not meant to."

"Well I know I'm going to break the rules. God should know that. He made me, after all, right?"

"I know what you're up to, Simon, and you need to stop. I'm here to tell you to let me go. God has granted me this moment . . . this one respite . . .

for your sake." Cynthia shakes her head from side to side again. "You don't know what you're doing."

Simon cups her face, brings her close. He kisses her hard, and she kisses him back. As he pulls away, "Do you love me?"

She sighs.

"Answer me, Cynthia." Simon's eyes well with tears. "Do you love me?"

"To death and back."

"Then trust that I know what I'm doing." Simon brushes his thumbs across her cheeks, once again wiping away the stream of blood as it seeps down from her eyes. "If God is truly about love, then He should understand."

She stares at him for a long time. Eyes reading his face as if trying to uncover some veiled secret encrypted in his expression. "Is this about love? Or about making a point?"

The hospital room door is kicked open.

Simon turns in the direction of the sound.

A figure is standing there, face obscured by odd shadows that act as a mask. He looks back to Cynthia. She's gone, his hands holding nothing but air.

The figure takes a step forward.

It's Travis.

He's brandishing that cursed kukri that sliced his face open.

"*You!*" Simon shouts as a sharp pain digs into his eye. He catches sight of his reflection in the mirror. An empty left eye–socket stares back at him. The jagged scar runs the length of his face, pulsing like a big red worm. He turns away in disgust, staring down the very man that took his sight, his appearance from him.

Travis Fucking Rail, Simon thinks.

Travis screwed him over. Robbed him of the Eyes of God. Took his money and his sight. How dare he show his face now? What he's doing is more important that what Travis wants to take from him.

This is a different Simon.

This is a man far from philanthropy and charity and entrepreneurship.

This is a man who lost his love, his life, and his looks.

He collects the treasures with a purpose.

For his Cynthia.

And this transient scumbag, Travis, who is just looking to score his next job, isn't going to get in Simon's way. Not now. Not ever again.

Travis charges at him, but Simon is ready.

Or so he thinks.

Travis sprouts wings, moves like a dragonfly, zipping around him from side to side. Stabbing and slicing him from every conceivable and inconceivable angle.

Simon tries to fight back, but Travis is too fast—slices his *other* eye, blinding him permanently as things go black.

Simon is jolted awake in his hotel bed, panting, skin sheening in a thin veil of sweat.

On his dresser sits a glass full of eye solution. Resting at the bottom of that glass is a prosthetic eye. However, instead of being made of glass, this one is made of platinum. And where the iris would be, sits a red garnet stone. He takes it out, dries it off, and pops it in.

A gust of air pushes aside the curtains that lead to a balcony. Simon rolls out of bed and heads outside to find Balco. Wings wrapped around himself like a blanket, he's perched on the balcony railing, peering at the world below.

"Balco."

The angel unfolds his wings and steps down. He moves with the grace of a butterfly, each movement flowing, almost dancelike. He stares blankly at Simon. There's a story behind those eyes, the eyes of an immortal being who has seen more in his existence than any man could imagine. "Yes?"

"Let's get to work."

Chapter 8 – On the Road Again

Beyond the cracked clouds that rake across the sky, a brilliant gradient of oranges and yellows reaches upwards. A semi-circle of light signifies the dawn of a new day. Sunrise in Tennessee is a daily work of art.

Travis grips the wheel as he speeds northwest on I-24. Nashville is pretty much a straight shot from Chattanooga. He'll be there in about two hours. The plan is to get a hotel. Spend some time looking for property. Find the right home – a home away from noise, bullshit, and prophecy – and be left alone. Hell . . . it probably wouldn't be the worst idea to ditch the cursed car and the cell phone.

Who does he really want to talk to anyway?

Amanda.

Travis shakes off the thought. She wants nothing to do with him, so he may as well change his number.

And hide.

Retirement.

Retirement from people, needs, and hopefully angels.

From behind him, a truck engine rumbles. He glances at the rearview mirror and catches a Dodge Ram souped up with chrome, dark tint and a pair of steel balls slung over the front grill. The truck closes in on him. Travis reaches for his gun.

The Rift found me again. Damn! I've got to get rid of this car. It's cursed.

The truck swings around to his left. The passenger side window rolls down. Travis grips the wheel with one hand, wraps his hand around his gun with the other. As soon as he sees the crusty, decayed grin of one of those pricks, he's going to blow them away—

A little girl with pink ribbons tied around two ponytails peeks out from the truck.

"Hey, mister," the girl's accent is thick with the local twang. "My momma said your taillight is out. Thought you might wanna know."

Travis relaxes his gun hand. Nods. "Thanks." He sighs.

Jesus, I almost took out a kid.

The girl grins from ear to ear. Yells, "Yer welcome!" as she holds up a Barbie doll, moving its arm, pretending the toy is waving at him.

The window rolls up and she disappears, obscured behind the tint as the truck speeds ahead.

Guess I need to get that fixed, he thinks. I need as few reasons as possible to get myself pulled over.

Travis inhales deeply, centering himself as he stares off at the passing mountains in the distance. Sloping green and brown hills dive and rise as far as the eye can see. The air is fresh up here. Untainted by persistent smog and pollution.

And it smells like peace.

That peace is promptly interrupted when the shrill ring of his cell phone breaks the serenity. He glances at the caller ID.

Duncan.

Man, he's stubborn. If only he were that persistent when telling the truth, the whole truth, and nothing but. No tests. No Covenant drama.

Just the plain old truth.

Travis debates not answering, but does anyway.

"Yeah?" Travis answers as he puts the phone on speaker.

"Travis?"

"What?"

"Look . . ." Duncan sighs. "I'm sorry. I can't apologize enough. I never meant to put you through what you went through. I had to be sure that your intentions were in the right place for the sake of the Covenant and the protection of its treasures."

Contempt flickers in Travis's eyes. "A word of advice?"

"Yes?"

"If you ever leave the Covenant, never consider a career in sales, because you would suck at it."

"First, I would never consider leaving the Covenant," Duncan insists. "And second, going into sales is of no interest to me. My heart is with God, not with achieving wealth."

"Actually, maybe you should consider a career change. I mean, you suck at what you do now."

"What's that supposed to mean?"

"That you're a devout do-gooder and nothing you've done so far has helped anyone."

"You must have a short-term memory, Travis." There's a shift in Duncan's tone; a change to that calm, collected, cerebral demeanor of his. "We kept the Eyes of God from the Rift—"

"*I* kept them from the Rift," Travis corrects him. "You didn't do shit but pretend to die."

"That's not fair. I did die "

"No. You faked your death so that you could test the loyalties of myself and your sister." A flock of birds in the formation of an arrowhead glides over the highway. Travis takes his eyes off the road just long enough to watch them fade into the distance.

"Call me paranoid, but I had to do what I had to do. My intentions were good."

"Your *good* intentions, however noble or divine, put me through Hell."

"But aren't you a better man for it?" Duncan asks. "You discovered who you truly are? *What* you truly are?"

"Yeah, I'm confused, lost, and wanted," Travis retorts. "Now do me a favor."

Duncan hesitates. "What?"

"Consider me dead." Travis ends the call. He stares ahead for a beat. Then hammers a fist repeatedly on the steering wheel.

"Is that what you want?" a voice asks. Travis nearly crashes the car. He turns to the passenger seat and sees Zach.

"Jesus!" Travis jumps in his skin, his heart nearly exploding within his chest.

"Please don't say the Lord's name in vain."

"It's not in vain if I meant it!"

Zach stares ahead, as if looking beyond the highway and seeing something else. His gaze is unwavering.

"What do you want?" Travis demands as he glances briefly at Zach. "I thought you were done helping me or whatever."

"Why would you say that?"

"Come on, old man. That's what you told me back in Miami, back in the elevator," Travis reminds him. "You said that you wouldn't help me a fourth time."

"Who said I'm here to help you?"

"Alright." Travis groans as if somehow that will quell the frustration that Zach tends to bring out in him. "Then what do you want?"

"Why did call me *old man*?"

Travis presses a thumb to his eyebrow. If anyone could incite a migraine, it's Zach. "You're answering a question with a question."

Zach says nothing. Eyes unblinking. Hard to tell if he's a living thing or something else.

Well . . . he is an angel.

And he is somewhat of a weirdo.

"I called you *old man* because that's what you are, right? Obviously, you weren't born yesterday, unless your definition of yesterday was about the same time as the big boom or whatever."

Zach cocks his head, eyes Travis. "And how do you know that you're not . . . *old*?"

Between the crazed dark angel, the Rift, Duncan and now Zach, it's as if the whole world can't seem to get by without some attention from Travis. The one person he *wants* to speak to—Amanda—he can't get ahold of.

"Travis?"

"Yes, I heard you." Travis shrugs, fingers splayed, raised off the wheel. "I don't know if I'm old, not old, whatever. Last I checked I'm still in my late thirties, and that's not old in human years. But then again, I guess it's all a point of reference, right? I mean, to a dog, I'm ancient."

"We are all made of the things that came before us, Travis." Zach looks toward the sky. "We are the debris of planets. The same elements that make up the universe, made us. The cosmos lives in us. We are star dust."

To himself, Travis mutters, "Ok, so you just went on the most random tangent . . ."

"Why you running away, Travis?"

"Easy. To escape the drama."

"Drama?" Zach tilts his head, curiously, as if the word struck him as peculiar.

"Yes, drama. The drama of you, the Rift, the Covenant, Duncan the liar. The drama." Travis glances ahead. There's construction. The highway traffic comes to a slow crawl. Several lanes are merging into one. Under his breath, "Seriously? They're doing construction in the middle of the day?"

"There is no drama. There is only life."

"And I want to live a life without drama. Wasn't it Jesus who turned the other cheek? Well, I'm turning the other cheek." Travis carves a circle in the air with his head. "I want to get away from all of this. I didn't ask for any of it. You know that."

"We don't always get a choice as to the life we are in."

"So, you're saying there's no free will?"

Zach rolls down his window. The crisp wind plays with his billowing mane. "As I've said before, you always have free will. It is the flow of life, the circumstances that come your way that you cannot control. It is that flow that forces you to make a decision, and therefore, allows you to enact your free will." Zach puts his hands together symbolizing prayer. "Of course, you can always pray for guidance and for an outcome. If it is His will, then so it shall be."

Travis exhales. If he could blow out steam, he probably would. "I'm not sure who's been more frustrating to deal with in the last twenty-four hours. Duncan or you."

Zach watches the traffic as it moves along at a snail's pace. There's nothing but a river of red taillights as far as the eye can see. Construction workers on either side of the highway are busy doing whatever it is that they're doing.

"Alright," Travis says as he turns to Zach, "so what do you want?"

"To make it clear that you can't run from yourself."

"And I want to make it clear that I don't want to be responsible for saving the world from itself. I want to get drunk on my porch, stare at the moon, and listen to the sounds of crickets and birds and nothing else."

"Then that is your choice."

Travis nods in affirmation. "Yes, it is. Free will, right? Saving the Covenant is not my job."

"It's not about the Covenant. It's about you."

"What about me?"

Traffic starts to move now. Several construction workers with flags wave everyone through.

"You know the truth now, Travis," Zach says.

"Dammit, what truth?"

Zach closes his eyes momentarily as if ingesting the word *dammit* like a jagged pill. "You know who you are now. You are a half-wing."

Travis winces as this conversation grows increasingly frustrating for him. "No, I don't know what that means."

"It means that the bloodline of our brothers flows within you. You are not just a mortal man, but one blessed by God and the angels."

Travis pinches the bridge of his nose. "Yeah, we covered that already. But what does that *mean*?"

"It means that yes, you may choose to run from your destiny. That is your choice, your free will at work, but the world around you may have other plans."

"If you know something I don't, then why not be useful for once and tell me what you're getting at instead of being frustratingly cryptic? You're really good at being all riddles and no answers."

Zach pauses. Says nothing for what seems like several minutes but is only seconds.

Travis wonders if he has finally offended the ascetic angel, but then Zach tells him, "The world is going to find you no matter where you go. You can either face your destiny and help those who reach out to you, or let the world come to your doorstep. That, and that alone, is truly your choice."

"And when you say *world*, who are you talking about exactly?"

"The world," Zach repeats flatly.

"Like who? The Rift? A coven of witches? Amway?"

"The world." Zach rolls up his window. "And what the world decides to do is not within your control."

Travis lets out a little laugh. Glances at Zach, his phlegmatic expression coupled with his manicured features.

Travis turns back to the road. "Well in that case, I'll still stick with Plan A, and by that I mean 'A' as in *alone*. If the world knocks on my door, I'll have a surprise waiting for them." Travis pats his holster. He looks back at Zach, who has vanished.

He shakes his head.

"See . . . all riddles and no answers."

Chapter 9 – Divine Ambitions

The faint thrum of jazz fills Simon's hotel suite. He's parked at the kitchenette table, hunched over, mindlessly thumbing a plush red velvet sack.

This will soon hold the most important treasures of all, he thinks. *Once I find them . . . then I'll find you.*

Simon stares at the sack, running his fingers along it.

Not even God can keep us apart.

"What the hell you doing?" Tizzy's shrill voice breaks his concentration. She's wearing a bathrobe that's a few sizes too big for her. Her hair is pulled back in a half-assed ponytail. Eyelids puffy as if she has been partying all night.

Simon glares at her. "Anyone ever tell you that you're about as subtle as a rash?"

"No, not really." The faint odor of cigarette smoke trails her as she drags her feet from the bathroom to the kitchenette.

Simon clenches his fists. "You mind walking like a normal person?" He relaxes his hands and takes a breath. "You know . . . perhaps pick up your feet as you walk?"

"Okie dokie." Tizzy searches the refrigerator, finds a carton of orange juice and drinks straight from it. "So . . . " She wipes her mouth with the sleeve of her robe. "What's the plan, Stan?"

"It's *Simon.*"

"Ok, *Simon,* what am I doing here? I already told you where those Rift hideouts are." Tizzy throws back her head, guzzles the rest of the orange juice, then plops the carton on the counter with an empty thud. "I mean, you're still keeping me alive for a reason . . . right?"

"Well, it's certainly not for your sparkling personality."

"Alrighty. Then what are you keeping me around for?"

"I'll tell you when I'm ready. I'm going to compensate you for your time and efforts." Simon pushes the red satchel aside and interlocks his fingers. "Meantime, it would benefit both of us if you'd relax. Perhaps focus on reining in that brash, irritable attitude of yours. I doubt it's been advantageous in your short, meaningless existence."

"Whatever. Look, I am who I am, and I ain't gonna change," she says with a smirk. "But I'll tell you one thing I *ain't*, and that's your hostage. You can't keep me prisoner."

Simon says nothing. Props his feet on the table and leans back in his chair.

"Unless you're some kind of perv," Tizzy folds her arms, "keeping me around for reasons that got nothing to do with the Rift or the stupid Covenant."

Simon glowers at her with his one good eye.

"I'm right, aren't I?" Tizzy asks. "You got me on standby in case you get horny. Employees with benefits, or some shit."

"First off," Simon holds up his hand, displaying his wedding ring, "I'm still married. Secondly," he takes his feet off the table, leans in, and with words dripping with acidity, tells her, "I'd rather set myself on fire than touch you."

Tizzy pauses. Digests his words. Then moves her head side-to-side and waves a finger in the air, as she retorts, "Well you're not my type either . . . with that *bougie* haircut, Gucci smile and that pink butt crack running up the side of your face." She laughs to herself. "So, I don't care how rich you are, I wouldn't fuck you if my life depended on it."

Simon nods, processing her derisive rant with an apathetic expression.

"Anyways . . ." Tizzy rummages through the refrigerator with an unwelcome audacity that causes Simon to shift in his seat. "You know, it'd be nice if you had some real food here." She retrieves a protein shake and studies it intently. "Instead of this organic, vegan crap." She shrugs. "Whatever.

I'm gonna choke this down and peace—"

The bottle barely makes it to her lips before Simon is in front of her, the refrigerator door between them. He smashes the door into her, and the container drops out of her hand. A green liquid spurts out of the bottle.

Before she can react, he grabs her, and drives her face into the pool of vegan shake protein that is rapidly spreading out across the tile floor. As he holds her down, the shimmering tip of a knife comes into her periphery.

"Would you like to know what it feels like?" Simon draws so close that his breath warms her cheek. His blade is centimeters from the wet skin of her eyeball. "To have your face split open and the fluid of your eyeball ooze down your cheek? To be rewarded with bright pain and eternal darkness?"

Tizzy squirms under him, but it's futile. She's in a bad spot.

Simon then asks, "So, would you like me to correct that attitude with an optical adjustment?"

Tizzy shakes her head *no*.

"Ok, then listen real close: You work for me. You're going to do *what* I say, *when* I say it, and *how* I say it." Simon gives Tizzy a jolt that rattles her jaw. "I'm fully prepared to die to get what I want, and no one is going to interfere with that. You tracking what I'm saying?"

Tears form, but Tizzy suppresses the urge to cry.

Fuck this asshole, she thinks.

"Do you understand?"

"Yes!" she answers. "Loud and clear."

"Great." Simon releases her, backs away. "The minute you wear out your usefulness, you're dead."

Tizzy pushes herself off the floor with a grunt. She turns to him, fuming. Her face is awash with anger and her robe drenched from the protein shake.

"Now, go put on some clothes," Simon tells her. "We have work to do."

Tizzy scurries away and slams the bathroom door behind her.

Simon tucks the red satchel into his pocket and walks out onto the hotel balcony to find Balco once more perched atop the railing, admiring the horizon. The sun is setting behind the hills.

"Beautiful sight," Simon opines.

"As are all of God's works."

"Hmm," Simon remarks with a wince. "I could think of a few thousand things in this world that aren't so beautiful."

Balco steps down, his movements lithe. "Tell me, Simon." He gestures to Simon's platinum eye, its red garnet glinting with the dimming light of the sunset. "Where did you find the Divine Eye?"

"I stole it," Simon replies. "From the Rift."

"And they stole it from the Covenant."

Simon shrugs. "Irrelevant to me. What matters is that it does what I need it to do: help me sense angels. Using it along with some intel Tizzy gathered, I was able to track down the Rift's stashes. That's how I found all of you, sparing you from whatever mess they had planned."

"And for that, I am grateful." Balco lowers his head. "But you should know where the Divine Eye is from."

"I guess." Simon leans back, rests his arms against the railing. "Enlighten me."

"The eye is from a fallen angel who challenged God, claiming that if God loved him, then God would show the angel His true face. The angel was mistaken, for the love of God is unconditional and so it should be in return. A baby loves its mother without question. A dog loves his master without hesitation. An angel should love His Father without expectation."

"And what happened?"

"God showed him His Face, and then Michael tore out the angel's eyes. One of them was lost. The other, the one that rests in your skull, was taken by the Covenant and preserved in platinum. Sealed with a red garnet."

"Sealed?"

"Have you stared into the gem?"

The question rocks Simon. He had never really stared deep into the eye. Or if he had, he didn't recall really seeing anything other than the glint of light reflecting off it. Simon removes the eye and examines it.

"Shake it gently and then look *closely*."

Simon does. A translucent glowing fluid swishes inside.

"The fluid is visible when angels are around. You no doubt have always had it in your eye socket while tracking us down, so naturally you never noticed it."

Simon makes a face. "What is it?"

"Our essence. It is how you can detect our presence. The core of the eye liquifies when we are near."

"Divine blood sealed in metal, corked with a gemstone." Simon reinserts the eye. "Fascinating."

"And highly volatile. The gemstone shatters easily. Toss it on the ground as you would a stone, and the light that escapes will be bright enough to blind all humans who look upon it."

"Thanks for the head's up, but I don't plan on dropping it," Simon tells him. "Now tell me . . . what do you know about the Manacles of the Messiah?"

"They're the keys to the next life." Balco flies back onto the railing. Glares pensively at the town below. "Forged from the very nails that penetrated the body of Christ."

"Yes, I'm familiar with that part. The Knights Templar disguised those nails in form of two objects: the manacles themselves and a cross," Simon says. "But do you know how they work?"

"Of course, I do. They must be combined to open the gate."

"And can you open the gate?"

"Perhaps. Why?" Balco turns back to Simon. "The manacles and the cross were lost centuries ago."

"Actually, the Rift have the manacles. Stolen from the dead hands of a Covenant's faithful transporter." Simon moves next to the great angel. "One of these repositories of theirs is bound to have them."

"How can you be so sure?"

"I found you guys, didn't I?" Simon asks. "It's just a process of elimination. Site by site."

"So, what kinda gate does it open?" Tizzy emerges, fully dressed now. Arms folded. "One that leads to the end of the world or something?"

Balco gives Tizzy a hard stare with his glossy black eyes.

"The fuck you looking at, Cupid?" Tizzy hisses under her breath. She turns to Simon and insists, "Hey listen, I'd just like to know what I'm into here, if that's alright?"

Tizzy shrivels slightly as Simon advances, dreading a repeat of what happened earlier. Simon shoots past her to grab a drink from the fridge. Downs it like it's the last beverage on Earth. He holds the empty bottle just above the garbage can and asks, "You want to know where the gate goes?" as he drops it. "Ok, I'll make you a deal." Simon lowers his gaze and raises his eyebrows, his face like the devil himself. "Get me to the next Rift hideout and the Covenant's headquarters and maybe then I'll tell you . . . and maybe then I'll let you go."

Tizzy tries to restrain herself, but her nature gets the best of her. "But what if I can't get you to either—"

"Both."

"—*both* of those places . . . then what?"

Simon glances at Balco, who steps forward.

"Then my friend here will take you on a quick flight," Simon gestures to the sky, "up into the beautiful starlit night above, high above the twinkling city. And then he'll open his arms and let you fall to your death. How does that sound?"

"Terrible."

"Then don't fuck up." Simon sniffs. "I need you to stay *useful*, Tizzy. You bragged about how *useful* you were when I spared you back in Miami. Told me that you've been working both sides." He spins around, eyes burning holes in her. "Well you'd better live up to that claim."

Tizzy looks away, notices Balco's dark orbs drilling into her. She recoils, that youthful rebellious angst waning. She mutters, "Got it."

"Wonderful. Now let's not waste any more time." Simon hands Tizzy a cell phone. "I need you to get me to the next Rift repository."

"But I don't know where that is." The words leave her mouth before she can catch them. Balco flaps his wings and is instantly upon her. He wraps his massive, slate-colored arms around her. She lets out a scream before he places his monstrous hand over her mouth.

"Have you ever been skydiving?" Simon asks.

Glossy terror flashes across Tizzy's eyes. She shakes her head frantically as her flimsy bravado sloughs off like dried petals from a dead flower.

"How's tonight sound?" Simon asks.

Tizzy shakes her head, managing to do so even under the grip of Balco's hand. She mumbles something.

"What's that?" Simon leans in, faking poor hearing. "I can't hear you."

Balco releases his grip on her face. A renewed scowl forms as her lips twist, gnarling with resentment. "Ok, ok, dude! I'll do whatever you need!"

"Simon. It's Simon," he tells her. "Not *dude*."

"Simon!" Tizzy huffs. "*Simon says jump and I'll fucking jump!*"

Somewhat pleased with her resignation, Simon motions for Balco to release her.

Tizzy steps away from them, rubs her face, and mutters, "Jesus, Cupid. You almost crushed my face."

From the depths of his chest, Balco warns, "Do not take the Lord's name in vain!"

"Then don't touch me again!" Tizzy stews. Says under her breath, "Asshole."

An unearthly grumble wallows up from Balco's throat.

Sensing the fragile ice she's treading on, Tizzy moves things forward, "Ok, so what do you guys need me to do?"

"I need you to find me their caches," Simon tells her. "If that requires a simple phone call or you banging every Rift employee under the sun, then you do what you have to do. I want to know where their next stash is . . . and I want those manacles."

Tizzy concedes. Not wanting to play all her cards, but not wanting to free fall out onto the pavement below, she offers up, "There is someone in the Rift. Met him through Lomak. They used to roll together."

Simon raises an eyebrow. Interest spreads across his face. "Go on."

"I hit him up from time to time." Tizzy glances down at the floor; a flash of shame that vaporizes just as quickly as it appears. "He sends me money . . . for favors."

Simon pulls out a chair. Props one leg up on it. Leans forward with growing fascination. He folds his arms neatly over his knee. "Continue."

"He's a big mouth. Suffers, you know, from big truck, small dick syndrome. He likes to brag when he's . . ." Tizzy's voice trails away. "Hanging out with me."

"Then don't let us keep you." Simon gestures toward the door. "Sounds like you got a date with a trucker."

Chapter 10 – Those of Shaken Faith

The Covenant hides in a nondescript building in an old Tennessee town.

There are maybe a dozen buildings here at best. Built sometime between the turn of the century and today. A hodgepodge of shops, boutiques, and a feed store. Situated behind them, away from the busy streets, is a brownstone building, about four stories tall, a skyscraper in its day. It sits apart from the other stores, with its brick frayed and cracking. The store front is as unappealing as it is uninviting, decorated with a chipped turquoise blue paint job that was last updated at least two decades ago. The windows are tinted, not by film, but by years and years of weathering, mold and age.

For most of the town, this building is largely invisible and written off as abandoned property.

But abandoned it is not.

Hanging at a slant above the entrance is a small wooden marquee with worn red letters that have seen better days:

Pastor Graham's Books.

Inside an elderly man pores over an equally aged book. The door chimes and he glances up from his book to greet his visitor. "Duncan," he says, a bit of surprise in his voice. A paroxysm of coughing seizes him. Eventually he declares, "Well . . . this is a treat."

"Afternoon, Pastor." Duncan slides a wooden chair over. It groans against the floor with a sharp complaint. "How are you feeling?"

Pastor Graham brings a handkerchief to his mouth and dabs. He's greeted by spots of blood, and quickly stuffs the handkerchief aside hoping that

Duncan will not notice, though it's clear from the flash of concern in the younger man's eyes that he was unsuccessful. "I'm fine." Playing it off, he clears his throat and asks, "What brings you by? Some light reading, perhaps?"

Duncan sizes up the bookstore. There's nothing *light* about this place, not the books nor the ambiance. Indeed, it is something out of the turn of the century, replete with floor-to-ceiling espresso-stained wood and bookshelves crammed with all things literary.

Books are stacked everywhere, some in crooked towers that rise toward the ceiling. Some in careless piles, strewn about on carts. Those books that rest on the shelves are a mishmash of titles impossible to discern since the place's lighting is so dim.

It's a miracle that anyone can navigate within the store, let alone find a book without tripping over something.

Upon noticing the young man's aloofness, "Duncan?"

"Sorry . . ." Duncan brings himself back to reality. He pulls off his glasses and wipes them with a microfiber cloth. "It's funny how we can put a man on the moon but can't create smudge-proof glasses."

Pastor Graham gently closes the book he was reading. Leans back in his chair. "What's wrong?"

"Travis," Duncan admits with a sigh as if the weight of the universe were on his shoulders. "He's what's wrong. There's no talking to him. He's upset at me for not telling him the truth about these," Duncan holds the gold beads around his neck. "And how they've kept me alive for the last six months." He tucks them back into his shirt.

Pastor Graham folds his hands together. The skin of his brow wrinkles with intent as he listens. "Go on."

"He's also mad that I didn't tell Amanda and kept her out of the loop. My loop."

"You had to be sure that we could trust them." Pastor Graham reaches out, lays a calming palm on Duncan's hand. "It was a necessary omission. I, myself, cut off all communication from everyone save for you, Duncan."

"I understand your caution, but perhaps Travis has a good point. A lie is still a lie." Duncan pulls away. "It's still a sin."

"This is true, and so we ask for forgiveness because we are human. Fallible. Unsure. Prone to err and of course . . . *sin*."

"I understand, but what if the forgiveness we need is from another man? From Travis. We need him to help us." Duncan's voice cracks, eyes widening with uncertainty. "Without him, we have no one."

"Then pray that Travis will forgive us."

"And if he doesn't, how do we take on the Rift? I'm not exactly street-fighting material, Pastor Graham. I can pray all day long and still my genetics won't change."

Pastor Graham takes a moment. Leans back in his chair again. "Seems your faith has been shaken."

"Tested, indeed."

"That is the nature of faith. However, we must trust that in the end, all will work out."

Duncan rises from the chair. He paces, fidgeting with several books on a nearby shelf. "The Rift continues to grow, Pastor Graham. They'll find us, rob us of the few treasures we have left, all while Travis fades into retirement." Duncan sorts the books based on size. "I'm not sure how it will all work out."

Pastor Graham lowers his head, lets out a chuckle.

Duncan pauses. "Pastor, this is not funny."

"No, it's not." He points at the books that Duncan has just rearranged. "But those *were* in alphabetical order."

Duncan stops. Takes a step back. Looks up and down at the bookshelf, then the room full of bookshelves. "No offense, but how do you know what is what in here? How do your customers know?"

"They ask, and I find." An easy smile warms the old man's face. "And as Jesus said, 'Ask and it will be given to you. Seek and you will find.'"

"Find what?" Duncan laughs to himself. "A book?"

"The answer," Pastor Graham replies. "Ask for it."

"Like how we will deal with the Rift?"

Pastor Graham spreads his arms, gesturing as if all of life's cards are laid before him. "Ask for help with everything. John 5:14 . . . ask for what you feel you need, and if it is congruent with God's will, then your request will be heard."

"I wish it were that simple."

"It *is* that simple. *We* complicate matters by trying to figure everything out, by trying to predict the future," Pastor Graham explains. "Our burden is heaviest when we trust in our own wisdom and not God's."

"Well, we need God's wisdom with this latest development." Duncan sits down. "I have an insider who works for the Rift."

"You do?"

Duncan nods. "And it is not Tizzy."

"Could this insider be exposing us to the Rift?"

"No," Duncan assures him. "We communicate using burner phones. The contact is only interested in money. I pay them for information. We never meet. It's all done digitally. I use a VPN so that my IP address can't be traced. I send them funds via cryptocurrency."

Pastor Graham stares at Duncan. "Forgive my ignorance, Duncan, but you did lose me there at the end."

"In short, I use the tools of the internet to maintain our anonymity from the Rift, since they are very adept at tracking our every movement." Duncan pulls out his cell phone. "And my source sent me some interesting footage."

"Is that so?"

"Yes." Duncan shows Pastor Graham several video clips of the first attack on the phosphate plant. "Someone has been pillaging the Rift hideouts. Pilfering what they have stolen from us over the years."

The footage is blurry. Brief shots of a hooded Simon storming the plant. Wreaking havoc and rescuing Balco.

Duncan goes on, "And this someone supposedly has been freeing an-gels—angels that the Rift had captured for who knows what sinister reason."

"Hmm . . ." Pastor Graham nods towards a roll of paper towels. "Could you pass me that please?"

Duncan obliges.

"Thank you." Armed with a bottle of furniture oil, the aged pastor methodically and painstakingly polishes a grand bookshelf adorned with wooden reliefs. "You know, Duncan, I have always found it interesting how certain woods soak up the oil in different ways." He rubs one particularly stubborn shelf with a little more elbow grease. "The splendor of variation in all of God's world."

"Pastor, did you hear me?" A tinge of frustration clips the end of Duncan's question. "This thief is freeing *angels*."

"I'm old, not deaf." He laughs inwardly. "*Yet.*" He continues to wipe down the shelf with long, caring swipes. Once satisfied, he steps back and admires his work. "The angels you speak of . . . they have a name." Pastor Graham's gaze meets Duncan's with a weighted seriousness now. "The Amissa."

"The Amissa?" Duncan cleans his glasses compulsively and then parks them back on the bridge of his nose.

"*The lost.*"

"Lost? From Heaven?"

"Yes. Tempted by man to seek more than the kingdom of God," Pastor Graham elaborates. "But they barely managed to escape. Michael showed up, scythe in hand. He took to them with the vengeance of God. The Amissa quickly went from having a hundred angels to several dozen."

"But if Michael was sent by God to strike these angels down, how was it that he failed at the task? God's will is absolute."

"Agreed. So perhaps God allowed those angels to escape so that some greater work could be done via their meddling in human affairs? This is only speculation as I cannot pretend to opine on God's intentions."

Duncan shakes his head in disbelief. "But why would they choose to leave Heaven . . . to come here? Who would want to leave God's side?"

"These are those who are full of pride. But now that they have had a taste of this corrupt world, and find it quite disappointing, they want to go back home. To do that, they will have to seek salvation and forgiveness from God." Pastor Graham sighs. "But since they are a prideful lot, asking for forgiveness is not in their nature. It would be to admit defeat and to say they chose poorly. So, they are looking for another way."

"Another way? There is no other way but through God."

"Oh, there is."

"You mean, the manacles? But we lost those in Japan."

"Well it looks like the Rift found them." Pastor Graham smiles gently. "Or at least part of them."

"What do you mean? The manacles are not complete?"

"Oh no; they are complete. But as with any such type of restraint, they need a key to open them, and that my friend, is something the Covenant lost long before you or I existed." Pastor Graham pulls out his phone. It takes him a few moments. "You know," sighing as he taps away at the touch screen, "I am not one for all of this technology. As you can see . . . I prefer books. Much easier on my eyes." He holds the phone up so that Duncan can view it. "However, I cannot discount the wonder of convenience that technology also brings. It would take me a good few hours, perhaps days, to reference where I last saw *the* key. Thankfully I took a picture of it."

Duncan stares at the picture.

It is a plain silver pendant in the shape of a cross, no bigger than a quarter.

"The manacles unlock portals to the next life. To access these portals, you need a key—the silver pendant. When we had the manacles in our possession, we effectively maintained half of the puzzle, protecting those sacred gateways from being opened. Now that we have lost them, all is fair game." Pastor Graham puts his phone away. "I imagine that the Amissa and their rescuer would like nothing more than to get their hands on both treasures."

"And the Rift?" Duncan asks. "Why have they been keeping these rogue angels imprisoned in the first place?"

"Perhaps they're seeking the key to the manacles as well? Extracting information from them? Or maybe they're using the Amissa for a more pernicious purpose—"

The front door swings open and a blonde woman stands before them. Her face is contorted by an expression of vile betrayal.

Upon seeing her, Duncan pales several shades as his skin goes pasty white.

"I thought maybe I was hallucinating when I saw you through the window," the woman hisses between gritted teeth.

To himself, Duncan stammers, "Oh . . . no."

"But I see that hallucination hasn't evaporated like I thought *you had six months ago!* So I guess you're really alive, then, huh?" Amanda spits his name like it's a curse, "*Duncan.*"

Duncan melts into his chair. "I can explain."

Chapter 11 – Cleverhill Realty

T ravis pulls into a gas station just off the highway. He's ten minutes south of Nashville. Inside he loads up on bottled water, beef jerky, and energy bars. At the counter a gruff young clerk with a Viking-worthy beard rings Travis up.

As the clerk scans his items, Travis's attention wanders. He catches sight of a home seller magazine:

Cleverhill Realty.

Nashville owned and operated since 1970. We know Music City.

Travis grabs the magazine and the clerk protests, "Hey, that's not free!"

Confused for a moment, Travis shoots the young man a look.

The clerk breaks into a smile behind the bushy tuft of his finely manicured beard. "Just kidding." He holds up Travis's bag. Travis promptly grabs it and storms out.

"Lighten up, man," the clerk says under his breath.

Travis pauses. He can almost sense the clerk freeze. He heads out to his car, tosses the bag of food onto the passenger seat, and then stares at the realty flyer.

He decides Cleverhill Realty is the name of the next destination on his list. Before going there, he calls to make sure they're still in business and when someone answers, he gives them a brief run-down of exactly what he is looking for.

No time to waste.

Just outside of city limits, it's an odd building, with a triangular roof and a narrow layout. Maybe it was a restaurant before, perhaps an old IHOP, now converted into a new use. The chimes on the door clang as Travis enters. He is greeted inside with the smell of mildew, the tang of ammonia, and the stale aroma of yesterday's greasy pancakes. He parks himself at a desk that is placed uncomfortably close to the door. The Feng Shui of this place is completely off. As he sizes up the room, he catches the old kitchen counter—no doubt once covered with eggs and stacks of French toast, now a sorry mess of towering faux wood accounting boxes and random three-ring binders choked with paperwork. Above the chaos of paperwork, several rusting AC vents with ribbons tied to their diffusers struggle to put out enough air to keep the place somewhat comfortable.

"Be right there," a woman calls from behind a makeshift wall. The sound of heels clacking against the weathered floor draw close. An older woman, early sixties with a beehive hairdo, emerges. Her hair is a murky brown, browner than it should be as it doesn't match her complexion, giving her an almost vampiric look. Horned rimmed glasses with lenses as thick as coasters give her hazel eyes an eerie magnified quality.

She looks like she just stepped out of 1969.

Travis feels like he's staring at a fish with bad hair.

She extends her hand, and he shakes it. "Name's Glory, Glory Cleverhill," she announces with a broad smile that lights up her face. Her southern accent is intense and as thick as it gets in these parts. "And you're?"

"Travis."

She pauses, waiting for him to say his last name, but he doesn't. Not missing a beat, she continues, "Well afternoon . . . *Travis*. How'd you hear about my office?"

Travis holds up the magazine he got from the convenience store.

"Great," she says as she seats herself and scoots her chair up. Travis examines the room as she gets situated. The place looks like a minimalist's worst nightmare: a jumbled office filled with boxes, files, and random stacks of paper strewn about.

Noting his expression, Glory chimes in, "'Scuse the mess. Just moved into the place."

Travis nods.

"At my age, moving is quite the ordeal," she admits with a chuckle. "My husband died five years ago, and boy do I miss him. Could've used his help with the move. He was a beast of a man."

"I'm sorry," Travis mutters.

"Oh, thanks, honey." Glory opens a laptop, her glasses slipping down her face as she cranes her neck forward. "He died doing what he loved." She types away, then looks up at Travis. "He died playing golf."

"Golf?"

"Yes, sir." She continues on the keyboard, typing for what seems like eons. "Had himself a widow maker on the eighteenth hole. Dropped dead as a doornail. EMT said he didn't feel a thing."

Travis says nothing. His sympathy for her loss quickly giving way to impatience.

"If you're going to go out, at least go out doing what God gives you the most joy doing."

Not sure what that would be for me, Travis thinks, *but maybe the answer lies inside a nice home in the country far, far away from the noise and needs of people.*

Glory pauses, then squints. Her eyes thin into black lines behind her thick lenses. "You know, I'm feeling a lil' lethargic this morning. I need a cup of Joe. Got an old Bunn machine in the back. You care for a cup of coffee as well?"

Travis nods. "Love one."

Glory smiles—a smile that says she's probably as happy to have company as she is to have a customer. As Travis eyes the place, he wonders just how busy she is. The place is in shambles. Smells like this room hasn't had human contact in two decades. He starts to wonder if she's really a realtor or posing as one.

I'm going to give her about the time it takes to make that cup of coffee, he thinks, *then I'm going to walk out that door and find me another realtor. Elderly or not, she moves at the speed of a snail and talks too freakin' much—*

An odd but familiar sensation overtakes him.

Time . . .

Slows . . .

Down . . .

"Tell me something," A voice says behind him. The door chime is never disturbed, which *disturbs* Travis. He jumps up, spins around, and finds himself face-to-face with a hooded man—the *angel* who ambushed the Rift back at the tattoo parlor. "Why are you hiding?" Travis reaches for his gun, but the angel holds up a hand. Reminds him, "You know that won't work on me."

Travis hesitates, still resting his hand on his Beretta even though he's equally positive that angels aren't as susceptible to acute lead poisoning as normal mortals. "I'm hiding because I want to stay out of trouble and be left alone. That too much to ask?"

The angel doesn't respond.

"Anyway, who are you?" Travis asks. "And why are you following me?"

"I'll tell you later . . . *maybe.*"

"Nah. You can tell me now."

The angel smirks.

"I'm not screwing around." Travis feels his body tighten and his patience wane. "Why are you following me?"

The angel steps forward and sunlight illuminates the lower half of his face. "Because it's what I've been tasked to do."

"You with the Rift?"

Without hesitation, "Fuck them."

Travis raises an eye.

"What? You think because I have wings that means I can't curse? This wicked world taints all who walk upon it." A smile bordering on a sneer widens across the angel's face. "You really don't know anything."

"Ignorance is bliss, right? But what I do know, is that I'm an angel magnet. Attracting the likes of Zach . . . and . . . *whoever* you are."

"Zach? You mean Zachariel?"

"Yeah. Him." Travis nods. "He's one of you."

"He's a foolish errand boy."

"You're all the same to me. Confusing, weird and pushy," Travis says with a dismissive shrug. "Anyway, what do you want?" Travis looks around, then back towards the kitchen, wondering what black hole Glory fell into.

But she didn't disappear anywhere.

She's stuck in the glue of Godspeed where nothing moves save for the celestial beings that have the supernatural ability to traverse it. Parked in front of her decades old Bunn machine, crusty carafe in one hand, mug in the other. A river of coffee is suspended between the spout and the mouth of the mug.

The ribbons tied to the AC vents are frozen horizontally.

There are several birds outside, formerly fighting over a scrap of what Travis presumes to be bread. They too are motionless in their pursuit of a meal—

"I need your help . . ." There's a measured pause. "*Unfortunately.*"

"Unfortunately? Hey, you're the one stalking me."

The angel glowers.

Travis continues, "And trust me . . . I'm actually not in the help-giving mood."

"You don't have a choice."

"According to God and Zach, I do." Travis says with a wink, "Free will, right?"

"You don't have a choice."

"I always have a choice!"

"Not this time." The angel's tone sharpens. "Time to think about more than yourself."

There's a flash – a brief image of Amanda wishing him well on his retirement – that pops in Travis's head, igniting a trace of anger that fuels his words: "It's thinking about myself that has kept me alive all of these years. Now stay away from me."

"Trust me . . ." the angel admits, "I wish I could." He backs toward the door.

The two of them stare at each other, locked in a competition of who will break their gaze first.

"Hide all you want." The angel glances in Glory's direction, then back at Travis. "I'll find you again."

Travis taps his gun handle in response.

The angel scoffs and fades through the door without touching it. "Stubborn man." He disappears just as time resumes a normal pace.

Travis feels the shift, almost like a thinning in the air.

The birds outside finish their scuffle over the indiscernible crumbs.

The ribbons on the AC vent flutter to life.

"I'm so sorry, hon!" Glory calls out from the former kitchen. "That doggone machine is slower than molasses in January." Glory's footsteps draw near.

"It's fine, Glory," Travis checks outside. The angel has vanished.

Glory rounds the corner, tray in hand. Two coffee cups rattle against a plastic container brimming with sugar, Splenda and Equal.

Travis sits down.

"I much appreciate your patience, but I promise you this coffee is worth the wait. I believe this is like a Sumatara . . . or Sumarta—"

"*Sumatra*," Travis says, wondering just how much patience he can afford. The sooner he can vanish, the better he surmises he'll feel. The anxiety of police, Rift, the Covenant, and now more angels, only reinforces his unease. Add Glory's lackadaisical approach, and that only serves to amplify his apprehension.

"Yes! That's it. A Sumatra blend. My friend, Mary Bell, says it'll put some pep in your step. She swears it's so darn good you might even see into the future!"

Wish I had some of that coffee years ago, Travis thinks. *Would've picked better Lotto numbers and left the transporting business a lot sooner.*

"I think when you first called me, you mentioned wanting a nice home in the country," Glory says as the sounds of ceramic cups clang together. "Some ideas popped in this old brain of mine. Far away from people, you said, right?"

"Yeah, that's correct."

"You know, in this day of cell phones and social media, everybody's in a hurry to get somewhere, do something or talk to somebody." She hands Travis a mug and sits. "I'm surprised you're not playing with your phone yourself."

"Glory, I just might be the most antisocial person you'll ever meet. That's *why* I want a house in the country as far away from people as possible."

"Perfect. I might not be the fastest realtor in the East, but I know my Nashville! And I got some places in mind!"

Travis gives her a thumbs up as he takes a sip of coffee. *I hope so,* he thinks. *I'm about half a cup away from leaving and finding someone else.*

"So . . ." Glory's gaze shifts away from the computer, eyes appearing huge behind those thick-lens glasses. "How's the coffee?"

Travis hesitates, wanting to say nothing more than *good.* It's just coffee at this point. His mind is somewhere else. But instead, he politely offers, "It's delicious. Thank you."

Pleased with his answer, she refocuses on her laptop.

"Come to think of it . . ." Travis nods towards her computer. "Can that thing tell you if they got any houses for sale in Sumatra?"

Chapter 12 – Duncan and Amanda

Duncan practically jumps out of his seat. "Amanda, seriously . . . I can explain!"

"Don't bother." Amanda is already back out the door.

"Amanda!" Duncan scrambles after her. "Wait!"

Amanda is almost to her car when he catches up. She spins on her heels and pushes him away. "Get away from me!"

Duncan is taken aback. Caught off guard by her strength. "Amanda . . . please." He puts his hands up in surrender. "Just calm down."

She stews. Eyes wide and glistening with anger.

Duncan reaches to gently touch her shoulder, hoping to console her—

"Don't touch me!"

Duncan reels from the outburst, her reaction. She's always been so cool, calm and collected. He offers, "I'm sorry." Then continues, "Look, I didn't expect you to catch up with me like this. You surprised me."

"I surprised *you?* Are you kidding me?" The heat of anger reddens her cheeks. "You were dead. Or at least I thought you were. And now, six months later, I find you alive? How?" She presses a palm to her forehead to try to suppress the rage. "And why didn't you call?"

Duncan surveys their surroundings. There's a few people on the street, walking, talking, and peering into store windows. A pregnant woman pushes a stroller. A postman fumbles with a stack of boxes that he's unloading from his truck. An old lady chats away on her cell.

Anyone of these people could be the Rift, Duncan thinks.

"Can we talk inside your car?" he asks Amanda.

She sighs. "Fine."

The two of them hop into her car, windows up.

"Speak!" she demands.

Duncan takes a deep breath as though he's about to dive off a cliff. "Ok, so in order to survive, I had to borrow something from the Rift—"

Amanda immediately digs into his shirt, pulls out the rosary beads. She leans back in her seat, face twisting in disgust.

"Jeez, Amanda!" Duncan says as he nervously glances at the passersby outside. He promptly tucks the beads away. "Now look . . . I had to do this in order to survive what Lomak did to me."

"It's dark magic, Duncan. You have no clue what you are messing with!"

"I know, I know, I know." His glasses slide slightly down the bridge of his nose, and he pushes them up, smudging the lenses in the process. "But I had no choice."

"Yes, you did."

"Would you rather I had died?"

"At this point . . . I'm not sure!"

The words bite. It takes a second for Duncan to recover. "It was a last resort. I barely came to, put them on, and escaped the house before it exploded."

Right now, I feel like exploding, Amanda thinks.

"Please. Cut me a little slack." Duncan reaches out, grabs her hand.

"I said *don't touch me.*" She jerks her hand away. "You didn't have to face Lomak alone. You could've asked for my help, but instead you chose to leave me in the dark. That's why I came out to see Pastor Graham. I needed answers. And boy, did I get them."

"Look, I didn't want to expose you to Lomak."

"A little late! You didn't have that psycho lick your face and kidnap you."

"No, I only had him gut me like a fish."

"And you waited six months to tell me . . . no hold on a second. You never *told* me. I just stumbled into you!"

"I needed the Rift to believe I was dead – and I darn nearly was – but the hope was that if Lomak thought I was done for, that perhaps he would assume that the Covenant had all but run out of members."

"What do you think?" Amanda asks. "They're keeping attendance?"

"I'm sure they know there are very few of us left."

"How do you know that?"

"Because there *are* very few of us left," Duncan says. "They killed off all of our transporters for starters!"

"They didn't kill Travis."

"Yeah and take a look around." Duncan gestures toward the street. "Where is he?"

Amanda eyes the people outside. A flock of pigeons mill about under a park bench as an elderly man tosses out seeds; a father and son eat ice cream as they stroll past; a shopkeeper sweeps the dirt from his patio.

"Amanda . . . he may as well have been killed off by the Rift. He wants nothing to do with us."

"You know that *how*?"

"Because I talked to him."

Amanda looks at Duncan squarely now.

"That's what Travis said? Those are the words he told you?"

"Seriously, Sis, I talked to him recently, and he's done."

"You talked to him, before you talked to me?" Amanda turns away, takes a deep breath. "I-I-I just can't believe this right now."

"I was going to tell you—"

"When?!" She looks back at him, acid in her words, "In another six months?"

"I had to meet with Travis first! I needed to see if he would help us. But he doesn't want to."

Amanda catches a glimmer of *more-to-the-story* in his eye and narrows her gaze, "And why's that . . . *Duncan*?"

"Because he's upset," Duncan sighs. "Because I . . . lied."

The fury in Amanda's face becomes more apparent by the moment. Her nostrils flare. Her breathing changes. She doesn't even seem to blink—she just stares at him like he's the worst person on the planet.

Duncan reads all of this. Offers, "Hey, I did what I had to do. I let the Rift believe they killed me, one of the Covenant's top people, so that they would never go after you. So that they would never realize you are even a part of us."

"You're way too late on that."

"What are you talking about?"

Amanda squeezes her eyes shut tight. This is like a bad dream. Her brother is a fabricator. And adding to that, he doesn't really know about *her* past. The Rift is very aware of Amanda, and Vanessa made sure to remind her of that fact before Travis killed her. "You think you know everything. Think you got it all figured out, don't you?"

"Amanda, what—"

"You don't know a thing about me! And you don't need to shelter me from the world! I joined the Covenant of my own free will, *not* because I wanted to follow in your footsteps and *not* because I was afraid to expose myself to the Rift."

"Ok, so I was wrong. I was just trying to protect you."

"The world doesn't revolve around you." Amanda grinds her teeth. Looks away.

"I never thought Lomak would find out about you."

"He found out about me because I let someone in that I shouldn't have. Someone I thought was looking to change their life, not take advantage of the kindness of strangers."

"Are you talking about Tizzy?"

Amanda nods.

Duncan swallows. "And . . . where is she?"

"Don't know. Don't care. She's a traitor, and she sold us out to the Rift."

Duncan goes cold.

Tizzy is the mole? He thinks as he feels his soul shrivel.

He had doubted his sister, kept her in the dark because he thought he could not trust her. And here someone else was to blame for the Covenant's betrayal.

Yet he betrayed his own sister.

Worried that Amanda can read the shame in his face, he turns away and catches sight of the pigeons at the old woman's feet, plundering the seeds beneath her.

"What?" Amanda asks.

Duncan watches the pigeons. With nothing left to eat, the winged scavengers take flight into the crystal blue sky above.

"Hey!" Amanda's voice makes him jump. "What's up?"

"Tizzy is the mole?"

Amanda acknowledges this with a nod. "Yes . . . and I told Jakob and Noam this when Travis and I delivered the spectacles to them."

Duncan processes this.

"I figured they would have told you . . . or Pastor Graham," Amanda says.

"I advised him to not reach out to anyone, to lay low, and I myself have not spoken with the brothers."

"Why?"

Duncan lets out an uneasy laugh. "You know . . . I'm paranoid. I don't know who I can trust."

"Well . . . you've done a wonderful job of proving that to me!"

But her words seem to go right over his head as Duncan freezes. Stares blankly at the floor of the car. "Tizzy . . ." His eyes widen. "She knows."

"Knows what?"

"Oh, my goodness." Duncan puts a hand to his face. "I'm an idiot. I should've pushed Pastor Graham to relocate! But with his illness and his stubborn opposition to moving, I didn't press him. This is his home after all. The books. The smell of the place. This quaint, little town. Still . . . I should've urged him to move, but it would have been like trying to uproot an oak tree."

"So, you mean if Tizzy knows about the bookstore . . ."

Their eyes meet, as Duncan finishes for her, "Then the Rift know."

Chapter 13 – Home Sweet Home?

Glory and Travis pull up to a log cabin hugging the side of a mountain. Trees cling desperately to the angled rocks and hills. The sun lifts from the east, spreading a gentle warmth along the property line. She parks and the two hop out. They are met with the distant chirps of birds and the hushed whistle of a soothing wind that carries with it the promise of peace.

Glory gives Travis a moment to take it all in. Then gestures towards the home. "What's your first impression of this one?"

The last few homes fell under several unappealing categories for Travis:

1. Too close to other people.
2. Not remote enough. Cell phones still worked.
3. A lack of southern charm.

Glory hopes she hit a winner with this home. As she studies Travis, asks, "Well, hon, what are you thinking? You like what you see?"

Travis sizes up the home. The nearest neighbor is at least a mile away. He takes out his cell phone. Cellular service is definitely weak. The fact that it was a log cabin screamed southern enough to him. While he was not a connoisseur of all things Americana, he knew what he liked and this place rang true.

"So far, so good," he answers.

Glory's smile stretches as far as the horizon. "Had a feelin' you'd say that."

"This place have a story to it?"

"Just two," she says with a laugh, noting that it has two floors. "Truth be told, the owners got tired of the serenity. Craved the city life."

"Sucks for them."

Glory shuts the car door and Travis almost tells her that she forgot to set the car alarm, but then remembers that they are far away from city life.

Things are going to be a lot safer out here, he thinks.

I hope.

"The place does have running water, right?" Travis asks, a hint of both sarcasm and seriousness in his voice.

Glory puts her hands on her hips and lets out a righteous, *humpf!* which pretty much answers that question. "Honey, I said I'd find you something nice. Might not be in the Sumatra or wherever in Sam Hill you mentioned, but it ain't no dump either. You're still part of the twenty-first century here, with running water, electricity, satellite TV, et cetera. However, if you are one of them porno addicts, I'll best be warning you that internet here is about as quick as moss growing on the north side of a tree stump."

"Glory, you had me at running water," Travis says. "Now let's see the rest of the house."

It's surprisingly bright inside considering the walls are all wood and the way the house sits huddled under the dense trees. It's welcomingly sunlit. The living room and kitchen are situated as one large room. The kitchen boasts a small window that looks out onto the side of the mountain below.

"When was this place built?" Travis asks as he marvels at the interior.

"Late eighties." Glory runs her hand along the concrete countertop. "But as you can see, it's been upgraded."

Stainless steel appliances. Custom counter. Commercial-sized stove.

Yep, it's definitely not 1985 anymore.

There isn't even a stale odor in the air that one would expect with an older home.

It almost smells like—

"New construction," Travis mumbles to himself.

"What?"

"Sorry." Travis eyes the upgrades. "It smells brand new in here."

Glory nods. "Yes, sir. You are looking at a well-cared for residence. They spent a pretty penny updating it."

Travis also notices that all the furniture, including wall art, décor, and electronics are still here.

"Do the owners still live here?"

"Nope. Like I said, they had an itch for the city. Left for Nashville months ago. Cabin's been vacant since." She adds with an eager smile, "These sellers are very motivated."

Travis waves a finger in the air. "What about all of their stuff?"

Glory shrugs. "The couple wanted a fresh start. If you want it, it's fully furnished. If not, they'll gladly remove everything."

"There an extra cost for the furniture?"

"A grand."

"*A grand?*" Travis scoffs. "They're motivated alright. Is it haunted?"

The question strikes Glory as curious. "The furniture or the house?"

"Well . . ." Not that Travis subscribes to that, but offhandedly jokes, "Both?"

Glory sighs. "There's no voodoo here. And I assure you that I'm not here to waste your time or mine."

"Fair enough," Travis says. "Can I see the upstairs?"

Outside Glory again asks what Travis thinks.

Travis stuffs his hands in his pockets and gives the house a long, hard look.

"You don't have to make a decision right now," Glory adds.

"I know." He runs his hand along the rough wooden exterior then completes a few solid taps. Nodding to himself, he looks back at Glory. "I'll take it."

Glory beams, eyelids fluttering with unexpected excitement. "R-really?"

Travis nods his head *yes*.

"But I do have a few other properties–"

"I said I'll take it."

"You sure you don't want to see any other homes?"

Travis glances back at the home once more. Scans the tree lines. The way the home nestles closely to the hill. The crisp blue sky above. Several birds flying overhead caw as they pass. They and the country air are the only things that can be heard for miles. "No, I'm good. When you know," he shoots her a smile, "you just know."

They hop back into the car and Glory asks "Gut instinct, huh?"

"Only fails me when I ignore it."

"And how about financing?"

Travis leans back in his seat. "How about all cash?"

Glory claps her hands together, giddy. "Oh, you're going to be so at home! I'm so glad I could find you a place so quickly. I wish all of my customers were like you."

As they drive off, Travis glances back at the house. "Trust me. You don't want that."

"Why's that?"

"Because I'm the most antisocial guy you've ever met."

"Well, you've been awfully cordial with me."

"That's because this is business." Travis offers her a grim smile.

It's the only thing I'm good at. Or at least so I thought.

An awkward moment passes, Glory starts the car. Asks, "So may I ask you a personal question?"

"Maybe."

"What are you running from?"

"What do you mean?"

"Well, you're obviously not wanting to be around many people, which I respect wholeheartedly, but just as you trust your gut, I trust mine and mine tells me that you're running from something." She gives him the side eye. "Am I wrong?"

"No, you're not wrong," Travis admits. "I am running from people trying to dictate my life."

"You don't have to do what they say, you know."

Travis says nothing. Stares out the window at the rolling green hills that swoop up and down like great waves.

"God done blessed us with free will," Glory says. "We're not here to please man, you know? We're here to please God first and foremost."

Travis plants his head in his hands. *Dear God, can I ever escape this never-ending fortune cookie, Bible-fueled life? If one more person mentions free will . .*
.

"If you don't mind, I'd rather not talk about all that. Be nice to take a breather from any kind of religious talk, to be honest." Travis looks at Glory whose face is . . .

Somehow softer, younger, and more angelic.

It's Zach.

Travis does a little hop in his seat.

"Then go on this journey on your own." Zach lets go of the wheel and folds his arms. The car begins careening towards the cliff edge; nothing but air is on the other side of the railing.

"Jesus! Zach!" Travis dives for the wheel, but not before the car smashes through the barrier and does a swan dive into the valley below.

There's an explosion of glass and metal and Travis is instantly reminded of his first encounter with Lomak and his Mustang careening off the road. That brutal crash. Everything floating in mid-air–

"You ok there, hun?" Glory asks.

Travis jumps. *What the hell? Where am I?*

He finds himself still securely buckled into his car seat.

Glory – not Zach – is at the wheel. They are safely parked in front of the realty office. She touches him lightly in the shoulder. "I'm sorry, hon, didn't mean to wake you, but you done fell asleep on the way back from the cabin."

Travis rubs his eyes. "I did?"

Glory laughs to herself. "Yes, sir. And you were snoozing all peaceful-like. These country roads will do that to you."

I don't know about all that, Travis thinks as he unbuckles his seatbelt. "Glory, why did you ask me if I was running from something?"

Glory stares at him like he's got two heads. "What?"

"Uhm, back there? When we left the cabin."

"Hon, last thing you and I were talking about was how I wished all my customers were like you. Next thing I know, your eyes are rolled up the back of your head and you gotta lick of slobber running down your chin."

"I guess I did pass out." Travis presses his fingers to his head. "And man, do I feel a headache coming on."

"Well, how about I make you a cup of that Sumatra coffee? Caffeine is good for migraines."

"Nah, I think I'll skip the coffee. My mind is stimulated enough."

They get out of the car and Travis shakes her hand. "Mind if we settle up the paperwork and stuff later? I think I need to rest."

"Of course, Mr. Rail. I completely understand. Last thing you want to do is fill out a bunch of forms or talk about mortgages and the like when you got a band playing drums in your head."

A band? It's more like a war zone.

"Well, you just come on back when you are ready." With a light chuckle, she adds, "But don't wait too long. I can't hold the property forever."

"Don't worry. My word is good." Travis gives her a thumb's up and just before he's at his car, he turns around and says, "Oh, and Glory?"

She's almost inside. "Yes?"

"Mind if we meet somewhere else to do the closing?" Travis motions towards his head. "Something in your office sets off my headache, I think."

Something as in some angel.

Or angels.

Glory smiles wide. "But of course, hon."

Travis fakes a smile, gets into his car and drives off.

Chapter 14 – Welcome Surprise

Rays of sunlight pierce the dusty interior of Pastor Graham's bookstore as Tizzy struts in. The door chime summons Pastor Graham from behind a shelf. As their eyes meet, he feels his skin go cold.

"Hey, Pastor G!"

"Tizrah."

"*Tizzy*." She looks back toward the door and then to him. "Were you expecting someone else?"

He was. Perhaps it's that obvious on his face. He frowns, trying to recover with a very limp, "No, no. I just didn't fancy seeing you here."

"What, you think I forgot where this place was?"

"I didn't think you cared."

"What gave you that impression?"

"Many things."

"I can read that judgmental look in your eyes like a fucking billboard, Pastor."

Pastor Graham clears his throat. "Tizrah—*Tizzy*, why are you here?"

"I'm more curious why you didn't relocate this place. Once you guys knew I wasn't," and she dances on the word, "*trustworthy*, why not up and leave?"

"What are you talking about?"

Tizzy freezes. "You serious?" She laughs mockingly. It almost sounds like a cough. "You mean, you don't know?"

Pastor Graham's eyes narrow. "Know what?"

Tizzy throws her hands in the air. "Jesus, you guys really suck at communication!" She steps closer to him and confesses, "I've been feeding the Rift info since I joined you losers."

The word comes out acerbically. "Why?"

"Because they pay better than you. I just needed a place to hang my hat until I found something better." Tizzy runs her hand along a shelf, tapping the tops of each book with her fingers. "And now I found myself an even better employer than you and the Rift."

"Who might that be?"

"None of your business, that's who."

Pastor Graham glares at her as she struts about the store, fiddling with anything she comes into contact with: pencils, books, an old globe. "I'm sorry to learn that nothing that Amanda and I have shared with you over the years has resonated."

Tizzy gives the globe a forceful jerk, and it spins wildly. "What are you talking about?"

"If indeed you were under that much financial duress, you could have just come to me. Or Amanda for that matter," Pastor Graham explains. "She took you under her wing. Tried to get you off the streets."

"Well, she failed."

"No, you failed yourself."

Tizzy shrugs. "Whatever."

Pastor Graham breaks into a coughing fit. He fumbles for his handkerchief, fighting to suppress the coughs as much as possible.

"Sounds like someone better start praying to God for some fucking better healthcare."

Pastor Graham ignores her as he wipes the blood from his lips.

"Aren't you part of AARP or some shit?"

"What do you want?"

"What do I want?" Tizzy laughs. "Well it sure as shit isn't your collection of dictionaries." She finds a book on a shelf at random and pulls it down. Flips through the pages, feigning interest. "I mean, who'd buy these old ass books?" She slams the book shut and a cloud of dust swirls up.

Pastor Graham's chest swells. He takes a step towards her, his shoulders arching forward. "So, then what are you here for?"

Tizzy tosses the book clumsily on a table where it slides off and lands on the ground with a thud.

"Are you here to kill me?"

"That depends on you," she says. "Do you have the pendant?"

"What pendant?"

Tizzy approaches him, stops short, then suddenly knees him in the groin. He's sent buckling over in agony. "Don't play dumb."

Pastor Graham exhales, takes a moment to allow the pain to subside, wincing as he rises. "I'm sorry, but the only treasure I possess currently is the gift of forgiveness."

Tizzy punches him in the face. A resultant crack echoes through the room. "Are you serious, Grampa? You think I came here to apologize *to you?*"

Pastor Graham recovers slowly. "There is no need to apologize to me for your trespasses against us." His bottom lip is split open. He touches it and glances down at the beads of blood on his fingers. "I forgive you, my child."

Tizzy delivers a right cross. This one knocks him to his knees. She pulls out her gun and presses it to his head. "I'm not your child," she growls. "And I'm not here to fuck around. I'm looking for that cross pendant. Where is it?"

The words are raspy, rumbling up from his throat. "I have no idea."

"Liar! I know you know where it's at." Tizzy swats him with the butt of the gun on the back of the head and he cries out. "You run the fucking Covenant." She pushes him to his knees. "So, tell me where the fuck it is—"

The front door swings open.

Amanda and Duncan rush in. Their jaws drop when they see Tizzy there, standing above Pastor Graham, gun locked firmly against the old man's temple.

"Tizzy?" Amanda asks.

"Check it out." Tizzy drives Pastor Graham towards the ground. "It's a family reunion." To Duncan, "Hey, I thought your scrawny ass was dead?"

"And I thought you had values," Duncan replies.

"Yeah, I do. I value money and opportunity."

"Why are you here? What do you want?" Amanda demands.

"The cross pendant. Where is it?"

"We don't have it."

"Give me a break," Tizzy insists. "I know you weirdos are all about hoarding God's shit."

"I'm telling you the truth," Amanda says. "We don't have the pendant."

Tizzy feels panic set in. She hadn't thought this far ahead. She figured fear and intimidation would motivate them to talk, but no one is offering anything useful.

Useful, Tizzy thinks. *I gotta stay fucking useful; otherwise that prick is gonna slay me with one of those flying freaks.*

Tizzy's hand betrays her. It starts to shake. She distracts both herself and the others by shouting, "Don't you assholes lie to me!" She grinds the muzzle against Pastor Graham's head. He grimaces as the weapon digs into his skull like a nail.

"Tizzy, stop!" Amanda steps forward, hand outstretched.

"Take another step and he's dead."

Amanda retreats.

Tizzy motions to the door. "Lock it. We're taking a short lunch break."

Amanda does as asked.

"Please . . . " Pastor Graham pleads. Gestures to Duncan and Amanda. "Leave them out of this."

"Shut! Up! They walked in on this shit." Tizzy points at herself. "I didn't invite them."

"They truly don't know where the pendant is," Pastor Graham assures her. "No one knows."

"You guys are trying to play me. Ha." Tizzy starts tapping her foot. She quickens her movements, backing away from Pastor. Alternates aiming the gun between the three of them. She then tells Pastor Graham, "And they call you the brains of this operation."

"God is the brains," he replies. "I am merely His servant—"

"Give it a rest!" Tizzy kicks him in the ribs. He flops onto the ground with a grunt. "We both know that the Rift has the manacles. They took them from your delivery boy in Japan. But *who* has the pendant?"

He wheezes out, "Not us."

Tizzy's cell phone rings. Without taking her eyes off the trio, she fishes out the phone. Answers with a curt, "Yeah?"

It's Simon. "Where are you?"

"I'm here with Team Jesus," she says, followed by a nervous laugh.

"What *team*? I thought you said there's just an old man," Simon demands. "That's why I sent you alone!"

"Guess I caught 'em during Bible study." Tizzy looks to Amanda, who stares her down with a blistering, vehement fire in her eyes. Tizzy feels something inside her quiver. She shifts her attention back to Pastor Graham.

"Whatever. We're on the way," Simon tells her. "I hope you have something useful for me. Understand?"

"Loud and clear, Mr. Simon."

"Thanks for telling them my name. Idiot."

Tizzy promptly hangs up. Curses under her breath.

Tizzy, girl, you gotta get your shit together. Get those nerves in check.

"So, who's Simon?" Amanda asks.

"You're about to meet him. And trust me, he's a real asshole." Pushing beyond the trembling nerves she's trying desperately to conceal by stiffening her body; she shouts, "Ok. Last chance! Tell me where the pendant is, or the old fart meets Jesus!"

"I told you, Tizzy, they don't know," Pastor Graham insists, his breathing labored.

You gotta do something; otherwise Simon's gonna take you out, Tizzy thinks. *They treated you like a kid anyway – like a damn stray rescued from the streets – so fuck them and their judgmental bull.*

There's a crazed spark in Tizzy's eyes, a shift in her countenance illuminating something menacing about her intentions.

Amanda reads it like a front-page headline: *Tizzy is going to pull the trigger.*

With a speed that even surprises herself, Amanda flings a book at Tizzy. It smacks her in the face, catching the young woman completely off guard. Tizzy brings the gun up just as Amanda slams into her, knocking her over

Pastor Graham.

The gun goes skidding.

Amanda dives for it, but Tizzy gets to her feet. With a roar, Tizzy catches Amanda by her shirt and throws her against a bookshelf. Amanda clips her chin on one of the shelves, stumbles, and crashes to the ground.

Tizzy goes for the gun.

As do Duncan and Pastor Graham.

The three of them collide. A tangled mess of arms and bodies reaching, twisting, fumbling for the weapon. Grunting and groaning amid the tussle—

The gun goes off.

There's a yelp.

Time slogs to a halt.

Amanda pushes herself to her feet. A red welt marks her chin, face stricken with worry as she wonders if her brother has taken a bullet.

But it is Pastor Graham who rolls onto his back, a crimson gash blossoming across his chest. His lips and teeth are vivid pink, slick with fresh blood. He moans and stares up at everyone with frosted eyes gleaming with trepidation.

Amanda drops to his side. "Pastor!" She takes his hand. "Oh God. Oh *no-no-no-no-no*." She turns to Tizzy and screams at such a pitch and with such ferocity that it makes both Duncan and the young woman jump. "Do something! Call an ambulance!" The fire hidden by Amanda's normally calm and professional demeanor has all but burned off. And what's left is someone, something raw.

Tizzy is at a loss for words. Stares on in shock as she thinks, *Holy shit! I did it. I killed him. Oh my god.*

This certainly isn't the first life she's taken – or at least attempted to take since Travis survived without her knowing – but the shock of killing someone rattles her, nonetheless. She takes a step back, watching everything unfold as if it were a scene from a horror movie.

Duncan comes to Pastor Graham's other side.

The old man can barely speak. He coughs violently, then utters, "We don't . . . have . . . the pendant."

Tears slide down Amanda's face as she squeezes his hands and tries to staunch the blood from his wound. "Just hold on, ok? We're going to get you to a hospital."

A hospital? Oh, hell no! Tizzy thinks. *They're not going to incriminate me. I gotta get the hell out of here. No doubt somebody outside heard the shot!*

"No one's going anywhere!" Tizzy shouts; her gun is trained on them. "Not until I get the pendant."

Amanda ignores Tizzy. Tells the old man, "We're not leaving you."

Pastor Graham gestures for Amanda to lean closer. He whispers, "The pendant is closer than you think." He grips her tight. "Don't let them have it." He releases her as tears well in his eyes.

Then his gaze fixes emptily on the ceiling.

"What are you guys talking about, huh?" Tizzy asks, then glances at the windows, wondering if someone outside indeed heard the shot.

Is someone gonna bust in here? If they do, I'm fucked, she thinks. *Simon, you better hurry.*

"Pastor?" Amanda shakes him.

He doesn't respond.

This man turned her life around. Spared her from a bleak future fulfilling ominous deeds under the guise of an unworthy cause.

And now he's gone.

Amanda turns to Tizzy. "You little monster!" A simmering rage, percolating from some shadowed depth of her soul surfaces to the top. Her gaze pulsates a volcanic bright white. Unearthly. Charged and roaring with an energy that is something that only thunderclouds above boast about, she yells, "I regret the day I ever met you!"

The hell is wrong with her eyes, Tizzy thinks. *This chick's coo-coo!*

Amanda moves, rising like a dark wave threatening to crash onto a small boat.

"I should've left you at that gas station to rot with the rest of the scum." The violent white in her eyes intensifies as she continues, "Because that is who you belong with. Not us. My reward for opening my heart and my little family has been met with death and disappointment time and time again. But not today! You've just resurrected the broken, dark half of me that has been asleep for too *fucking* long."

Duncan nearly jumps out of his skin at the sound of his sister cursing.

Tizzy stares, mouth slung open. She points the gun at Amanda's face, but Amanda grabs it, gripping it with every ounce of strength in her body.

The gun turns a searing, pulsing white.

Tizzy screams and releases the weapon, cupping her hand as if she has touched a burner on the stove. "What the fuck's wrong with you?!"

Amanda takes her by the throat. With eyes sparking like firecrackers and a voice that echoes like it's from another dimension, she tells Tizzy:

"I'll show you what's wrong with me."

Chapter 15 – Mr. Gladius

Nestled within the rolling hills of Dade City, a small town just north of Tampa's urban sprawl, sits a mansion that could have been plucked off a wine bottle. It's replete with a Spanish tile roof, peach stucco walls bordered by generous wood trim; grand archways are framed by sun-blemished terracotta tiles.

As the heat of the morning sun spreads across the acres of his property, Marcus Gladius opens the double doors leading onto his second-floor balcony. It overlooks a sizeable garden of bougainvillea, hibiscus, and oleanders. Above him, a series of planter pots cling to the ceiling. On either side of him, large stone pots erupt with fresh pearl-white lilies.

Compared to the lush, healthy, flourishing greenery surrounding him, Marcus's appearance is anything but. His sunken, sallow eyes are a distant shade of hazel. His face is a wrinkled mess, with a set of jowls that droop cruelly downward. His hair, once plush and sable black, is now an oily mess of silver strands that cling to his scalp.

Marcus dons a velvety red and purple robe, reminiscent of the late Hugh Hefner, only he's not as agedly handsome. Sporting a pronounced potbelly and wide hips, the robe makes him appear like an eggplant with legs.

Moving at the speed of turtle, he drags his feet across the uneven tile floor of the patio and rests his arms on the artisan stone railing that lines the balcony. He takes a moment to appreciate the simplicity and tolerable temperatures of the early morning, knowing the impending heat and humidity will soon overtake the day.

"Sir."

Marcus takes one more breath, savoring the aesthetic resplendence in front of him before turning to face the source of the interruption:

Quell, his top lieutenant, is a broad shouldered, fit, African American woman who is equal parts stunning and deadly; her beauty is blighted, hidden beneath an opalescent mask that covers half of her face.

When Quell was a teenager, she was tasked with stealing a rare Bible from a local church. She failed, and Vanessa made an example of her by hanging her upside down over a bed of candles. The flames licking at Quell's face would have completely disfigured her if not for Marcus's intervention. He put an abrupt end to Vanessa's wicked punishment, sparing Quell from further agony. Marcus reasoned with Vanessa, making the case that if the Rift tortured or killed off all their employees for the most minute of infractions, the ranks would default to desertion or suicide, neither of which was going to help grow the organization.

Vanessa vehemently disagreed. She reveled in torture and inflicting pain.

She also saw the Rift as wholly expendable for a greater cause, a perspective which Marcus would later find fitting and deliciously ironic, given that – *thanks to Travis* – she was permanently retired.

Marcus rejoiced that her reign was over, though deep inside, he feared the repercussions from Viola, Vanessa's much wilder and brutally chaotic sister.

Marcus preferred to employ the approach of taking care of his agents and treating them, to the best of his abilities, as worthy and respected. Not that he wouldn't sacrifice agents if he needed to, but this would only be done in a calculated way, not simply to whet some appetite for revenge or to purge himself of frustration at their expense.

And that's how he gained Quell's loyalty.

The young woman would cut the heart out of the Pope for him, if Marcus were only to ask. No hesitation. No more failures.

Over the years, Marcus began to see Quell as the daughter he never had. He'd never want to subject his offspring to the dark, soul-corrupting effects of the Rift. Where Vanessa danced on the line of chaotic evil, Marcus maintained his sense of lawfulness and wanted to raise Quell through the ranks of the Rift in that same vein.

Quell never gravitated towards learning dark magic, drawn instead to study martial arts. Marcus recruited the best underground fighters and put her through a grueling training regimen. He molded her from an emaciated, aimless teen, to a pit bull with unquestionable devotion.

Should something happen to him, Quell could possibly succeed him and take the Rift off its self-destructive, Vanessa-inspired path to one of simply chasing and eradicating the Covenant. Marcus envisioned the Rift taking a wiser approach.

The caustic promises that Vanessa and Viola campaigned for – controlling God's treasures in order to crusade against every Christian in the world – no longer had to be realized. That was a myopic, wastefully vengeful approach.

Marcus's plan was much greater—not global domination or retribution, but *global influence.* With Vanessa dead and Viola ousted, a new direction was on the horizon. Vines of Rift hegemony could creep into every major political decision, every popular "cause." The religious values of man could be questioned, broken and overshadowed by new knowledge awakening them to the malevolent powers that he believed truly run this universe.

To him, lambs need something more present than God to follow, and the Rift with their ability to tap into unadulterated power could be the shining light to lead them into a bigger cause.

One person at a time.

A steady trickle of people converting into the beliefs and whims of the Rift. Slow and steady wins the race.

Conservation of energy. Striking only when needed.

This is the way of Marcus.

Yes, he may move at the speed of a turtle, but the turtle eventually crosses the finish line.

"Sir!"

Marcus shakes off the trailing thoughts.

"Are you alright?" Quell asks with a bit of concern in her tone.

Marcus nods. "Never better." He turns back towards the sun timidly rising above the lavish vegetation below. "So, what is it, my dear?"

"Agent Riley has a lead for us."

Marcus brings his pinky up to his teeth. His fingernails are long, sharp, and tinged yellow. He scratches the plaque off his tooth and glares at the tiny white glob as if it were a lab specimen. "Go on."

"He's been informed by a source close to those who have been stealing from us. They plan to strike his repository next."

Marcus wipes his nail off on his robe. "How reliable is this information?"

"May I be honest?"

"Please."

"Sir, Riley is a lot of things." Quell takes a moment to choose her words carefully. "He's a chauvinistic pig, and he treats our witches like garbage. Honestly, at some point, I would like your approval to castrate him."

"But?"

"But he's not one to mistake a tactical decision. At least not in my experience."

Marcus grabs a handful of the lilies and prunes their stems using a small knife. "Did you know that you and Riley nearly shared the same fate? Vanessa was going to burn him alive for failing to steal *back* the Rosary beads from the Covenant." He brings the flowers to his nose, inhaling their scent before continuing, "Fortunately, I was able to pay her off and indenture his service to me."

"How did you pay her off? You mean financially?"

"No." Marcus squeezes the bouquet so tightly that the flowers crumple. "I had to give up some of *my* treasures."

"You traded treasures for *us*?" Quell tilts her head, a look of pure confusion in her eyes. "Why?"

"Because I'd rather sacrifice a few items to a fellow councilman for the undying loyalty of my men and woman." Marcus shoots Quell a wayward glare. "Are you not loyal to me?"

"Without question."

"And look at how things played out." Marcus opens his hands and tosses the ruined flowers over the railing, "Vanessa is dead, and we have ransacked her stores. Everything I gave to her, you got back for me. Funny how that works, right?"

Quell nods in affirmation.

Marcus gestures to one of the plants that hangs above. "Do you know what kind of plant that is?"

Quell eyes it curiously. "No clue."

"It's a pitcher plant." He runs a finger along the rim of the oblong plant's gaping maw. "It lures bugs, flies, anything with wings, into it. These tiny creatures think they are getting delicious nectar; however, the very thing that draws them in becomes their undoing." Marcus fiddles around inside the belly of the plant. Plucks out a fly, where it dangles lifelessly by its tiny legs. "And unfortunately for them, they're slowly digested."

Quell nods, starting to piece together where he is going with this analogy. "So, Riley's stores?"

"Our pitcher plant." Marcus flicks the fly away. "Let our winged friends get what they want."

Quell approaches the plant, fishes inside, and rescues a beetle from its watery grave. Though it's struggling to move, the beetle is still alive.

"I want to know what those angels are after," he continues. "And I have a strong suspicion I know what it is."

Quell brings the beetle close, watching it twitch. "And what's that?"

"The keys to Heaven. I have one half." He walks Quell over to a glass display case where the Manacles of the Messiah are perched on a red pillow. They are non-descript, ordinary metal cuffs that could be mistaken for a theater prop. "If this is what our friends are looking for, I want to know." Marcus seizes the beetle from Quell with surprising speed. He pinches it between his fingers and a yellow goo spills out. "If indeed they are on a quest for the manacles, there might be a chance they have the other half—the pendant. And of all we've stolen and collected, that is the only treasure I care about." He looks up at the sky as several clouds shift by. "What's more powerful than having control over the very gates to the afterlife?"

"What if they don't have the pendant? What if that's not what they are even looking for?"

"I have looked into the black depths of the eyes of the Amissa," Marcus says with a hiss. "I've seen the desperation and regret buried within the bottomlessness of their souls. They made a mistake coming here, and now they would like nothing more than to go home. I doubt there is any treasure in this world that they would covet more. Now, instruct Riley to thin out his guards. We need a skeleton crew running his repository."

"Understood." Quell then asks, "Should we canvas the Council? See if perhaps they can aid with any information?"

Marcus lunges and seizes Quell by her throat, nearly choking out her last breath. Says with a hiss, "Say nothing to the Council about this! We don't need them."

Quell is physically strong enough to break Marcus in half, but a quiver of fear strikes her heart, and she locks up.

"If we involve them, then we inevitably involve Viola." Marcus feels her body trembling against his. He releases her and steps back.

"I don't understand," she admits as she rubs her throat. "How would Viola get involved if she's been excommunicated from the Council and put under that enchantment spell? She shouldn't even know who she is anymore."

"I appreciate your faith in our magic, my dear. However, don't underestimate the vehemence of that woman, and what her wrath can overcome. There are cracks in even our sorcery that an alpha witch like Viola can sense, no matter how potent the spell that has been cast upon her. She has a volcanic personality that teeters on insanity and would blindly wipe out everything in pursuit of eradicating Christians from the face of the Earth. No cost is too great. Not even her own life." Marcus leans over the rails and stares out at the sun, now hotter and higher than it was before. "She demonstrated her manic nature once, nearly exposing the Rift by openly slaughtering so many of the Covenant's transporters."

"All but the one that counts, I suppose."

Marcus glances back at her. "Travis Rail?"

"Yeah." Quell's eyes narrow. "I'm not sure if I should thank him or kill him for wiping Vanessa out."

"Agreed." A grin curls up on the corner of Marcus's mouth. "So, for right now, let's keep this issue to ourselves." Marcus turns back, places both hands on the railing. Stares down at the sprawling garden below him. "I want to know what our band of feathered thieves are after. And I want to know something else, too."

"What's that?"

"If our experiments will finally pay off."

Quell lowers her head. "The Shaker witches? But they're not ready."

"Well . . . this would be a good time to find out, now wouldn't it?"

Quell nods.

"And speaking of being ready," he says, "are you ready?"

"I am."

"I need to be sure that you can take them on. You know that."

"I'm not afraid."

"This test could kill you." Marcus hangs onto the last question: "Are you sure you are ready?"

Her terse response comes out with an impatient quickness. "I said *I am*."

"I hope so." Marcus turns away, a smile growing on his face. "You should go prepare while you have time. The training room is open, as always." Without looking back at her, he makes for the door. Glancing over his shoulder, he adds, "If you die during your test, please know that I have always loved you like a daughter."

Quell says nothing as she watches him leave. She moves to the balcony and glances out to the garden. A million thoughts run through her mind. She turns away, feeling an itch in her soul. Something is afoul. She can sense Marcus's veiled fear a mile away. What is he afraid of? The Amissa? The Rift?

She turns to leave and catches sight of her mask in the reflection of the windowpane of the French doors leading to the balcony. The mask speaks to her, seemingly having a voice of its own. Reminding her that she is unlovable. Unworthy. Ugly.

She smashes her fist into the window, shattering it. Several tiny glass fragments twinkle back at her from the hills and valleys of her knuckles. Hand shaking, she stares at the sparkling shards and the seeping streams of blood from her wounds.

But I am loved, she muses.

Marcus loves me.

And whatever he is afraid of, I will destroy.

She removes the fragments from her knuckles.

Just as he saved me, with every ounce of my being, I will protect him.

Chapter 16 – Dark Magic

Amanda lifts Tizzy off the ground by her throat. The young woman kicks wildly as she tries in vain to pry Amanda's hands free.

The door shakes. The flimsy deadbolt holds in place, but not for long.

Several angels burst in, along with Simon who files in from behind. "What the hell is going on here?"

Amanda lets out a roar that could set off car alarms as she hurls Tizzy across the store. Her body flies through the air and slams into Simon, taking them both down.

Balco and another angel rush in and charge Duncan, who dives clumsily over a small bookshelf.

Amanda's face goes dark, as if a permanent shadow were cast upon her. It's a stark contrast to the thin white beams of light that escape from her eyes. One of the angels lunges at Amanda, flying at her with astonishing speed, but she manages to dodge it deftly—a feat normally impossible for a human.

Duncan peers timidly above a bookshelf, and as he witnesses her unusual agility, feels confusion mixed with dread welling within him.

Before the angel can react, Amanda spins around and impales him with her bare hand. He wails at such an anguished pitch that the other angels cover their ears in unison.

There's an explosion of light and all things, both angelic *and* mortal, are knocked down

That angel is no more.

Duncan finds himself sailing through the air, then lands so hard on his back, his jaw rattles and his glasses shoot off his nose. Between the pain and the celestial detonation, the world becomes a blur. Something oozes from his ear. Still in shock, he wobbles shakily to his feet. He touches his earlobe, then eyes his fingertips.

Blood.

Before he has time to digest what just happened, a hand grabs his wrist. The blurry, shadowy face with penetrating white eyes hovers in front of him like some distant ghoul materialized to take his soul. He barely has a second to scream, speak or make noise when the dark face before him brightens and he can somewhat make out:

Amanda?

She yanks him towards the back of the store. Still reeling from the explosion, ears ringing, his world devolves into a stumbled mess of pandemonium as she pulls him along.

Then things move even quicker.

Amanda ushers him to a car.

He's shoved into the passenger seat.

Car doors slam.

Something is yanked across his torso.

Seatbelt?

The engine roars and he's pressed against his seat.

Amanda reaches over to him and he jumps. There's something in her hands—glasses. He puts them on, which proves to be quite the feat given how shaken he is.

She comes into focus. Her skin color is normal again. Face taut with emotion, she stares dead ahead at the road as they speed out of town and towards the highway.

"What?" Duncan is amazed he can even form words at this point. "What just happened?"

Amanda looks at him for a moment. Her face may be normal, but her eyes are as neon-white as full moons.

"They woke me, Duncan." Amanda focuses back on the road. "They woke something up in me that I didn't want back."

Chapter 17 – From the Treetops

From high atop the dense trees that surround an old Victorian-style hotel, Victor watches the cars flow in and out of the parking lot. Hidden between clenched fists of leaves, balanced effortlessly on a large branch, he surveys the activity below.

A muscle car swerves in, engine rumbling. Victor stiffens at the sight of it. The driver side door swings open and Travis emerges, a cup of coffee in one hand, a manila folder in the other.

"Victor," a woman says softly next to Victor's ear.

Victor turns to the voice next to him. It's a face he recognizes. "Mom?" He utters the name like it's a long-lost secret finally revealed to the world at large.

"You still long to bring me back. I can feel it."

"Of course," Victor admits. "I screwed up. Not that it matters now since neither of us are of this world anymore."

"But you won't let it go."

Victor watches Travis. "I could've done more." Victor grinds his teeth. "I panicked, and because of that, you're gone—"

There's a flash of bright light that blinds Victor.

It's just after dusk.

A woman sprawled on the asphalt is gasping for air. A crimson puddle finds a crooked path from the back of her head towards a dip in the parking lot. Above her a tall, lurching figure stands, crowbar in hand shimmering with blood. From behind the smudged windshield of his mom's old Chevy Nova, Victor watches from the front seat. The glove compartment sits open. The light of the setting sun provides enough illumination to outline a revolver that rests inside. His mom was always paranoid of being robbed or kidnapped. She'd told Victor that she had a premonition that the "bad people" were going to come for her. When Victor asked her why the bad people would want her, she never went into detail, only saying that it's because of what she carried. Then she would caress her belly, bulging with a child who was created out of a forbidden love, considered blasphemous by some and revered by others.

This was too much for a then ten-year-old Victor to swallow. Nonetheless, she once told him that if they were ever in danger to use this gun to protect them.

Victor steels himself. Then picks up the revolver with a trembling hand and stuffs it into his pants. His heart slams against his chest. His breathing becomes shallow. He slips out from the car and cowers behind bushes that edge a band parking lot.

A random car pulls up, headlights cutting across the lot. The tall man sees it, then tosses the crowbar and makes a run in the opposite direction.

Straight towards the bushes.

Straight into a young Victor.

The two collide.

To Victor, it feels like he just got hit by a truck. He goes flying back. There's a forceful crunch as his skull smacks into the ground. The pain is instant and intense.

"Whoa, whoa, whoa!" The tall man's voice is penetratingly deep and echoes in Victor's jarred mind. "What the hell you doing out here, kiddo?"

Victor shakes off the blow, sits up.

"You lost or something?" The tall man stands before him, towering like a skyscraper, knife in hand. Past him, Victor's mother lay dying, sprawled out and gasping for air.

Victor starts to crawl away, moving backwards until he stops against something solid—an oak tree. He tries to push himself to his feet but slips on a crooked knot of wood, landing on his butt.

"Wait a second." The tall man glances back at the dying woman, then Victor. A remnant stripe of the fading sunlight catches his face as he concludes, "You're not lost, *are you, kiddo?*"

Victor can't seem to speak. Trembling at the towering ogre in front of him.

That ogre is Lomak.

Walter Lomak.

Victor whips out the revolver, but the gun quivers in his hand.

"Oh, now that's cute." Lomak advances quickly, taking long, deliberate strides. "Where'd you get that?" He looms over Victor as if he were a tower of bricks poised to topple over at any moment. "Here." He extends a hand. "I won't hurt you if you give me the gun."

Victor squeezes his eyes shut, screams and pulls the trigger.

There's a loud crack, followed by two powerful hands clutching his shoulders.

He opens his eyes to see a massive palm connecting with his face. The smack is so loud, that it makes Victor's ears ring.

"You can't hit your target with your eyes closed, dumbass!"

Reeling from the pain, Victor's head flops back. He's lifted off his feet.

"You wanna know what it feels like to be shot?" Lomak asks, his breath so close, Victor can smell the last thing the man ate, and it must've been rotten.

"Hey!" someone calls out from the parking lot. "Hey, what are you doing over there?"

Lomak sees shadows approaching. Victor lands a solid kick in his nuts.

"Ah!" He drops Victor, and the boy scurries off. "You little shit!"

"Hey, you!" The voice and shadows draw closer.

Lomak growls and takes off running.

Victor races through the darkness and the denseness of the surrounding woods. Tree limbs and branches smack him in the face. A subtle ray of moonlight scarcely illuminates the path of wherever it is that fear is driving him to—

He runs into something and bounces backwards. He looks up, and at first, he thinks it's a tree, but the "tree" lights up, glows with the uncanny effervescence of the stars above.

His mother stares down at him. A frosted white haze twirls along her body as if she had taken a dip in a pool of starlight.

"It's not your fault, Victor," she tells the boy. "You were just a kid."

The image of his mother, the dark woods, his own body, all fade out like the cutscene of his life-movie.

Victor blinks several times.

He's back within the canopy of the tree, obscured by the crisscross of branches that camouflage him from the cars and people below.

His mother is still next to him, radiating with that unspeakably soft, gossamer beauty. A wispy, butterfly-halo of light swirls around her body. Coffee brown hair flows with a surreal buoyancy, drifting as if immersed in invisible water.

"I didn't need a replay of that night." Victor pulls away with a frown. "Seen it enough in my head. I should've just walked to the ATM with you instead of waiting in the car."

"You didn't know that was going to happen."

Victor takes a moment as though letting the emotions from the rerun of that nightmare night pass. He then asks, "Why'd you show me that again?"

"I want you to finally understand that you can't bring me back."

Victor turns away.

"You need to let it go," she tells him.

"No, I don't."

"God forgives you."

"For what?" Victor watches Travis disappear into the main lobby of the hotel.

"For being angry at Him. It's understandable to feel the way you do, but God's ways are higher."

Victor glares at her. "God let me escape Heaven."

"Maybe. Nevertheless, you were the one who chose to leave because you saw an opportunity with the Amissa. You went along for their ride, their exodus, but you had your plan, guided by vengeance," she says, "but that's why I'm reminding you, *yet again*, to let it go. You died once for me. God may not be so gracious a second time."

Victor puts his head in his hands and lets out a groan. "How many times do we have to go over all this?"

"How many times do I have to tell you that you don't need to avenge my death?" His mother reaches for him, lifts his head up by his chin. "My, son, the Rift is not your concern. Your brother is—"

"You mean my *half-brother*."

His mom says nothing.

Victor shrugs. "And he doesn't know we're related."

"The time will come when he needs to know."

Travis emerges from the hotel. Heads back to the car. His mother watches him from above, emotion brimming in her eyes.

"Do you feel sorry for him?"

"No." She looks at Victor. "I miss him, and I miss you."

"Then why aren't you guiding him, instead of hounding me again?"

"Because God wants me to work through *you*."

"Tell Him I'm fine. I know what I want."

"Yes. Retribution, but it's a lost cause," she says. "Your brother should be your cause."

Victor grips a branch, squeezing it so tightly that the wood begins to snap. Travis glances up, and Victor pulls away. Travis stares intently, and for a moment, Victor thinks he's been spotted, but then Travis turns to his car, reaching for something—his cell phone.

Victor's mother goes on. "Travis is not ready. He needs your training, and he's not strong enough to face the Amissa. Especially when he harbors so much doubt."

As Travis heads back inside the hotel, Victor studies his brother with renewed curiosity. He wonders why hasn't he sought his brother out sooner? Perhaps in his pursuits for tracking down the elusive Lomak, he lost sight of more important things, like the family that was still alive on Earth.

"Victor, once you move your focus off revenge and onto our family, you'll see that the way back to Heaven is much more accessible than you think."

Victor smiles to himself. "You want me to completely give up on wiping out every last one of the Rift scum that walks this Earth . . ." Let's out a huff as he narrows his gaze at the horizon. "You're asking a lot from me."

"I know. That's why God sent me to talk to you once again. He knows your stubborn nature." She says with a laugh, "It's a Rail family trait."

"So's anger." Victor turns back to his mother, but she has vanished.

If God sent me to save a man who doesn't want to save anyone, he muses, *then we just might all be screwed.*

Chapter 18 – Angel Chase

Amanda's sedan races towards the highway. She swerves clumsily onto an onramp. Duncan's seatbelt locks as his shoulder bumps against her.

"Whoa, Sis!"

Amanda ignores him, presses harder on the gas. Her knuckles whiten as she clutches the wheel. They cut between lanes, heading north on I-95, moving as quickly as the traffic will allow.

"Are you listening?" Duncan straightens his crooked glasses. "Amanda!"

"Shut up!" She roars with a guttural intensity that causes Duncan to do a double-take. He catches her eyes flash an incandescent white as she commands, "Just shut up and let me think."

Still shaken by the pyrotechnics show back in Pastor Graham's bookstore, the old man's murder, and his sister's new visage, Duncan leans back in his seat. Takes a moment to try to comprehend all the madness. Then barely ekes out, "What . . . what happened back there—"

"They pushed me. That's what happened."

"What do you mean?"

"Everything has a boiling point. Water. Volcanoes," she explains. "*Me.*"

"That wasn't a boiling point. That was a nuke." Duncan wipes the newly formed beads of sweat off his brow. "I mean, what you did to Tizzy and to that angel . . ."

Amanda stares ahead. "I didn't want this to happen."

They pass through a cloud of traffic.

"Want what to happen?"

"*This.*" Amanda gestures to herself with her hand. "There's something inside me I don't want out, but the world seems determined to unleash it." She squeezes the wheel with such force, the plastic begins to crack.

Witnessing this, Duncan swallows the growing lump in his throat.

"It's been a lot to absorb in just twenty-four hours," Amanda continues. "First, I think you're dead, but then I find out you're not. Then Pastor Graham dies right in front of me, and he doesn't come back." She glances down briefly at her shirt. "I mean, look at me. I'm covered in his blood!"

Duncan does. He hangs his head, then stares out at the passing scenery.

"And now . . ." Amanda says, "Now, I've got the . . . the *burn* inside me. It's back."

Only the hum of the motor fills the air now. The two share a lengthy moment of silence.

"The burn?" Duncan asks.

"Yes, it's like . . ." Amanda struggles with the words. "It's like an uncomfortable heat inside of my chest. It feels like I swallowed the sun, and that sun is only getting hotter as we speak."

"This *burn* . . . is it because you have been dabbling in the black arts, or something?"

Amanda shoots him a sideways glance. "That was a long time ago—"

The roof above their heads squeals as it is peeled back like the top of a sardine can. The two share a scream and look up, face-to-face with a furious angel. His brow is furrowed and eyes as black as tar. His hands grip the thin sheet metal with such voracious strength, it dimples under his fingers.

"They followed us!" Duncan yells.

"Yeah, I see that!" Amanda cranks the wheel left and the angel flops onto his side. Tires screech and a car ahead dashes out of the way just in time to miss Amanda's bumper. The angel rights himself and swipes at Duncan, barely brushing the top of his head.

Amanda blares her horn at the cars in front of her as she pushes this sedan beyond its everyday limits. Other drivers honk back in anger and confusion, yet she weaves between them with almost perfect timing.

The angel swats again and his claws connect with Duncan's shoulder; he cries out in agony.

Amanda reaches over, grabs the angel's arm. As her eyes burn that caustic bright white, she tells Duncan, "Hold on." She jerks the wheel, takes a hard right.

The car launches off the highway, goes bounding up and down through rivers of weeds and tall grass, carving a wake of dirt and debris as it starts to spin sideways—

They slam into a tree.

The rear passenger door crumples inward. Amanda and Duncan are jarred in their seats. Chunks of plastic and shards of glass rain from every direction. The hissing smoke of all iterations, both chemical and amorphic, steams upwards.

The angel has vanished.

Amanda leans back. A jagged streak of blood seeps from her forehead. Her ears are ringing. She looks to Duncan, who is out cold, head slumped to one side.

Hands trembling, she reaches over and gives him a shake.

No response.

"*Duncan?*"

Still nothing.

She unbuckles her seatbelt and leans close. "Duncan," Her voice trails off as she grasps his face in her hands. Blood runs down the side of his head. "Oh, oh, God, please. Come on, Duncan!"

The escaping odors of gasoline, charred vinyl and burned rubber attack her lungs. She begins to cough uncontrollably. She grasps his collar and pulls him close, "Duncan, talk to me!"

Nothing.

She catches an imprint of the rosary beads through his shirt.

What good are these beads if they don't protect you, she thinks.

But then again, it is dark magic.

No guarantees.

They are not sanctioned by God.

Something grabs her from above, tearing her out of the car as if she is a stray weed caught in the wrong garden.

She's airborne.

Wind whips past her ears. Suddenly the crack of the ground greets her, followed by a heaviness upon her entire body. The angel has thrown her, then clamped his body down on her, crushing her with a weight that no mere man of similar stature could emulate.

Her face darkens and her hands spark to life, but the angel pins them to the ground.

Gasping for air, she tries to push him off her, but he proves immotile.

The angel speaks words that twist in her brain, a tongue as foreign as a language long dead yet revived through something far more numinous than she can comprehend. He mutters in tones and choppy phrases that make it sound as if he were talking in reverse.

Barely able to breathe now, she thrashes futilely under him, then utters, "What . . . do . . . you . . . want?"

The angel's lips tighten like a belt pulled beyond its limits. He's about to speak when black metal connects with the side of his face.

"Get off my sister, you!" Duncan shouts. "You jerk!"

The angel hops off Amanda, propelled by a single flap of his now expanded wings.

Duncan glances down at the tire iron severely bent by the impact with the angel's head. With a frown, he mutters, "Crud." The tire iron falls from his hand.

The angel rears back, a moment away from pouncing on Duncan.

"Hey!" Voices call from the highway as people close in. "Hey, are you guys ok?

The angel turns in the direction of the incoming voices—

Amanda jumps the angel from behind. He whirls around to grab at her but fails to shake her off. Her hands flicker to neon-blue life, and she digs her fingers into his wings.

Light pulses between the two of them as the angel stares up into the sky, wailing so loud that Duncan drops to the ground, arms pressed against his head.

Amanda's hands push further into him as if his body is comprised of clay, not the solid object that bent metal upon impact.

The two of them are locked in a screaming embrace. The sound is thunderous, though not as booming as the blast that expands outward from the angel as he bursts into a sphere of fulgent energy.

The shockwave from the angel's death spreads in an ever-widening circle.

The approaching voices from the road are suddenly silenced. Amanda is not sure if those people, whoever they are, are dead or just knocked unconscious.

Her ears are met by nothing but silence.

Everything goes silent.

No birds. No wind. Nothing.

Covered in sweat and shaking like crazy, she brings her hands up to examine them. The darkening of her skin subsides; her natural tone returns.

Duncan is writhing on the ground. A thin rivulet of blood leaks from his ears.

"Duncan!" Amanda throws an arm around him and hoists him up. She catches sight of their would-be rescuers wriggling on the ground. They too have blood spilling from their ears.

"C'mon," Amanda insists as she rushes past them. "We got to go."

"W-w-wait," Duncan stammers, "Where are we going?"

Something urges Amanda to look straight up at the sky.

High above, two more angels circle overhead and then shoot off in opposite directions.

"Assuming our car still works," she replies, as she helps him into the front seat; the door creaks as it is opened and closed, "we're going to get help."

Chapter 19 – Beatific Revelation

Travis steps out onto the front porch of his newly purchased log cabin dream home. Coffee cup in hand, he leans against the support beams propping up the roof and stares off into the sky. A brisk wind disturbs the treetops, sending a ripple of leaves fluttering downward in delicate waves. The air is crisp and carries the hint of a scent of firewood. Travis closes his eyes and takes in a deep breath, savoring the long-sought halcyon atmosphere.

This day has taken too long to get here.

Just a few feet away, a cardinal braves the wind and perches itself on a tree stump.

"Hey, buddy." Travis salutes the bird with his mug.

It cocks its head to the side and stares back with an inquisitive gaze.

"It's just you and me up here."

The cardinal does a slight hop closer to him.

"And I plan on keeping it that way."

A familiar voice from behind him breaks the silence. "You know that cardinals are a sign."

Travis jumps. "Jesus!" His coffee cup slips out of his hand and lands with a wet thud on the grass. The cardinal flies off.

Travis whirls around, Beretta drawn on a well-manicured angelic figure standing before him.

"No," Zach informs him, "I am not Jesus."

Travis frowns.

"You know that won't hurt me," Zach tells him.

"That's too bad." Holsters the gun.

"You wish to harm me?" Zach asks and Travis interprets this as the oracular angel being somewhat offended.

"No. I just wanna be left alone." Travis waves him off. "We've covered this a hundred times."

"Not a hundred."

Travis rolls his eyes.

"God doesn't want me to give up on you."

"You don't say." Travis steps off the porch and retrieves his coffee mug. As he wipes off the dirt, he nods toward the vacant tree stump. "You scared away my new friend."

Zach floats down the steps and stops just shy of the stump. "He knew I was coming."

"The bird knew you were coming?" Travis puts his hand to his head, feigning a headache. "Actually . . . don't answer that." He tilts the coffee cup upside down and shakes the last drops out of it. "I was really enjoying that cup too. Not sure if it's this Sumatra blend," Travis waves a hand towards the rolling, lush green hillside behind him, "or the mountain water, but it sure did taste like Heaven."

"And you know what Heaven tastes like?"

"I imagine it's pretty close." Travis dries the mug with his t-shirt. "After all, God made the coffee tree, which made the coffee beans, which I *was* enjoying." He moves back towards the porch, but Zach lays a firm hand on his shoulder stopping him short—

"Are you happy?"

"With what?" Travis shakes himself free of Zach's grip, but only because Zach *lets* him.

Zach motions to the cabin. "With this?"

"I'm still getting settled. I mean, I just moved in," Travis says. "And now you show up . . . *already.*"

"You wanted to run away. Here you are."

"Can't seem to run away from you."

"You can't run from God."

"You're not God," Travis reminds him. "You're—what did that creeper angel call you?" He snaps his finger several times, trying to recall, "His *errand boy*?"

"Who is this angel that you speak of?"

Travis shrugs. "No clue, man. Didn't exactly catch his name, but he was one of your crew."

"Only a chosen few of us, selected by God, may travel between Heaven and Earth. If he came specifically looking for you, he is no longer of Heaven but possibly one of the Amissa."

"The who?"

"The Amissa. The Lost."

"I must be part of them too, because I'm always lost—"

In the blink of an eye, Zach is suddenly upon Travis, eyes ablaze with lightning and a face as emotionless as the sea is vast. Travis finds that, for the first time in a while, he's feeling something stirring in his bones.

Fear.

Zach floats, face-to-face with Travis. "Never speak of the Amissa in such a way." His voice echoes in that unearthly bellow that makes Travis's stomach churn.

Travis freezes up. Seems he found Zach's last nerve and clearly tap danced on it with that comment.

"They are blinded by pride," Zach explains. "They've gone their own way, forsaking God for the promises of the wicked."

Travis takes a cautious step back, finding his back literally against the wall of his house. Zach glides uncomfortably closer.

"Never align yourself with them," Zach warns, "whether in jest or in truth."

"Alright. I got it."

The storm in Zach's face subsides, and he moves away.

Travis exhales, realizing he had been holding his breath.

"You cannot risk the temptation to join them. They will try to convince you to join their plight."

"I have no idea what you're talking about."

Zach suddenly presses his palm on Travis's forehead, and everything goes dark—

Then light.

Eyes opening, all is a blur. Travis blinks repeatedly, struggling to focus. It's as if he is witnessing the world for the first time, though the world does not make any sense. In every direction, he sees a vast expanse of clouds, painted in varying degrees of yellows, whites and grays.

Travis takes a step forward, but his feet swim freely through the air—he freaks, arms grasping frantically, though finding nothing to grab onto. He peers down to find that he is floating through a sea of clouds. Below him, a thin gold stripe cuts across the dense floor of clouds, and these clouds open like a great mouth, revealing a swirling mass further below that he mistakes for more clouds.

He's pulled towards the opening by some invisible hand gently urging him closer. The swirling mass comes into focus, and he finds that he's not gazing into a raging storm, but a flurry of angels encircling a much larger angel anchored in the center. The large angel stands before two ornate, solid gold posts.

Travis drifts even closer to the angelic activity without being noticed.

The large angel speaks, and at first, it is the most inane and unintelligible language he has ever heard. Yet somehow the words transform in Travis's mind and he is able to discern what is being said.

"After eons of dutiful worship and service to the Father, we are no more loved than the smallest of vermin that crawl upon the earthen floor," the large angel declares. "I have spoken with a dweller of Earth, and he made the case for our freedom."

The chaotic churning cyclone of angels slows.

"And so why should the Father be upset if we leave our posts to dwell below with the very creatures – *the humans* – he favors so?" The large angel grabs the poles, taking one in each hand. "By unbinding the gate, we are free as the birds to fly, the dolphins to swim, and the bison to roam. We are free as man, who wanders aimlessly beneath our wings. We are free to understand why the Father adores man more than he does us. We serve God obediently;

yet man has the freedom to make his own choices while still enjoying the benefit of our Lord's love."

The angels abruptly halt, hovering about like hummingbirds awaiting the nectar that is their promised freedom.

From high above the endless levels of clouds, a single angel hurtles downward: Zach.

Travis's eyes widen as he looks on.

Zach lands in the middle of the commotion.

"Zachariel?" the large angel asks.

"Balco?" Zach responds.

"Are you here to stop us?"

"You know why I am here. You are being tempted by the forked tongue of crooked men for the promise to comprehend that which does not need comprehension. You do not need to understand love. God's love simply *is*."

The large angel unsheathes a massive golden sword. "Don't preach to me about God's love."

The other angels follow suit, brandishing their respective bladed weapons.

For Travis, it is a sight to behold. Zach is outnumbered well over a hundred angels to one.

Balco rests his arms on the poles. "We each have our roles, Zachariel. Yours has been to attend to the prayers of man and convey them to the Father." He taps the poles. "Mine has been to guard these gates."

"And a fine job you have done. God is grateful."

"Grateful . . . but does He truly *love* us?"

"Indeed, He does, Balco." Even in this vast expanse of clouds and sunshine and fog, Zach's voice is crystal clear. "Why do you question that?"

"Because His preference is still for the mortals. Is that not so? Has He not given them their own world to do with as they please?"

"Jealousy is unbecoming of you, brother—"

"Do not call me, brother." Balco's voice darkens, "Unless you plan to stand by our side!"

"In your plan to flee Heaven? To dwell amongst the lost? What is Hell but a place void of God?"

"And yet the Father still shines His love on them. More love than He shines upon us."

The angels tighten the circle. Zach is unphased.

"You deliver prayers to the Father, and what do those mortals do for us? They do nothing and are loved more, forgiven tirelessly," Balco asserts. "We should be down there, among them, living in a world that He prefers."

"The tongues of the wicked have tainted you," Zach admonishes. "You have given into temptation, to a man's iniquitous lies, and you will be disheartened with what you find."

"We will learn why He loves them so. We are stronger than they are. More worthy. The divine living amongst sheep." Balco takes the poles with his free hand. "Now we may join man, instead of merely attending to his needs."

"Balco, you are wrong. Should you leave this world, God's true kingdom, you will no longer be divine. You and your blessings will spoil. By attending to the needs of man, you are honoring God, therefore loving Him. And in loving Him, He loves you."

"Your clever words will not sway us. We have made our decision. If men can entertain their free will, then so can we." Balco pries the poles apart and a kinetic whip of electricity arcs between them. "Keep to your occupation and tell Father that we shall reside amongst His beloved humans."

Zach closes his eyes and nods his understanding. "Know that I love you and forgive you, but I cannot let you go."

"It's too late for that. You can't stop us." Balco spreads the poles open. "Now leave!"

The electrified field between the poles intensifies. Crackling and buzzing with energy as the gate is slowly opened.

"I said leave us!" Balco shouts above the crepitating sounds of the poles being forced apart.

Zach folds his wings downward, chin up, and flies off.

Travis has barely a moment to blink, when suddenly Zach flies back to Balco's side.

However, this time, he is not alone.

There is another, a much more herculean angel accompanying him.

Michael.

This great angel wears opulent golden armor with immense shoulder plates adorned in beatific reliefs. Underneath his breastplate hangs a cloak of gold chain mail that runs from his neck down to his waist. A stark contrast from his aureate armor, his wings are a fiery neon blue, flickering violently as if powered by lightning.

Travis feels the hairs on his entire body stand. Something is about to go down.

Balco's voice eclipses the noise of the gate as he asks, "Michael?"

Michael arms himself with a scythe; its blade is comprised of the same electric blue energy that is emitted from his wings.

"Forgive me, Balco," Zach says before zooming off into the infinite cloud space of Heaven.

Balco watches him leave, then turns to Michael. Tells the great angel, "We have served the Father for eons. It is time for us to make our own choice."

Michael readies his scythe.

The circle of rebellious angels closes in, armed with a hundred blades.

"Let us pass in peace," Balco demands, "and we will not fight you."

Michael moves so quickly there's only two visible streams of hot blue light carving figure eights, weaving between the horde of angels, creating a string of death. Bursting in succession like grenades of pure light, at least thirty or so angels have perished in that one attack.

Michael continues to mow down the angelic mob at an incredible rate.

The angels raise their blades to strike but themselves are cut in half, their bodies sliding apart with a resultant explosion of refulgent energy. There's a waning shriek as each one detonates into nothingness.

For Travis, it's reminiscent of the Rift agents turning into black dust when they die.

Though not all the angels are struck down.

Nearly two dozen take off towards the gate. Balco holds the poles open wide, the frightful static sparking between them in a chaotic pattern. The angels vanish as they dive into the hissing field of energy.

Upon witnessing this massacre, Travis feels every inch of his being on fire;

a ripple of trepidation travels through him.

Oh, great. Am I next?

Can Michael see me?

Travis tries to move away, but he is stuck drifting in this one spot.

Fortunately, Michael never notices him and instead continues with the attack. Within no time, he has withered the winged crowd down to an unlucky few who abandon their weapons and rush the gate. Some make it through. Some don't as Michael lands between them and their freedom. With his blue swath of death, they meet the same end as their brethren.

Only Balco is left now. He asks Michael, "Why have you butchered us so? Can we not experience the same love as the humans that scurry like roaches below?"

For a beat, there's nothing but the sizzling sound of the gate and the jangling of Michael's chain mail. His lip curls into a snarl. A scowl pushes his eyebrows down. He lowers the scythe towards the poles. "You chose the promise of a man over God. Your pride leads you." He raises the scythe level with Balco's throat. "And by your own pride, you will fall."

"Then fall, I will!"

Balco releases the poles. As they draw together, he slips into the sizzling energized field—but not before Michael drops the scythe, catches one of the poles with one hand, Balco's face with the other, gripping it with the fullness of his massive palm. A bright burning red emanates from Balco's skin as he cries out in pain.

Strong as Michael is, he struggles to keep the poles apart. With only one hand holding one pole, the other pushes against him. In a matter of moments, the poles will snap shut, cutting both angels in half.

Michael stares down Balco, who looks back at him between his fingers, eyes wide and unblinking. With a reluctant roar, he releases Balco and the pole, and the gate slams shut, snapping the end of his scythe off in the process. The blade disappears into the ether, vanishing along with Balco and the other absconded angels.

Michael pauses, staring at the gate in hollow silence as the sizzling sounds of the poles quiet. He throws his broken weapon aside with a huff.

Then he looks up to see Travis floating above, watching him with eyes wide.

Travis feels his heart slam against his rib cage.

Oh crap. I'm next!

Michael flies up, right at him. There's a blast of light.

And the blinding white light fades.

Zach steps back from Travis, who lets out an exasperated gasp. He's back on his porch, in front of his new home. Breathless, he sways from side to side. Zach steadies him and helps him sit.

Travis's heart thrums steadily. He takes a minute to catch his breath. "What the hell was that?"

Zach sits next to him. A twinge in his expression conveys disapproval of the mention of the word *hell*.

"Sorry." Travis wipes away the sweat pouring down his face. He dabs his forehead with his shirt. "So, what did I just see?"

"You saw what started this journey for you."

"So, a bunch of angels got massacred by a monster angel, and the ones who escaped here are somehow my responsibility?" He shakes it off. "That's too much to swallow."

"You've felt that way before, Travis."

Travis nods. "I felt a lot of ways before, but you just took me on a psychedelic trip to cloud city and now I'm supposed to digest that?"

"Yes."

"And let me guess. You want me to be inspired to somehow save the world?"

"Yes."

"You're the world's worst life coach; you know that?"

Zach's deadpan expression matches that of a dog unsure of what its owner is saying.

"Zach." Travis snaps his fingers. "I'm talking to you, buddy. Stay focused."

That far off look in Zach's face fades. "I am focused. Are you?"

"I am." Travis glares. It's as if he's arguing with a tree stump. "But you really suck at explaining things." With a laugh, "Along with the whole motivational thing."

A bonfire ignites in Zach's eyes.

He drifts upwards, an aura of light swirls outward, surrounding him. His voice echoes as if it were being broadcast across multiple stadiums: "Do you want to know what life is, Travis?"

A pang of fear stabs Travis as he surmises that his petulance has finally earned him an abrupt end by this prophetic and now pissed-off angel.

"This life is a filter, from which man is sifted. The clean from the corrupt. The prideful from the humble. Those who love, hate, and are vacantly neutral. Man is judged by God based on his actions and therefore permitted or denied into His kingdom." Zach's booming voice travels across the hillside with a thunderous resonance. A flock of birds shoots out from the trees and takes flight at the sound of his words, which makes Travis wonder if animals really can see angels. "In the end, it's who loves God that rises upwards to Heaven. This is not man's process. Nor a decision of the angels."

Zach makes a sweeping motion towards the horizon. Travis feels an earthly quiver in his body. It's rare that he gets scared, but Zach's intensity gives him extreme pause.

"The unconsecrated man and recusant angels who get into Heaven carry with them corruption and an unclean heart," Zach explains. "These are the very apples that will spoil the rest of the fruit."

"And God can't stop that? I mean He can stop anything. He's not going to let that happen."

"That's right. God *can* stop anything. That's why He has you."

Travis lets out a laugh. "He's about to be disappointed."

"So, you would let all that you love wither and turn black?"

"All that I love?" Travis looks around as if Zach is talking to someone else. "I don't really love anything."

Zach waves his hand, and a faint image of Travis's grandmother appears next to him.

Travis jumps. "Grandma?" He moves towards her, but she evanesces.

Zach waves with his other hand, and another version of his grandma appears.

Travis moves closer, reaches out, but his grandmother's image darkens. Her eyes swirl like black holes, a dark liquid seeps from them. She smiles and her teeth lengthen, sharpening unnaturally. Head twitches as if being intermittently zapped from within.

"What are you doing to her?" Travis demands. "Stop it!"

Grandma pops and jerks with the furtive movements of a malfunctioning robot. She opens her mouth, a thin snake-like tongue unravels outward.

"*I said stop it*!" Travis shouts, but Zach does nothing. He watches almost absently as she finishes her transformation. Losing all her hair. Skin sinking inward and cracking like a thin film stretched beyond its breaking point. She squeals, her head flopping from side to side like a spring.

"Zach, god dammit, stop!"

She stops indeed.

His grandmother stands before Travis in full form, blistered, mangled and smelling of decay and filth. She extends a crooked finger to him. "Travie?" His name, uttered from her creaking throat, sounds like a caliginous and prehistoric secret finally excavated.

Travis clenches his fists. *What did Zach do to her?*

"Travie, why do you look at me so?" She reaches towards him, but he recoils. "You don't want to taste the darkness?"

"What?"

"The darkness." She licks her sallow lips with a forked tongue. "Vanessa showed me."

"Vanessa?"

Grandma extends her other hand, which is scrunched tight. "She wanted to show you, too." She opens her hand, revealing an eyeball.

Travis is at a loss for words. What kind of madness is this? His grandma is a wretched, haggard mess of what he last remembered.

"You took this from Vanessa." Grandma's voice deteriorates like a distant phone call with terrible signal. "But she is willing to forgive you for what you did to her. However, you must first taste the darkness."

"What did you do to her?" Travis asks Zach.

"Nothing."

"You did something!"

"No, I have not. She is still your grandmother."

"This is some kind of Rift trap!" Travis pulls out his Beretta, fires at his grandmother and she withers away. He turns to Zach and fires, but the bullets zip right through him.

"I am not the Rift," Zach assures him. "And this not a trap."

Travis takes a breath. Lowers his gun. "Then what did you do to my grandmother? If that was even her."

"That is her, but it is her in the future."

Travis swallows hard, trying to make sense of all this. Something about Zach's visits always fry his brain and now, no matter where he tries to hide on this Earth, the stubborn angel finds him.

"Travis, that is what will become of all of us in Heaven. We will taste the stygian darkness. Like a virus brought in from the cold, it will be carried on the backs of man and angel, spreading through Heaven in a maddening sweep. The lies of the enemy will pour out of the mouths of every soul in Heaven."

Travis's gaze falls to the floor.

"And your mother, grandmother, and everyone you know will fall under the influence of the Rift." Zach's frenetic energy abates. "But you can always just hide away here in your new home."

"So, in plain English, if I don't help, what happens?"

"The angels and souls of man will open their ears to the unclean interlopers. There will be no delineation between Heaven and Hell and Earth. It would all be impure and imperfect. There would no longer be a contrast of black and white, but an ever-expanding gray," Zach intones. "Heaven will fall."

"And God would stand by and let that happen?"

"I guess that's up to you to find out."

Travis is taken aback by the comment. "What does that mean?"

"It means, whatever you decide to do next will answer that question for you." And in token Zach fashion, he folds his wings, and launches skyward.

This would normally be a moment where Travis would wise crack to himself about the peculiar enigmatic nature of Zach, but for once, he genuinely understands the angel.

He has a decision to make.

He can choose to be left alone. To see what happens. If what Zach opines will come to fruition, his respite will end abruptly. As Heaven and Earth blend into chaos, the Rift will finally have their day.

Or he can choose to jump back into the fight. This time not for financial gain or for some vision quest of his own, but to spare his loved ones, both dead and alive, from having their souls soiled by darkness. If that happens, then his mother, his grandmother, and even the few he cares for on Earth fall to the grips of evil. Then the Rift, unopposed, wins.

Travis closes his eyes. He must decide whether to stay in his personal bubble of peace and let God, man and the Rift work it out.

Or to get off his ass and jump back into the fray.

Chapter 20 – The Tortured Plight of the Winged

S imon pours himself a shot of rum as he makes his way to the balcony of his hotel. He takes a sip, relishing the caramel notes as he stares out at the ominous clouds that smother the sky and choke out the sun.

Balco joins Simon on the balcony.

Simon glances over his shoulder at Balco, then looks back towards the creeping darkness of night. "So, what's the deal with the red birthmark all over your face?"

Balco cocks his head to the side, curious.

"The handprint," Simon adds.

"A parting gift from Michael."

"Ah." Simon takes another sip, then gazes pensively out to the horizon. "Care to elaborate?"

Balco takes a moment to respond. "No."

"Fair enough."

Balco stares at Simon as he drinks absently from his glass. "Why do you ingest that poison?"

"Everything in this world is poison, Balco." Simon tilts the glass, making sure that even the last drop makes its way down his throat. "From the air we breathe, to the food we eat. At some level, everything we touch, visible or invisible, kills us."

"And yet, you knowingly imbibe?"

"We're going to break into Heaven . . ." Simon pours himself another shot. "And you're going to chastise me about drinking? God knows what we are about to do, but He clearly isn't stopping us. Nothing is going to stop us."

"You wear your pride on your body like a second skin. I would be wary of being so confident that the Father doesn't find a way to stop us. Perhaps He is even allowing this to happen for some greater purpose."

"I couldn't care less about God! He let my Cynthia die." Simon shakes his head, fighting back emotion as it roils up from within him. "She and I wasted years contributing to hospitals and churches; yet not a single fucking pill or prayer prevented her passing. God abandoned us in our time of need, and now I no longer need Him. But *we* . . ." Simon whirls around to face Balco. "We need each other so that we can find those treasures. You and your brothers want back *into* Heaven, and I want Cynthia *out*." Simon pauses, then adds, "But if you want to go about things on your own, you can go. I will not stop you."

Balco stares at him with the unwavering gaze of an owl. "You freed me, Simon. Therefore, I will assist you. Indeed, I want to go home. I do not want to reside among you and the rest of the unclean of this world. While I will never understand why God adores you so, I no longer care."

Another of the Amissa alights from the vast expanse above. With one swoop of his wings, the angel lands gracefully next to Balco.

Balco greets him. "Edos."

Edos. A silver haired stalwart consistently by Balco's side, he had guarded the gates dutifully since the dawn of man. He was the first of the Amissa to escape Heaven.

He was also the first captured by the Rift.

He was tortured while enduring their experiments. His skin is marred with scars. His wings are crooked and tattered, appearing more like the weathered sails of an old boat than the majestic appendages of his kin.

Edos bows to Balco. When he speaks, it's raspy, almost indiscernible if one isn't within earshot. "Dumahl is gone. The bewitched woman has slain him just as she did Ardiel in the bookstore."

Balco frowns, but his taciturn nature prevails, revealing no other traces of

137

emotion.

"She knows dark magic," Edos continues, "and therefore may be conspiring with the Rift. Perhaps they are looking to recapture us and continue with the conversions."

"What do you mean, conversions?" Simon asks.

"Many of the Amissa were turned. Forced to endure the sins of man at the hands of man until they aligned with those sins." Edos squeezes his hand into a fist so tight it shakes as if it's about to explode. "Those who did not expire were stripped of their wings. A tortuous pain that no human – and barely an angel – could withstand. These wingless remnants were then discarded into putrid cells, bereft of light and noise. Made to suffer in pain and silence. Comforted only by the lingering, repetitive thoughts and images of humans exacting foul horrors upon other humans." Edos grimaces, his angelic mind at a loss as expressed through the snarling movements of his face. "The free will God grants you seems to only enable your wickedness. Why God chooses to love you is something that we will never comprehend."

"You don't have to. You just have to help us reach into Heaven." Simon finishes the glass and plops it down clumsily against the stone railing. "Anyway, so what happens to those angels after they are thrown into solitary? Are they just left there to die?"

"We don't know," Balco admits.

"Aren't you interested in rescuing them?"

Balco lowers his head in shame.

Edos answers, "Even if we could find them, they are far too corrupted to be brought into Heaven. They are *tainted*, if you will."

"And you guys aren't?"

Without flinching, Balco responds, "Of course not! We still love our Father and we have no taste for the befouled temptations that man delights in."

"If we were to bring these fallen into Heaven," Edos explains, "they would spread their infection throughout God's kingdom."

"And you guys won't?" Simon asks with a self-assured laugh.

"Our Father will take us back without question," Balco answers.

"And you're a hundred percent sure of that?"

What Balco fails to share is that Michael might be waiting for them on the other side of those gates. He and his brethren will race to reach the feet of God and beg for salvation, forgiveness for their folly. There is no guarantee that one or all may make it, for Michael will make every effort to strike them down.

Aside from the threat of Michael's wrath, there is a gnawing guilt that weighs upon Balco. He steered his angels astray. He convinced them that there was abundance and an understanding to be had on Earth. He inspired so many of his brothers to abandon their place with the Father.

And for what?

To have most of his followers slaughtered by Michael?

To be captured by man and forced to wallow in their sinful ways?

Balco has run a fool's quest, and ironically, he led the Amissa into *becoming* the Amissa.

"Balco?" Simon asks.

Balco's eyes shine with a deathlike gravity, as though he just read a devastating letter that crushed his soul.

Simon snaps his fingers in the angel's face. "You good?"

"No."

"*No?*"

"The answer to your original question, is *no.*" Balco trades glances with Edos. "I am actually not a hundred percent sure we will be let into Heaven."

"You're not? Why?"

"It doesn't matter," Balco replies as he shakes off the sticky uncertainty that clings to him. "What does matter is that we get the gate open and free your wife, thereby relieving us of our debt to you so that we may focus on seeking redemption from God."

"To do that we still need the pendant and the manacles," Simon reminds him. "I'm sure that couple who got away knows where we might find them. It's just too bad we lost them."

"Actually," Edos says, "our brother Zolash was not harmed by her magic. He is following her as we speak."

Simon's face brightens at the news. "That so?"

Edos does a slow nod.

"Then, perhaps we should send more angels his way," Simon muses. "To aid him, should he need backup?"

Edos smiles, exposing his jagged teeth. "Zolash should be fine on his own against the witch and the human."

"Oh really?"

Balco interjects, "Zolash can turn himself into his own army."

"Literally," Edos agrees, as his mouth twists into a rictus, forming something closer to a sneer than a smile. "Zolash can handle himself. He can fight them off if need be and report to us."

"I hope so," Simon says. "Just because they are two *humans*, doesn't mean they can't be a threat."

"I, too, bore witness to what the witch did to Ardiel," Edos says with a hiss. "I assure you. He will not fail us!"

An abrupt sound comes from within the hotel room.

A door slams.

Tizzy struts onto the balcony. "What? Did I miss the angel convention?"

The angels eye her with displeasure.

"Yes, and you weren't invited," Simon says, his speech somewhat slurred. "So there better be a reason for your bravado."

"Bravado?" Tizzy huffs. "I'm surprised your drunk ass came up with a big word like that."

In an instant, Balco catches Tizzy by her leg and slings her over the balcony edge like a Yo-Yo. Squealing and squirming, her hands flail about aimlessly. As she dangles high above the street, blood rushes to her head, veins bulging to the point of bursting.

"What the fuck!?" Tizzy yells.

Simon folds his arms and peers over the railing at her.

Balco holds his arm out without so much as twitching. She struggles high above the looming street below like a trapped rodent. "You're equal parts stubborn and dumb. You killed that old man and left us to clean things up. I'm not looking for extra work; you got that?"

"Yeah!" she insists, "I got it. I'm sorry, alright!"

"Sorry?" Simon clenches a fist. "If one of the old man's neighbors heard the shot and the cops get involved," he shakes his head before warning, "I'm turning your sorry ass in."

"Ok got it. No more mistakes. Won't happen again, ok?" she assures him as she struggles not to look at the distant street below.

Simon glares at her. For a moment, he debates giving Balco a thumbs up to drop Tizzy to her death.

We don't need more bodies. We don't need the cops getting any more involved than they probably already are, Simon thinks. *But if she fucks up again, I'm going to have to make an exception.*

Tizzy gives in, glances momentarily at the dizzying drop below. She promptly shuts her eyes and begs, "Ok, can ya put me down? I've got good news for you."

Simon nods to Balco who hoists her back onto the balcony. "Speak."

Tizzy straightens her hair and her clothes as she tries to gather herself, doing her best to shake off the nerves. "You guys should be thankful. I had to sleep with that Rift pig, Riley, to get the info. Guy smells like a fucking dump truck." She eyes the bottle of rum. "Mind if I have a shot? Not sure what's got me more shook—Goliath here nearly throwing me over the edge, or the flashback of Riley's naked body."

Simon hands her the bottle.

Tizzy takes a swig straight from it. Then she continues, "I got him to tell me where the next hideout is, the one *he's* running. He told me that since their hideouts have been ransacked, the Rift have put him in charge and upped the security. So, Riley invited me to his hideout. Says he's never fucked while on the clock. Says he hasn't banged a chick my age since Gun and Roses was still on the radio." She shrugs. "Whatever that means. Any-who, we exchanged numbers. Said he'll text me the address. Told me to wear something cute. Like a thong or some shit under a tiny ass skirt. I don't even own a thong."

"We'll take you to Victoria's Secret," Simon says flatly.

"No thanks." Tizzy waves her finger in the air. "I ain't screwing fatso a second time."

Simon shoots Balco a look.

Balco moves like he's about to grab her again.

Tizzy shrivels up. Takes a clumsy step back.

Simon gestures for Balco to back down. "I'm joking. Don't worry," he assures her as he takes the bottle back. "You won't have to do double-duty. But you'd better be sure he answers your call when you set up date night, because you're going to lead us right to him."

Chapter 21 – Empty Retirement

The house is a little lonelier than Travis anticipated.

No one knocks at the door.

Even his mailbox is a solid hike from his porch.

His only company lately has been a mix of birds, squirrels, and the occasional wild turkey. Otherwise his world is a genuine ghost town, devoid of activity and people.

Just like he wanted.

Even with the spotty cell service, his phone hasn't rung. No one is asking him to track down or drop off some beloved or cursed artifact that promises to bring eternal peace or death or lotto numbers to its possessor.

Nothing.

It's just what he's longed for all these years.

Yet deep inside, he is unsettled. As of late, he has been battling a gnawing sense of unfulfillment.

This house, this promise to himself, has been frustratingly lacking. The sense of vacuity prevails in his core. It chews at his soul like a small rodent—not significant enough to cause disaster, but enough to cause discomfort.

Why do I feel this way? Travis muses. He makes himself tea. Earl Grey. Black for the discontent in his soul. *This sucks. When does that peace that Zach drones on about kick in?*

He did his job.

He stopped Lomak.

Gave Vanessa a long overdue dirt nap. Returned the Eyes of God to the

Covenant. He proved that he thought about others more than himself.

Or did he?

Is this palace of isolation and absence of feeling his prize? Is this sour gift of "freedom" soiled with the knowledge that he left cards on the table? That, despite their flaws, he let Duncan, Pastor Graham and Amanda down?

What about man itself?

He is half-angel, half-human.

Zach foretold his gifts. He is fully healed from all his physical injuries. But what of the scars in his mind? The dreams? The thoughts of Grandma? His mother? The fight in Heaven?

Travis takes a sip of tea, and it is so hot that it scalds his palette. He spits it out. With a frustrated sigh, he sets the cup aside. Feeling the chaos of emotions and questions swirl inside of him like an unwanted storm, he drops to his knees and resorts to the most basic, rudimentary thing he can think of.

The practice both Zach and his Grandmother went on about.

He drops to his knees and prays.

He folds his hands, closes his eyes, and rests his forehead against his thumbs.

"God, I'm going to be really honest," Travis begins, "I've done what You needed me to do. I saved Your Vision. Got it in the hands of the Covenant. I've sworn off cussing, though I'm going to admit that I'm still working on that, but You know that." He takes a deep breath, an attempt to calm the swell of exasperation in his throat that's knotting within him unexpectedly. "What I can't understand is why You can't let me enjoy my peace?"

There's a soft silence.

Nothing stirs in response. He awaits an answer but is met only with the vapid sound of emptiness. A variety of noises fills the air, though nothing that would supplant God answering from the thundering heavens above. Or wherever He resides.

The only sounds Travis hears: the sound of his own breath, the distinct tick-tick-tick of the quartz clock on the wall, and the occasional stirring of the ice maker jettisoning its next load of cubes into the freezer tray.

Travis laughs at himself. What did he expect? Sure, he has seen some supernatural things. Had his body heal in unimaginable time. Seen the world as God sees it. And spoken with angels, albeit frustratingly confusingly . . . still . . . angels nonetheless.

But here in this moment, there is no heavenly epiphany. No unearthly clarity. Zach is conveniently absent.

As always.

No, the only thing in his presence right now is an itchy emptiness and unsettling dissatisfaction with his new home. What he wanted hasn't brought him the happiness and solace he wanted, and it's a real pisser.

Travis leans back, unfolds his hands, and sighs.

"Who am I kidding?" he mutters to himself, but that's when his phone buzzes on the counter. Not once, but several times. He nearly dives for it.

How ironic? Here's a man longing to be alone, yet killing himself to check his phone for some sign of life. A missed call. A voicemail.

Or a text?

A text?

A text!

From Amanda. Not one, but several.

Where are you? The text reads. *Where are you?*

Where are you?

Where are you?

Where are you?

How many times has she texted him?

His question is answered as his phone displays NO SIGNAL.

And then the signal is back.

And then out again.

He was so eager to get away from humanity, he wrote off the very thing that kept him – however loosely – in touch. His cell phone.

"Amanda?" Even speaking her name brings a peculiar warmth to his soul, a feeling that that log cabin was supposed to deliver but hasn't.

Amanda.

Travis holds the phone up in the air as if it's somehow going to lead him to water. He paces about the living room, then the kitchen.

NO SIGNAL.

He moves about, waving the phone as if it's some kind of magic wand, but rather than seeking to cast a magic spell from it, a magic text is all he wants.

NO SIGNAL.

Travis bursts outside, holds his cell up in the air like a lightning rod trying to encourage some semblance of a connection.

NO SIGNAL.

"Dammit!"

Yes, the very thing he wanted, he got . . .

He got to disappear.

But not now!

For some unexplainable reason, Amanda is the only person he wants to hear from. Probably because she's the only one who's been straight with him. She's the only one who hasn't demanded anything more of him, more than to step up, grab his *cajones*, and help her stave off the Rift.

He got what he wanted: solace and solitude. But is this the meaning of free will? What we think we need, we don't? And what we don't realize we need we do? Travis wrestles with these thoughts as he practically jumps in the air with his phone.

"Come on, come on, come on!"

The cell signal rewards him with one bar. He frantically types: I'm here!

She replies: Where's here?

He hesitates. Begins a mental argument with himself: *Think fast, Travis! This could be a trap. What if it's not Amanda? What if it is? It is her number, but that doesn't matter. Her number could have been compromised. Perhaps she got a new phone? Maybe another burner?*

She replies again: Where's here?

Think, dammit!

An idea hits Travis. He texts her: What's the last thing you told me? In Miami?

NO SIGNAL.

"Shit!" he shouts with a groan.

The signal returns.

Then her reply text comes through: I told you that I hope retirement finds you well. How's that working out?

Travis feels that warmth grow inside him, a sensation that catches him off guard.

He texts her back: It is you!

She answers with: Yep. Sure is. Now where are you?

And he responds as quickly as the angels fly above the heavens.

Chapter 22 – Quell's Test

The great room in Marcus's mansion is nearly pitch-black, save for a sparse number of candle-lit sconces mounted along the opposing stone walls. Between them, several flagpoles are propped at forty-five-degree angles, bearing artwork that is indiscernible under the pale light.

There's a resounding crack as an LED spotlight rains a shaft of yellow onto a woman decked in all black.

Quell.

Positioned at the center of the room, she readies her sword. The harsh light from above gleams off the slick surface of her porcelain mask.

Marcus's voice booms from speakers cloaked within the shadows above. "Are you ready?"

Quell nods, the hilt of the sword held firmly in her grip. She knows that she must conserve every ounce of energy to survive her trial, so she makes a concerted effort not to grip her weapon too tightly.

A single word echoes from the speakers: "Begin."

Quell looks in every direction in anticipation of what is going to leap from the darkness. Wherever her attention goes, the tip of her sword follows. Chattering noises resonate from every shrouded corner of the chamber.

"Few have seen the Cleaners up close." Marcus's voice, amplified by the sound system, is more punctuated. "Let alone taken them on."

The chattering closes in from all directions, intensifying like a symphony of wall clocks, all clicking steadily and unnervingly.

Quell steadies herself, all while spinning continuously, scanning for the slightest movement.

There's a blur of motion.

A gray arm emerges from the shadows and claws at her. A red stripe of blood trails down her arm. She winces and turns in the direction of the attack.

Another arm lashes out.

Quell is struck again. She whirls around, sword aimed squarely at the suffocating darkness in front of her.

The chattering draws closer.

"I have confidence in you, Quell."

Quell is economical, deliberate in her movements, guarding her tight circle, in constant motion, checking and re-checking over each shoulder as she turns left, then right, then left again.

"If you can take on the Cleaners . . ."

Several arms lash out from both in front and behind her. Claws scrape down the center of Quell's back. She arches forward; the pain is blinding, but she chokes it down with a muffled grunt. She wheels herself around and lunges, her sword cutting nothing but empty space.

"Then I'll have no doubt you can take on an angel."

Another claw zips through the air, but this time Quell avoids the strike. She responds with a solid thrust forward but again, hits nothing.

She's fighting with ghosts.

"For the Cleaners are nothing more. . ."

There are several loud pops in succession, the snapping sounds of something shifting into place. Or turning on.

". . . than fallen angels."

More LED spotlights burst to life, exposing three figures surrounding her.

The Cleaners.

Grotesque versions of their former angelic selves. Their skin tone is pallid, ashen, and cadaverous. Their freakish eyes, big as eight-balls, bulge as if these creatures had been squeeze-toys in a previous life. Their mouths are equally exaggerated, stuffed with oversized teeth that clatter relentlessly.

One of the Cleaners yanks a flagpole off the wall, opens its clacking mouth and feeds itself the entire length of the pole, chomping away with the efficiency of a woodchipper. As it finishes with an unapologetic blank expression, its vacant black orbs glare at Quell with empty regard.

Quell does not flinch. Wherever the creature's meal vanished to is no concern to her. She is ready to strike it down.

Heads angled to one side, ears parallel to the floor, the Cleaners step forward in unison studying Quell with their vacuous expressions.

"We have taken these fallen angels," Marcus continues, "and given them a new purpose. They are no longer the Amissa. The lost. They are found. They are the Cleaners of the Rift."

The hungry Cleaner snatches another flagpole and consumes it in a matter of seconds as well.

Quell's will does not falter. She is steadfast in her readiness.

The hungry Cleaner stiffens. His arms lock at either side. Hands splay as if holding invisible basketballs. It advances, charging Quell so fast that it nearly grabs ahold of her, but it misses.

Two bright flashes of light carve an 'X' in midair.

Quell steps aside as the creature slides apart, diced expertly by the heavenly blade she wields. The hungry Cleaner explodes, a disc of expanding fulgid light, and with a shriek it evaporates before its twisted body hits the floor.

Quell is already back in position, elbows high, but close. The end of her sword is aimed with a deliberate clarity. She keeps a measured distance from the other two Cleaners, who, upon seeing their fallen kin, split up, arms and fingers spread wide and ready. They circle her, but she matches their pace; her attention shifting from one Cleaner to the other.

Then she darts between the two.

Swipe-swipe-swipe.

Even the air hisses as her heavenly blade, once wielded by the archangel Michael himself, turns this monster of a former angel into a light show.

Quell moves on to the last one standing.

The remaining Cleaner is lankier than the others with the gaunt build of a scarecrow. To the untrained, a slender physique could be seen as a weakness. But Quell, in her years of fighting through the ranks of machismo and sexism through the Rift, has found that all opponents should be treated equally. Make no assumptions.

Yes. Make no assumptions. Such as those foolish men of the Rift had of her. Because she was a woman, some of their men thought they could take her.

They were wrong.

Dead wrong.

Black dust wrong.

She dusted her way to the top.

Then Vanessa recruited her. Stuck her working with a shitty crew of Rift boys who didn't want to listen to her. They did things their way. The mission failed. She took the fall.

A snarl forms on her lips as the memories bubble up in her mind.

She paid the price with her face. She had never been vain, but now she was disgusting to look at. Marred. Beautiful only from one angle. Disgustingly disfigured from another. No man or woman would want her.

And in turn, she wanted no one.

Only the one who believed in her, the one who spared her from losing her face, her life entirely.

Marcus.

He had no agenda.

He did not want her body.

He did not want her soul.

He only wanted to inspire and mold her to do that which he could not physically do himself. Vanessa's self-centered, chaotic ways cock-blocked Marcus's genius and leadership, but now she was dead, and the Rift was primed for a new order.

Nothing was going to stand in the way of their running the Rift their way. *His way.*

Quell's way.

This is no longer a *man's* world, and in time, this could be *her* world.

Until then, her loyalties were first and foremost to Marcus. He spared her life and asked nothing in return. She could not turn on him. She was going to see this through the end.

Neither man . . .

Nor Rift . . .

Nor angel . . .

Was going to stop her.

The Cleaner's mouth chatters maniacally as it closes the distance. She tries to adjust, taking a step back but finding herself against the cold walls of the room. Jaws snapping away, it reaches out to bite her, but instead takes in the blade of her sword.

Unlike the flagpoles, the blade does not vanish from existence.

A screech follows.

Then bright light.

And the Cleaner is no more.

Quell's chest is heaving. She pivots on her heels. Left, then right, then left. *Are there more?* She wonders.

Out of the darkness of one of the entryways, a lone figure wearing a long elaborate cloak claps his hands together in awe. "Well done! Well . . . done!" Marcus smiles as he applauds her performance. "I was not the least bit worried."

Catching her breath, she swipes the sweat from her forehead. "Sir, that was almost too easy."

"Indeed." He takes a corner of his cloak and dabs at the sweat on her face. "But that is only because you have trained so hard and for so long." His gazes lowers to her sword. "And with the Angel's Blade, nothing can stop you, whether natural or supernatural." He caresses her face, sensing the doubt in her eyes as they shift uncomfortably from side to side. "But the tool is only as good as its master."

"Why are we doing this?" She leans back, resting her body against a pillar.

"You know why."

"The Amissa."

"And whatever else God brings our way."

"You mean like Travis Rail?" Quell sighs. "I'm not afraid of him."

"You should be. Don't underestimate him or any of the Covenant. They are insanely devout to their . . ." Marcus makes quotes with his fingers, "beloved Father."

"If you don't believe God exists," Quell takes a moment to catch her breath then asks, "then why do you want the keys to His kingdom?"

"Because if we control the entrance to Heaven, we control the world."

"That doesn't answer my question."

Marcus snorts, turning away in frustration. "It doesn't matter what I believe. All that matters is that you are prepared in the event that the Covenant, the Rift, or the Amissa shows." Marcus looks back at her. "You're the only one I trust on this wretched planet."

"For that, I am grateful sir. I owe you much."

Marcus talks over her, goes on, "This is why I have been training you all of these years. You are next in line to take over, so long as Viola does not come back into power." He closes in on her; she pulls back slightly. "The Raven sisters have it all wrong. You do not need dark magic to control the world." He taps a finger against his temple and elaborates, "You only need a sound, resolute mind. That, you have. The magic you lack will be supplanted by our witches."

Quell ponders his words, then asks, "And if Viola awakens?"

"If she awakens from her spell and finds out that her sister died, she will go on a rampage. But again," he gives her shoulders another squeeze and continues, "if you can take down a Cleaner, you can take down an angel, and you most certainly can take down a witch, no matter how powerful."

There's a flash of doubt in her eyes and she tries to look away, but Marcus grabs her face.

"Travis killed one of them," he tells her. "And he has no idea who or what the fuck he is. So, if he can do it, you can surely take Viola or anyone else on, ok?"

Quell nods.

"Are you with me?"

She nods again. "Yes."

Marcus breaks into a smile. Then relieved laughter follows. "Good." He hugs her. "Good. Good. That's all I needed to know."

"Sir!" A voice from behind them breaks in.

Both Marcus and Quell cease their embrace to find one of his Rift agents at the entrance to the room.

"Yes?" Marcus asks.

"We have confirmation," the man reports.

"Of?"

"The next hit. The Amissa took the bait. Riley is prepped and waiting."

"Really?" Marcus rises, elation in his tone. "Tell me more."

Quell wipes the last bit of sweat from her face with her forearm and sheathes the sword gracefully in its hilt. Not a trace of blood or fluid on it.

"Well, sir," the agent explains, "they are going to strike soon. They believe they will find the manacles at Riley's warehouse."

Marcus claps his hands together. "Perfect. Then let's give them something worth finding!"

Chapter 23 – Old Friends and New Issues

A car pulls up to Travis's cabin. He peeks through the windows and sees two figures step out. Beretta ready in case this is a Rift trap. Even texting her the address was a stupid, emotionally-driven move. If it isn't Amanda, then he led the Rift right to him.

Screw it, he muses. *Let's settle this anyway.*

The figures approach.

It is Duncan and Amanda, at least from their outward appearance. Sure, this could be a setup, but his gut screams otherwise. As she draws closer, he feels a sense of peace. Something he hasn't felt in a while, not since she practically bolted from his car back in Miami, leaving him with a growing dislike of himself.

Duncan and Amanda marvel at the house as they approach. Travis watches them as they hesitantly trade glances. Amanda is the one brave enough to knock.

Travis gives it a moment. Gulps hard. He hasn't seen her in six months, but it feels like years.

She knocks again.

Travis chokes down the hesitation, then asks, "Who is it?"

"Travis, it's us," Duncan replies. "Duncan and Amanda."

"How do I know that?" Travis asks.

"Well . . ." Duncan searches Amanda for an answer but is only rewarded with a shrug. "Ask me something."

Travis turns away, mind reeling. Then, "What's the last thing you asked of me?"

Duncan pauses.

Amanda squints, tries reading her brother.

"At Dunkin' Donuts." Travis adds. "What's the last thing you asked me *not* to do?"

The wheels turn in Duncan's head. Then he sighs, remembering. He looks to his sister, then back at the front door. "I asked you not to tell Amanda that you spoke with me."

"And why's that?" Travis prods through the door.

Duncan swallows. Amanda shoots him a look.

"Why's that, *Duncan*?"

Duncan turns to Amanda. "Because I didn't want her to know that I was alive."

Amanda bites her lip, holding back the resentment that is resurfacing inside her. Duncan reaches to console her, but she swats his arm away. "You made me cry for you. You lied to protect *who*? Me? From what?" Her eyes burn hot white. Her voice deepens an octave lower. "You've seen what I am."

Duncan says in nearly a whisper, "I didn't mean to bring that side out of you."

"It never left."

The door creaks open. Travis steps aside to let them in. "What was that?"

"What?" she asks, her voice normal again.

Travis hesitates. "Never mind." He shakes his head.

"So," she questions as she brushes past him, "are you growing paranoid in your old age?"

"I had to be sure you guys were actually *you* and not something else."

"How do you know I'm not?"

"What?" The comment catches Travis off guard. Maybe that little voice change outside wasn't in his head.

With a half-cocked smile, she throws back, "*Never mind.*" She drops on the couch like a bag of bricks.

Travis injects as much sarcasm into the words as possible, "Yeah . . . so . . . go ahead and make yourselves at home. And yeah, it's great to see you," looks at Duncan, "both."

Duncan grits his teeth as he slowly settles next to his sister.

"Can I get you guys something to drink?" Travis asks.

Amanda glares at Travis.

Duncan clears his throat.

"Right." Travis rolls his eyes as he pours himself some water. He finds a spot on a leather loveseat across from them. A staring contest begins between Amanda and Travis. Duncan trades glances between the two. No one says anything for a while and the air thickens with awkwardness.

Travis treads carefully with this question, arching an eyebrow as he asks her, "So, did you come here to give me dirty looks?"

"I'm sure you don't care, since you didn't exactly know him," she says flatly, "but Pastor Graham is dead."

Travis searches Duncan for confirmation, who nods. "I'm sorry." Travis sets the glass of water aside and folds his arms across his chest. "The Rift?"

Amanda stares at the floor. With a distant gaze, she answers with a soft, "No."

"Then who?"

Amanda turns away.

Duncan answers for her. "Tizzy."

"Tizzy?" Travis puts his face in his hands, hangs his head over his knees, and lets out a long sigh. "I never liked that little jerk. She shot me, lied to all of us, and now you tell me this."

Amanda glances at Travis. Eyes narrowing, she asks, "So how does it feel to be right? Does it feel good?"

Incredulous, Travis jumps out of his chair. "I don't care about being right! Ok? I just never trusted her. I wasn't wrong, and now the old man's dead. I'm not the bad guy here."

"You're right. You're not." She looks up at him, eyes boiling with emotion. "You were just out here . . . in the boonies . . . minding your own business. Nice and retired."

"I got it." Travis sits back at the edge of the cushion. "You're upset that I didn't stick around and help you. Trust me when I say that I have thought about that moment in the car every day."

"Yeah, well you had other plans," Amanda reminds him. "Can't say I blame you. I mean look at this place." She sizes up the room, scanning the wooden furnishings. A pang of jealousy laces her words as she admits, "Your hard work paid off. You got what you wanted."

"I know you're upset, but please don't blame me for the pastor's death. Blame Tizzy."

"Oh, I blame her plenty. Along with myself."

"I didn't mean to suggest that you were to blame."

Amanda holds up her hand, ceasing the conversation. "I didn't come here to talk in circles. I came here . . ." She sighs, looks to Duncan, then Travis. "I came here because we have no one else to turn to. And if you're willing to help us . . ."

Travis approaches her, kneeling close to her side. The heaviness that has weighed on him since Miami seems to finally lift now that an opportunity to escape from his own selfish needs presents itself. Amanda has done something that not even the angels of Heaven could inspire him to do.

Help.

"Look," Travis hangs his head as he confesses, "I'm sorry for being a selfish prick. I let my own ambition get in the way of helping." He looks up at her, her eyes crystalline with a mixture of fear, anger and sadness. "I saw that look in your eyes back in Miami and I should've helped you then. I'm sorry I didn't and now Pastor Graham's dead." He takes her hand. "You have my help." He glances over at Duncan. "Even if your brother here has lied to me."

Amanda lets out a little laugh. "Join the club."

Duncan protests, "For the record, I did what I thought was right."

"Yeah, by leaving things out." Travis rises. "But we won't get into that again. Like she said. No talking in circles." To Amanda: "So, if you want me to hunt down Tizzy, I'm all in. Just tell me where she is and I will end her myself."

"It's not just about Tizzy, and this is not about vengeance. This is about something bigger."

"You might want to sit down for this, Travis," Duncan warns.

"Alright." Travis plops back onto the loveseat. Smacks his knees and asks, "What's up?"

"Tizzy is not working alone," Amanda explains. "She is working with someone named Simon."

"Simon?" Travis runs the name through his brain. "Simon who?"

Duncan shrugs. "We didn't have time to interview him."

Travis points at Duncan. "I'm not talking to you."

Duncan deflates, settles deeper into the couch.

"I don't know." Amanda stares absently into the floor. "That's just the person Tizzy was talking to on the phone, and then a man showed up with . . ."

"With what?"

"A group of angels."

"How many?"

"A few. I think. I can't remember. It was a blur. I only remember everything going black. I grabbed Tizzy and threw her at them, and then we ran."

"Wait. What?" Travis replays her words in his head, blinking several times as if processing what he just heard. "You *threw* her?"

Amanda begins to rock back and forth in her seat, attempting to console herself. "Yes."

"Like, did you throw her over your shoulder or something?"

"No," she answers, not making eye contact with him. "I . . . I picked her up and chucked her at them like a throw pillow."

"A throw pillow?" Travis chuckles inwardly. "How?"

"With hate. That's how." Amanda locks eyes with him now. They pulse a bright white. "She woke something up inside me."

"Ok," Travis says as he points at her and laughs uncomfortably, "now that's new."

"Not really." Amanda inhales deeply, as if mustering the courage for what she is about to say. "I helped Tizzy because I saw myself in her. I was running the streets too when I was her age." She looks to Duncan. "Ask him. I was never home. I hated being home because we didn't have a home."

"What do you mean?" Travis asks.

"We were foster kids, Travis." Duncan winces after he speaks. "We don't know who our parents are."

"We bounced around from house to house," Amanda goes on, "and each home seemed worse than the last. Duncan sought refuge with the church. But, like Tizzy, I found refuge on the street; only the Covenant didn't recruit me . . ."

"The Rift did," Travis finishes for her.

Amanda gently nods her head *yes*. "I wanted to be out of the foster loop so bad, I jumped into the first group of people who took me in like family."

"How exactly did you run into the Rift? It's not like they've got signs up all over town."

Amanda laughs at herself, mocking her own foolishness. "I was waitressing at this seedy club in Downtown Miami. It was a busy night. The manager and I were the last ones to leave . . . only he had other plans. He locked me in his office and tried to have sex with me. I fought back. One thing led to another and I ended up on the ground with this monster about to rape me. Then a very attractive woman with the blackest of hair burst in the door. She had glowing, emerald green eyes—eyes that commanded your attention. I couldn't look away."

"Vanessa?" Travis asks.

Amanda nods.

"But she acted like she didn't recognize you when she had her goons bring you out back at her office in Miami."

"It had been ten years. Guess either I grew up a lot since then, Vanessa grew more senile, or both. She was recruiting big time back then. I was one of many, many women that she groomed." Amanda sighs and continues the story, "Anyway, Vanessa killed that pig. Placed her palms on the guy's head and his eyes went black. Blood slid from his nose and ears as though she nuked his brain."

"Maybe she did."

"Probably," Amanda agrees. "Vanessa told me she owned the club and had been wary of this manager. He'd been *casually associating* with the other help. Now that she caught him, she sent him to the dark place. Part of me

160

was scared. Part of me was fascinated. Then, she told me that she had been eyeing me and promised to teach me if I was willing."

"And why would you want to learn that crap?" Travis asks.

"Because I was eighteen, angry, and lost."

"But," disgust seeps into Travis's words as he reminds her, "*it's the Rift.*"

Anger flashes in her eyes. "Are you judging me?"

"No, I just hate the Rift."

"Well at the time, I had no idea about the Rift or what she was all about until it was too late!" Amanda jumps to her feet.

"Look, I'm sorry. I didn't mean to sound like I was judging you."

"I couldn't care less if you were or not." Amanda walks to the window and looks out.

"Either way," he tells her, "I'm sorry."

"No, I'm sorry." Amanda touches the glass pane on his window. "I'm sorry I let them teach me. They fed off my angst and exploited it, grooming me to enrich their coven. She was creating a small army of elite witches, known as the Shakers. Super witches who could effectively shake the soul out of living things." Amanda rests her hands in front of her, palms facing up. "They had me train in the dark arts so that I could kill people they didn't want around. I did it. I hated every minute of it. The more I killed, the more the hate grew, but there was this still small voice inside telling me that I was losing touch with myself." She opens and closes her fist. "It wasn't until I was supposed to kill Pastor Graham that things changed."

Duncan shoots her a look of surprise. "What?"

"Yeah. You didn't know that, huh?"

"No! He never told me—you never told me!"

"Sucks being lied to, huh, Duncan?" Travis asks.

"That's not being lied to," Duncan corrects. "That's having the truth held back. Leaving important details out." He catches himself. His words falling upon an indignant audience. Both Amanda and Travis frown at him, and he shrinks.

"Anyway," Amanda continues, "when I was sent to kill Pastor Graham, he was the one who turned things around. When I was about to nuke his brain, much like Vanessa nuked that pig, Pastor Graham began to pray." She pauses. "I thought that was the oddest thing. Then that still small voice spoke to me again. Told me that Pastor Graham was going to change me. And that voice was right. He did." She squeezes her fist and it ignites with fiery blue light, then fades.

Travis's jaw drops.

"Ironically, I ended up using the very things they taught me." Amanda clenches her fist so tight, it shakes. "That rap sheet Vanessa mentioned that I had . . . well she was referring to the crimes I committed against her. The people I killed. I started wiping out Vanessa's Shaker witches. They were just as young as me, neophytes in black magic. I dusted them one by one. But the more of them I killed, the more of myself I killed. Vanessa was right. I joined the Covenant out of hate for the Rift."

Travis stares at her in pure awe.

This is nothing he would have ever expected her to admit to. A far cry from the woman he had helped save from the Rift back in Miami. "So, all that time you were with Lomak – when he held you captive – you had the capacity to kill him, but you didn't. Why?"

"Because I made a promise to Pastor Graham that once I left the Rift, once I left behind that dark magic, that I wouldn't kill again. I wouldn't open the door and go down that path of losing myself. But clearly, I have broken those promises. And now that I have had a taste of the black magic again, the craving has returned. It's kind of like giving an alcoholic a drink after years of sobriety. There's a renewed feeling, a retired comfort that returns." Amanda closes her eyes and sighs. "You feel dual emotions simultaneously. Shame and euphoria. Magic, this disgusting vile magic, is like that shot—once you have it again, you remember. You miss the power, and you despise the helplessness that comes without it."

"I never realized that you went through all of that, Sis."

"You never cared."

Duncan winces. The words sting. "What?"

"Yeah, you were too busy pursuing righteousness. Your eyes were fixed up above. Not on any of us right in front of you."

Duncan holds his tongue. Gaze falling to the floor like a scolded child. The moment hangs in the air, uncomfortable and weird.

"Well . . . speaking of alcohol," Travis rises and goes to grab a beer before asking, "anyone else want a drink?"

Duncan holds up his hands. "You know I don't drink."

"Maybe you should start," Travis responds.

"No, thank you. Life has enough temptations."

"You mean like whether or not to lie or to withhold the truth?" Amanda asks and Travis makes a face that says, *she said it*, not me.

"If you guys want me to apologize, I will a thousand times over." Duncan makes the point with his hands. "I'm sorry for not telling you both the truth. The full truth. I didn't want to expose either one of you to information that could hurt you."

"We're past the hurt stage," Amanda answers. "And whatever your selfish reasons were, trying to protect me or not, really didn't matter. I still had to face Lomak and Vanessa. I was bait for Travis. I didn't want this blackness to resurface. I have tried so hard to bury it, but it has resurfaced and now this is no longer about you, *Brother*."

Duncan swallows hard. His omissions have withered away his sister's trust like weed killer on a precious flower. "I didn't mean to hurt you, either of you. I had only good intentions. I figured less is more."

"What's that cliché?" Travis muses. "The road to Hell is paved with stupid intentions."

"Good intentions." Duncan pushes his glasses up the bridge of his nose. "*Good* intentions."

Travis scowls. "You need to get yourself some new glasses. Clearly those don't fit anymore."

"I've been a little busy."

"Yes . . . lying."

"Shut up! Both of you!" Amanda's voice reverberates around the room. The two men exchange looks.

"I didn't come here to argue. I came here for your help, but I'm not going to beg for it. If you're not interested, then continue your hermitage. I'm

163

perfectly—"

"I already said I'll help you!" Travis exclaims, holding both hands up in surrender. "Now just tell me what's going on."

"Fine. I'll get right to it. Tizzy is working with Simon and his gang of rogue angels to find two pieces of a puzzle: the Manacles of the Messiah and a silver cross pendant."

Anxiety ripples through Travis at the mention of the pendant.

A voice within him utters softly, *It's your pendant.*

He shakes off the voice and the sudden coldness he feels throughout his body.

"The pendant is technically the key that opens the manacles," she continues, "which inadvertently opens a backdoor, if you will, into Heaven."

"This Simon. . . does he have a slick, well-dressed demeanor? Like a manicured asshole?"

Amanda sighs. "Don't know. I was a little preoccupied. What are you getting at?"

"What did he look like?"

"It was quick, ok? I mean, I didn't get his inseam and shoe size, but I can tell you his appearance was the opposite of what you described. Rough. Face full of stubble. And a nasty scar that ran up the left side of his face."

"Did the scar go from here," Travis traces a finger from his chin to his eyebrow, "to here?"

"Yeah, it was pretty prominent."

Travis nods. "Well . . . I gave him that scar."

"You what?" Duncan asks.

"He was the one looking to buy the Eyes of God off Lomak, but instead left with one less eye. Thanks to me."

"Guess it's too bad you didn't kill him," Amanda says.

"Oh, I was busy dying." Travis makes a face. "So does Simon have the manacles?"

"Don't think so. I believe that the Rift does, and he's been ransacking their warehouses and safehouses on a rampage looking for them and the pendant. Meantime, he's been freeing up these angels and building himself a small army."

"Well if he has Tizzy working for him, then she must know something that he doesn't; otherwise that prick would have killed her." Under his breath he mutters, "Not that he's the only one."

Amanda cocks her head to the side, and grimaces. "That makes two of us."

Travis shoots her a look. "Did Pastor Graham know where the pendant is?"

"If he did," Duncan says, "he didn't tell us."

"Well, since he didn't tell you," Travis pulls at his necklace, unveiling the silver cross pendant, "I will."

There's a shimmer of awe in Amanda's eyes. "Where did you get that?"

"My grandmother. She gave me grief once, in a dream, about not wearing it. I used to keep it in my wallet." He taps it. "Now I keep it close to my heart."

Amanda looks at it, then searches his eyes. "May I?"

With a shrug. "Sure."

Amanda eyes the silver cross. The way the light gleams on it makes it seem almost translucent. She goes to touch it, and as soon as she does, a tiny spark forms between her hand and the pendant.

Both she and Travis jump.

"What was that?" Duncan demands, his eyes wide with shock.

"I don't know." Travis tucks the necklace back into his shirt. "I never had that happen before."

Amanda recoils, wiping her hand against her jeans. "It's me. God knows I'm not . . . *pure*."

Travis laughs. "Honestly, ain't no one on this Earth pure."

"He does have a point, Sis."

"You guys don't get it." Amanda opens her hands, palms up. "I've been corrupted by the Rift, by my own choice, no matter how young and stupid I was at the time." Her hands ignite like the blue-tinged flames of a gas stove. "And now that I have killed angels, I have delved even deeper into the darkness."

Travis watches her sink into depression. Shoulders slumped forward, head hung low, she's in a downward spiral, a mental abyss of her own making.

"Actually, what is the point of trying to stop them from opening up the gate to Heaven?" She's talking to herself now. "What am I fighting for? None of this matters."

"Stop it!" Travis grabs her; shakes her hard. "That's bullshit and you know it!"

Duncan raises an eyebrow at the curse word, and Travis points at him without looking, gesturing for him to stay silent.

"Whatever angels you killed, if they were working with Simon, then their intentions were no longer pure either," Travis reminds her. "They were just as corrupt as Simon."

Amanda stares at the floor, as if she were looking through the wooden slats and not at them.

Travis kneels in front of her, stealing her attention. Their eyes meet. "There's still good in you, regardless of what you did in your past. A screwup like me is proof of that. I've done a lot of things I'm not proud of, and yet, God, for some strange reason, keeps me around. Wants me to help Him out. Between you and I, we got some work to do." He squeezes her shoulders and softens his tone. "So, tell me, what do you need?"

"I need your help stopping Simon and these angels from combining the pendant and the manacles."

"Well, they're not going to get the pendant from me, I can assure you of that."

"Travis," Duncan interjects, "You're talking about angels."

"So?"

"Rogue angels."

"So what?" Travis shakes off the comment with a *what does that mean to me?*

"They're not just any angels. They are the Amissa. They are the tainted. The misplaced. The corrupted. The . . . lost," Duncan explains.

"Oh, so, they're just like us?" Travis asks. "Like . . . people."

"Yes, but they don't want to be lost anymore. They want the pendant and they want to get back to Heaven. It's that simple."

166

"I know. Trust me. I saw the movie!" Travis says. "Saw how it all went down. How some escaped and some didn't. It was a massacre. These guys thought the grass was greener on the other side of the clouds; only they got here and found nothing but weeds. Worse yet, they ended up more confused as to why God loves weeds so much."

Duncan stares at Travis in awe. "That is the most profound way of putting it I've ever heard."

"I never knew you were capable of sarcasm, Duncan."

Duncan searches for the words, "I-I-I actually meant that."

"How do you know all of this?" Amanda asks Travis. "And how did you see it go down?"

"Let's just say not all the angels upstairs would like them to come back home."

"That's why we have to stop them," Amanda insists. "We can't let them get ahold of both treasures."

"And not just the Amissa," Duncan reiterates, "the Rift. Or man at large. If anything, we need to get back the manacles and get them to Jakob and Noam. To our vault overseas."

"Well, I'm ready." Travis taps his Beretta. "Let's do this."

"That won't work on angels," Duncan informs him.

"No, but it will work on anybody else who gets in my way." Travis holsters the gun.

"Wonderful. So, what's the plan then?" Duncan asks.

"Well my first thought is that we hunt down the manacles, assuming the Rift still has them," Travis answers. "Since the Amissa are making their rounds, we'll undoubtedly run into them. Take them head on—"

The front door explodes and all three are knocked to the floor.

There's dust and noise everywhere.

Zolash enters.

He is a peculiar angel, with pale, almost translucent skin that radiates thin, iridescent pastel colors. His hair stands on end, as if energized by all things static and volatile and electrically charged. If a lightning bolt were made sentient, it would be this frightful atrocity of an angel. Perhaps his time on

167

Earth — or whatever experiments and torture the Rift had put him through — has brought some darker portion of his angelic duty to the surface. If he were a soul searcher or slayer in his position above, that duty has now permeated itself throughout his angelic being but with a sinister twist.

"There's no need to hunt us down," Zolash pronounces, "if we are already here."

"Who are you?" Travis asks as he gets to his feet. Duncan and Amanda follow suit, dusting themselves off.

"I am Zolash. Scout of the Amissa. I can be everywhere at once. I can spread myself across the corners of your world."

"Ok, ok, ok." With a dismissive wave, Travis interrupts. "You can stop right there. I stopped caring about two seconds ago."

"Interesting." Zolash leans forward, studying Travis like a target he's about to take down. "Seems your home was visited by our brother. I can smell the traces of his essence."

"No clue what you're talking about, dude."

"Yes . . ." Zolash licks his lips. His teeth are devilishly sharp. He says the name so fast; it sounds slurred: "*Zachariel.* He was here."

Travis readies himself.

"Zachariel is quite the pontificator. Promising this world peace through prayer." Zolash's tongue flares like a snake's, sniffing the air. "But he is enamored with the Lord's every whim. He is one of God's favorites. His door-to-door salesmen of promise."

"You sound jealous." Travis winks at him. "Just a little."

"I love the Father. How dare you minimize that?"

"And yet, you want Him to take you back after you ran away?" Travis quips. "Talk about daddy issues."

Zolash snarls, his tongue quickly retracting behind a wall of crooked enamel. "You blasphemous half-breed!"

"Half-*wing.*"

"How dare your abhorrent tongue refer to our Father as *daddy.*" He brings up his fingers, claws stretching outward at impossible lengths, sharpening at the ends. "I'm going to sever that monkey-muscle from the floor of your mouth and grind it between my teeth." Zolash points at Amanda. "And then I'm going to dine on her beating heart. Char her soul just as she did our brothers."

"Bring it on, *motherfucker*." Travis pulls out his Beretta. "I'm not afraid of you."

Chaotic energy flickers out from Zolash and several copies of the angel fan out from either side of him.

The wave of anxiety that hits Travis is almost instantaneous.

Deja vu.

His first encounter with Lomak.

Does this angel possess the same intoxicating poison that Lomak had?

No.

Travis's gut – his angelic senses – tell him that this is *not* Rift magic. This is what Zolash meant when he said he can be everywhere at once.

One of the Zolash clones whirls around and flies outside.

The rest march in on them like the jaws of a closing trap.

Chapter 24 – Riley's Place

There is a *For Sale sign* outside the battered and rusted warehouse tucked under I-75. The realtor's numbers are obscured thanks to the wrath of summer's unyielding heat.

Inside, several agents sit attentively at a camera bay. Ten screens alternate between varying angles of the warehouse. There are more cameras in play than the Super Bowl. Any trace of movement and the surveilling team is instantly notified. Given the recent string of robberies, this crew was not going to take any chances.

Not so much as a feral cat was going to break in.

One of the surveilling agents, a young man barely in his thirties, catches something on the monitor. He leans forward in his chair, vision narrowing through thick Coke-bottle glasses as he studies the screen. He swivels around to face a burly agent dressed in black fatigues, sporting a thick ginger beard and a wool turtleneck.

Riley.

"You ever get hot in that thing?" the young agent asks.

Riley delivers a curt, "What?" With his Australian accent, the word ends up coming out more like, "*Wot?*"

"Dude, we're in Florida. You gotta be dying."

In one swift motion, Riley unsheathes a knife and lands it inside the agent's nostril so deftly it doesn't even disturb his glasses. "If I cut off your nose, you might not die." Riley's eyes swell with crazed excitement as he threatens, "But I guarantee your glasses won't fit anymore."

The young agent trembles and his glasses begin to slide.

"If I wasn't already shorthanded, you'd be ash right now." With a quick flick of the blade, Riley catches them and gently pushes them back up the bridge of the young agent's nose. "Take your eyes off the cameras again and see what happens." Riley gives the man a kick and the chair rolls into the desk, causing all the monitors to flicker. He then addresses the other agents who look on from their respective corners of the vast room. "We're on red alert, chaps. The lot of you got that through your noggins?"

Silent agreement washes across the men.

"Be a damn shame if this place turns into a dog's breakfast, letting it all go to shit. Whoever is ripping us off, is making sure to wipe out every bloody drongo in their wake." Riley taps the blade against his chest, and it clinks against one of his shirt buttons. "So, I'm making sure that we don't end up dusted."

"But Riley," a voice calls out.

Riley's head snaps in the direction of the agent talking.

"Are we just going to sit here and babysit these fucking boxes?" The agent steps forth from the cover of a rusted shipping container. An automatic weapon is slung across his chest. He gestures towards a stack of wooden shipping crates piled neatly in the center of the room. "I mean, how long are we supposed to wait?"

"How long?" Riley takes a step in the man's direction. Clenching his teeth, he lowers his gaze as if he were about to strike his boot across the floor and charge. Louder, "*How long?!*"

Sensing the clear display of aggressive body language, the agent promptly raises his arms in surrender. The gun dangles now from his shoulders like a clunky necklace. "I'm just asking. That's all."

"Until the trucks show up, that's how long! What we need you to do is nothing but a piece of piss. It's easy shit. You're getting paid to fucking babysit whatever the Rift wants," Riley says. "Now, is that alright with you?"

"Yes, sir."

"Fan-bloody-tastic."

"But when's the truck coming?" another agent asks.

Spittle flies from his mouth as Riley barks, "Who just asked that?"

From high in the catwalks, a single, brave agent raises his hand.

"Do I look like a fucking secretary?" Riley asks.

"No, sir, we're just . . . a little on edge, that's—"

"Apples she'll be, mates! Everything is going to be peaches and tits as long as when our friends show up, you pricks are on your toes. Not messin' around on your video games or jerking off." Riley stuffs the knife back into its sheath. "You sods are not paid to ask daft questions. You're paid to make sure those bastards don't take our shit. That clear?"

There are several acknowledgments from around the room.

"Alright then, how about this, gents . . ." Riley holds up his cell phone. "Since the lot of you are in a fat rush to get on, I'll give the old HQ a call and find out when the trucks are coming. That fair?"

Silence.

"Bloody wonderful. Nothing better than calling Marcus and botherin' him, but I'll do it for you all, since you babies need reassurance." Riley scans the room. "Now, are there any more stupid questions?"

No more questions. Only the occasional throat is cleared, which echoes awkwardly through the room.

"Right then." Riley takes a cigar from his breast pocket, clips it, and sticks it in his mouth. "I'm going to throw my headphones on and enjoy my smoke in peace. When I'm done, I'll ring HQ and tell them to move their asses." Riley hops down from his post and heads towards a makeshift office. He gestures towards the large bay door at the north wall. "Now, none of you bother me unless Jesus himself walks through that door. Got it?"

"Yes, sir, we got it!" one of the men shouts.

"Right, then." Riley slams the door behind him so hard the thin-walled office shakes, but that shuddering is quickly replaced by another sound. A louder sound.

The massive bay door buckles as if God himself were knocking. The guards grow edgy, guns raised as they set their sights on the impending interlopers at their door.

Without taking his eyes off the quaking door, one of the guards asks the young agent at the camera bay. "What the hell is out there?"

The young agent checks each monitor, flipping between views. Every single shot shows a full-color, high definition scene of empty alleys, windswept fields of trash, corroding metal barrels, and amber lights shining muddy cones of yellow down onto patches of broken concrete and cracked asphalt.

The agent studies the camera on the exterior door as it dimples inward, almost as if being assailed by an invisible hammer. "I'm literally watching the door fold in on itself."

"What are you talking about?" another agent demands as he approaches the buckling door. "You sure the cameras are even working?"

The young agent taps frantically at his keyboard, and he appears on one of the screens. He waves to himself just to be sure it's in real time. "Yeah, they're working."

"Then what the hell is outside?"

The question is answered as the massive door implodes, slamming into a group of guards. It takes them a moment, but they collectively kick it off in one solid heave. Up on their feet, they raise their guns, expecting to see something or someone standing in the doorway, but nothing is there at the threshold.

For a moment.

This moment is followed by smears of white streaks as the Amissa invade the warehouse, zig-zagging like wasps targeting their prey. The Rift agents open fire, but their ammunition is wasted. They may as well be shooting at ghosts, as not a single angel is affected by their gunfire.

The Amissa descend upon these agents with the fury of God's wrath—or at least a wrath of their own. They thrash about the place delivering precise, lethal cuts. There are screams and shouts from all corners of the room as agents are diced at impossible arcs with a speed and accuracy that no man could possibly execute. Mouths open, shrieking in horror, they're rendered into black dust, bursting in succession like fireworks, as the Amissa make their way from agent to agent.

Riley kicks open the office door, automatic in hand, a cigar clamped between his teeth, headphones dangling around his neck. He hikes up his pants, having just finished watching porn or whatever entertainment helped him pass the time spent managing this outpost. He scans the room and catches wisps of smoke everywhere. The fowl stench of singed flesh invades his lungs.

Riley coughs, choking on the stink. Then he calls out, "Thomas? Robertson? Ellers?"

No response.

"Bloody hell!"

There's a flurry of wind, a miniature tornado that twirls down from the maze of catwalks above, as Balco makes a hard landing on the cold pavement. Wings unfolding, he approaches Riley. "We don't like that word."

"What word's that, you snake-eyed banger?"

"You know which word," Balco replies, "monkey."

"Oh, you mean *Hell*?" Riley chucks aside his cigar. "Well, that's where I'm gonna send you, Nancy." He pulls the trigger, automatic roaring.

But Balco is already in the air. He lands on top of Riley, knocking the man down. He spreads his wings open as if he were a great trap about to ensnare its prize.

Riley breaks out into uncontrolled laughter.

Balco hesitates, somewhat intrigued.

"You stupid, feathered-fucks," Riley growls through gritted teeth as the winged behemoth weighs down on him. "You think we weren't prepared for you and your fairies?" He grins, bearing a mishmash of crowded, cavity-riddled teeth. "I'm not the only one here who knows about this."

Balco eases back so that Riley can breathe.

"Knows about what?" Simon inquires as he enters the room. "That we were coming?" The other angels file in alongside him, as well as Tizzy, who is disguised behind a ski mask.

"Yeah, ya' bloody dongo! We rolled out the red carpet for ya!" Riley sneers, tries to catch sight of Simon, but can't since Balco has him pinned. "We been expecting you."

A swath of yellow light cuts a diagonal beam across Simon's face, but under the cover of his hood, only his chin and mouth are exposed. "You have?"

"Yes, that's right. What? You think you can just waltz into our hideaways, looting 'em like it's a free-for-all at a riot?" Riley cackles. "You got a rude awakening coming. The holy-fucking lot of ya!"

Simon turns to Tizzy. "Did you know about this?"

"Of course not!"

Simon glares at her, unconvinced.

"Seriously, I didn't know shit about this!"

"Hey," Riley cranes his neck to catch sight of her as he declares, "I know that voice."

Tizzy ignores him. To Simon, she insists, "You wanted me to find you their next hideout. Well I did." She flattens her hand like a dagger and aims it at Riley, who is lifting his head as high off the ground as he can to see her. "I fucked that retard just to get you the address of this dump. So, cut me some slack."

"Bloody fucking knew it!" Riley lets a chuckle slip. "Tizzy! Lovey! It *is* you!" He motions with his head for her to approach. "Come 'ere so I can get a good look at ya, all dressed up like a *coppa*." He sticks out his tongue and wags it. "Would love to see you wearing that next time I'm plowing into you. You're heaps good in bed, you know?"

Tizzy storms over to him, winds up with her leg, and kicks him across the face. There's a sharp crack of her foot against his cheek. "Ain't happening again, asshole."

Riley smirks as he licks a sliver of blood from his split lip. "I'm callin' police brutality." He looks to the others. "Sorry, boys, but this twat walked you Angies right into our trap."

Several electrified gates drop down in place of where the metal bay door formerly stood. One of the angels attempts to fly through it but is zapped backwards.

Another angel folds its wings, and rockets up to the roof, only to crash into it. Sparks explode at the point of impact. The angel drops to the ground with all the weight of a car plummeting from a skyscraper.

The fallen angel is quickly scooped up by his brethren and helped to his feet.

"What wretched sorcery is this?" Balco demands. "You have cursed this building."

Riley cackles. "It's called dark magic, ay."

There's a hiss from the far side of the room. The angels steady themselves. Simon and Tizzy take a step back.

"Speaking of dark magic . . ." Riley nods toward the commotion. "You fairies are in for a lovely surprise."

In the center of the room, the wooden crates shake and whir. Their lids pop open as if pushed off their hinges by a high-pressured pump. Three feminine shapes with rail-thin builds rise from the boxes with the deliberate, measured paces of mummies awakened from slumber. Their bodies snap and twitch, as though their bones are realigning themselves but in a jostled, hurried fashion. Dressed in ribbons of ancient cotton, their heads are shaved. Only a single lock of hair tied in a ponytail is coiled around their skull. There's a blackness in their eyes that mirrors those of the Amissa, except that a distant twinkle winks back at whoever locks eyes with them.

They move in unison.

Their lanky legs shift forward in economical, quick strides, stepping carefully from their containers. There's a stutter in their presence. A single frame in the reel is missing, and they seem to skip forward, practically teleporting a millisecond of movement. Heads cocked at crooked angles, their gestures are fidgety, with elbows bent, arms tucked at their sides. Their hands hang forward as if pushing some invisible cart; the skeletal frame of a human, hung improperly onto the body of a praying mantis.

As they come into the light, it does little to improve their famished and wan appearance. Their skin is a shade darker than bone. Lips purple and full. Hands raised now, they approach in one solid wall of peculiarity, mouths open but completely lacking in sound or breath.

"Who're these crazy ass bitches?" Tizzy mutters, as she pulls out a gun.

"No clue," Simon replies. "But they're definitely not human."

"Actually," Riley, adds, somewhat amused, "they used to be."

The floating trio closes in on them.

"We call 'em Shaker witches," Riley tells them. "Or just, *Shakers*."

"I don't give a shit what you call them," Tizzy says. "We got them outnumbered and outgunned."

"Ha! Good luck with that, love!"

Tizzy aims and fires at the Shakers, but the bullets vanish as they strike some invisible field surrounding the women, resulting in blurred circles that ripple outwards just inches from their anemic, vacant faces.

"Ok . . . screw these freaky bitches." Tizzy unloads her clip, though the result is the same: not a single bullet harms the witches. She might as well be shooting into the ocean.

The Shakers advance. Teeth gnashing. Bodies convulsing erratically. Eyeballs glinting with the moist vacancy of an insect's gaze.

Tizzy throws the gun at them. It too smacks an invisible wall, ripples and then evaporates.

Balco motions for one of the Amissa to advance. An angel obliges, making a mad dash towards the Shakers, but disappears into their invisible field.

"What in the entire fuck?" Simon turns to Balco, who shares an equally unnerved, almost bewildered look.

"Jesus Harry Christ!" Riley gloats. "That was beautiful, mates!"

Balco looks down at Riley with disgust and hatred for this human flooding his gaze. "Never speak His name like that." Balco digs his hands into Riley's innards as if the man were made of sand, forcing an unearthly scream out of him.

Blood erupts from Riley's mouth as that smug expression of his is replaced with pain and dread. He grunts out, "Do what you want to me. You're all dead anyway!"

There's a glimmer of motion, and now the Shakers surround the angels.

Balco gestures to the other angels to form a tight circle, back to back, wing against wing, with Simon and Tizzy hunkering down at the center.

"That's why we call them Shaker witches," Riley explains as his mouth froths over with pink spit and blood. "They shake reality. Shake the souls out of you." He throws his head back, then shouts, "They send you to the empty place!"

"You are a disgusting creature." Balco stares at Riley with disdain, nostrils flaring, eyes simmering with contempt. "I will never understand why the Father favors you so."

"Where they're sending you . . ." Riley chokes, blood gushing from his lips as he mutters, "there ain't no Father."

The Shakers close in at twelve, four and seven o'clock. One of them lashes out at an angel, who responds by trying to grab her, but instead the witch grabs him and pulls him into their portal to the unknown.

The angel vanishes.

The Shakers fan their claws, making listless attacks, hissing and taunting the Amissa.

The angels strike back but the Shakers are unaffected, protected by their supernatural barrier, and those unfortunate enough to get too close are pulled into it, disappearing instantly.

The ranks of the Amissa quickly dwindle.

"What are we gonna do?" Tizzy asks aloud. "They're killing us!"

The witches tighten the circle. Their personal bubbles of protection are now too close for comfort.

"I mean, we've come this far, only to lose to a bunch of stank ass bitches!" Tizzy shouts.

"Well then maybe we shouldn't rely on magic," Simon muses. "Balco, do your wings protect against fire or man's other manipulations of nature?"

"Indeed."

"Then put those wings to use. Make us a wall. Let's test my theory."

Balco signals for the others to close the circle around Simon and Tizzy, expanding their wings to form a feathered wall.

"The bloody hell?" Riley asks, followed by more bloodied coughs. "You think you can stop them with your fucking quills?"

Simon ignores him, retrieves several grenades. Waits until the witches are just close enough. He tells Tizzy to get down as he pulls the pins and launches the grenades over their heads and then ducks.

The grenades detonate behind the Shakers. Rather than being absorbed by their fields, the explosive force flings them forward, sending them screeching across the floor, face first. Seems that what Simon hypothesized was correct:

their auras of protection could only be focused in one direction.

Ears ringing, air singed with a burned quality, Simon and Tizzy rise and survey the damage. The Amissa remain firmly planted, unphased by the cannonade.

"How did you know that was going to work?" Tizzy asks Simon.

"I didn't."

There's a thundering at electrified gates.

Something begs to be let in.

Simon looks to Balco for reassurance, and Balco gives him a nod indicating that what raps at the gate is something more welcoming than the trifecta of evil they are dealing with now.

The three witches slowly rise, convulsing with agony, their bodies snapping and jerking. Whatever dark energy animates them is clearly at work, empowering them beyond the shock and awe of grenades discharged at close range. The fact that their frail bodies were not ripped apart at such a close proximity reinforces the magnitude of the dark magic that fuels them.

The pounding continues, and the gate ceases to sizzle with electricity. It falls and another angel enters:

Zolash.

"Hurry." Zolash signals for the humans and the Amissa to flee.

Just then, the Shaker witches recover from their injuries. Palms out, fingers splayed, they focus their powers like a wave of doom aimed at the escaping angels.

Simon tosses several more grenades in the Shaker's direction, but this time the Shakers are prepared for the attack. They spread their arms wide; electrified currents flare between their hands, receiving the explosive offerings. Like distant thunderstorms, radical waves of light pulse above the witches as the combustible energy of the grenades are absorbed and dissipated into another world. However, the explosives were merely a distraction, buying time for Simon, Tizzy and the Amissa to escape.

Zolash waves them outside, and the group of them turn and make quick work of the exterior of the building, tearing strips of metal and construction from the fascia to imprison the Shaker witches inside.

Riley is dragged out by Balco. Looking like a tattered dog's toy, he's tossed outside onto the wet grass, wounds aggravated by the impact of the landing.

Balco lands on top of him. "Where are your precious abominations to save you now, monkey?"

"Fuck you, fairy!"

Balco sinks his hand into Riley's stomach, stuffing it deep into the man's ribcage.

Riley's eyes turn bloodshot as he cries out.

Simon sets an explosive outside the building. The countdown begins for the building to be reduced to a pile of concrete dust, shredded metal, and the bones of Shaker witches.

The charge goes off and there's a resultant boom. All but the angels flinch at the explosion. Once the smoke and dust clear, Riley stares in shock at the near flattened building.

Simon looks down on Riley like the smug dying roach he is. "Where's that cocky attitude now?"

Riley tries to spit in his face, but the pink saliva doesn't make it far, instead dribbling down his chin.

Simon kneels, studying Riley as if he were a trapped rodent. "Where are the manacles?"

"Sod off!" Riley blurts.

Balco digs deeper into Riley's stomach, grabbing hold of something. Squeezing his entrails with gentle, yet exquisitely painful precision ensures that the pain grows more and more unbearable.

"Hurts, huh?" Simon asks. "I can end the pain. Just answer my question."

"Fuck you!" Riley shouts.

Balco squeezes something, earning an instant and violent jerk from Riley's body. Whatever organ Balco is messing with is driving him mad. Veins bulge along the sides of his neck. Brows furrowing, he lets out a gasp and a roar.

"Now where . . . are . . . the manacles?" Simon asks again.

Blood oozes from the corners of Riley's mouth. He utters, "Marcus . . ."

Simon leans in.

"M–Marcus . . . Gladius," Riley says. "He has the manacles."

"Where do we find him?" Simon asks.

Riley lets out a wheezed chuckle. "Up your fucking arse!"

Balco squeezes Riley's entrails and the man shrieks.

"Where?" Simon presses.

"There's a chateau south of the highway." He nods towards his pocket. "Use my cell. Take you right to him."

Simon frowns. "Is he expecting us?"

"If I failed . . ." Riley fumbles; his words are labored. "Then he knows . . . you're coming." He still manages to smile through the pain. "But I can . . . I can tell you one thing . . ." Coughing up blood, his teeth are stained with crimson as he grins. "Been grooming them witches to kill everything including fairies."

Simon glances back at the heap of rubble. Not a pebble or bit of concrete moves. The only thing animated is the dust from the debris swirling up into the sky. "If you're talking about your shakers, I don't think things worked out for them."

"There will be more of *them* . . . and maybe something worse . . . waiting for you."

Simon grabs Riley's jaw and squeezes tightly. "I'm not afraid of you or the Rift. I'm going to get my wife back, no matter what."

"A bloody fool's errand." Riley shouts out through his gritted agony, "You're all dead! The fucking lot of you."

Riley lets out a brief shriek as Balco squeezes his heart, killing the man instantly.

"If this Marcus Gladius has the manacles," Zolash informs them, "I know where the pendant is."

Balco rises, his arm stained with blood.

"Continue," Simon says.

"It is with a half-wing. Born of angel and man. His name is Travis."

"What?!" Simon snaps. "Travis?"

"Yes, and he was with that woman, Amanda, who killed our brothers."

Simon's gaze falls to the floor. Lost in thought, he runs a finger up the length of his scar. "He owes me an eye." To the other angels: "Let's pay

Travis a visit."

"No need," Zolash assures them as he holds up his hands. "You guys focus on retrieving the manacles from Marcus." His eyes flash a gleam of shimmering silver white. With a devilish smile, he adds, "I'm taking care of Travis as we speak."

"What do you mean?" Simon asks.

"That is his gift," Balco explains. "He can be in multiple places at once."

Simon looks almost frustrated that he can't join in and deal with Travis personally. However, his efforts are best focused on pursuing the manacles while the lead is still hot. Even if they are walking into another trap, the chance to see Cynthia again is worth any cost.

If he must kill everyone – mortal or otherwise to do it – so be it.

She is worth it.

"Do what you have to do," Simon tells Zolash, "but get me that pendant." To Balco: "Now let's go visit Mr. Gladius."

Chapter 25 – Travis Entertains the Clones

Zolash and his ghostly copies close in.

Amanda points towards the stairs. "Duncan, go!"

"Right!" he says as he rushes up to the second floor.

Travis gestures for Amanda to go too.

"No way!" Amanda opens her arms wide.

"What are you doing?"

Amanda's hands spark to life, emanating that bluish-white aura. "What does it look like?"

"We're outnumbered!" Travis yells as the Zolash clones charge in. "Just get out of here!"

However, Amanda holds her ground, and as the angels flank them, she lets loose an outpouring of energy. Chaos ensues. Some of the clones burst into light. Others are thrown about the room.

Travis is knocked down too, but something yanks him up by his foot. Several of the clones lift him above their heads

"We're going to enjoy . . ." one clone begins.

". . . tearing you apart," another finishes.

Travis is tossed across the room, where he lands on a table. They advance, but Amanda jumps in front of them, palms out, eyes ablaze. Out of nowhere, another Zolash clone slams into her, knocking her off her feet. She crashes into the back of the couch, her head snapping backwards, rendering her unconscious.

The lead Zolash clone spreads his arms. More copies emerge from either side of him, filing out like fanning cards from a mystic deck. There must be two dozen of them. "Your woman-friend can't save you now," he informs Travis.

Travis hoists himself off the floor. Wipes the blood from his nose and the weeping gash above his eye. "You just can't get enough of yourself."

The army of clones descends on Travis like a zombie horde. They grab ahold of him, pulling his arms and legs in opposite directions, stretching him with all their individual might.

"A regular monkey would have ripped apart by now," one of the clones tells Travis. "But since you've got our blood in your veins, I guess that means you get to savor this pain that much longer."

Something in that statement strikes Travis wrong.

Why can't a dozen angels pull me apart? he thinks.

A cold hand grabs his head and Travis catches sight of the inverted frown of this devilish cherub that has him strung up like a trampoline, pulled taut at each angle.

"You have a gift, Travis. You have our blood in you," the clone tells him. "You could join us in returning to our kingdom. To where we belong."

Momentarily, Travis is in too much pain to focus. The tendons and ligaments in his body cry out for respite.

"Did you hear me?" the clone asks.

"Yes, I did," Travis says with a pained grunt, "and fuck you and your fairytale gang."

The clones suddenly drop Travis onto the ground. The pendant necklace spills out from his shirt and the lead Zolash clone catches sight of it, beaming with glee.

"Nothing is going to stop us from going home." The clone approaches Travis, eyeing the necklace with an almost lustful elation.

"Actually," Travis says as he pushes himself up onto his knees, "I can think of one thing."

The clones simultaneously shoot him a look of bemusement. The lead Zolash asks, "And what's that?"

"Me." Travis closes his eyes and prays.

It takes Zolash a moment to figure out what Travis is doing. "A prayer?"

With a trailing laugh he asks, "For what? For Zachariel to swoop in and save you?"

Travis ignores him, continues to pray.

"Well he won't! Zachariel is apathetic, indolent, and doesn't care about your paltry requests as much as he'd have you believe." The clone kneels to face Travis. "The only thing he delivers is false hope."

Travis keeps his eyes shut tight, mouthing his request to God.

"What are you praying for?" There's a hint of irritation growing in the vile angel's tone.

Travis continues praying as if the clone is not even there.

"Answer me, monkey!" The clone grabs Travis's head, digs his nails into Travis's cheeks.

Travis's eyes snap open. "I'm praying that you fail."

"I'm sure even Zachariel taught you that not all prayers are answered."

"Guess I'll leave that up to God then."

"While you wait for your response," the clone taunts as he reaches for the cross pendant on Travis's neck, "we'll be on our way." And the second his fingers touch it, the clone bursts into a fulgent ball of light.

The other clones go flying backwards, slamming into the walls, over furniture, and colliding into one another. Travis himself crashes against a framed picture of a generic landscape on the far wall.

There's a moment of shock.

The air is acrid and smells of ozone.

The clones come to, examine one another and note that the lead Zolash is absent. The copies talk to one another:

"It doesn't make sense."

"We should be able to take the pendant from him."

"What is wrong?"

"Are we not worthy? We are of God."

"I think you all got ahead of yourselves," Travis informs them with a rough laugh as he recovers.

The clones look in Travis's direction.

Travis gets to his feet. He tucks a thumb behind the pendant and shoves it in the clones' faces. "Come on, you bunch of pricks. You want it? Then come get it!"

One of the clones reaches forth, but another clone swats his hand away. "This aberrant monkey is taunting us!"

Another responds, "He figured it out."

And another, "Yes, a conclusion that we should have arrived at as well."

Amanda slowly comes to and sits up. Head spinning, she lets out a groan as she presses her fingers against her temples.

"It's this world," another clone adds. "This Earth has tainted us! Our time on this wretched rock has soiled our worthiness."

"That or maybe when you all skipped out of Heaven," Travis implies, "God branded you deserters as unwanted."

"How do you know about that?" all the clones ask in unison.

"Because I watched it happen," Travis informs them. "He showed me the whole thing."

"Who?" one of the clones asks.

"Zachariel," another offers. This clone motions to one of the others, who promptly zips upstairs and returns with Duncan in his clutches. Two other clones hoist Amanda up off the ground. Both she and Duncan are brought in front of Travis.

All the clones smile in unison.

"Did our beloved brother, Zachariel, show you the future as well?"

Duncan chimes in, "Only God can do that."

One of the clones grabs the rosary beads on Duncan's throat. Glaring at it, he hisses, "This is black magic. You and this witch will suffer for endorsing such malignant sorcery." To Travis: "Allow us to tell you about the future of your friends here." The clone tugs at Duncan's necklace; his eyes widen as he stares down at the strained string holding the enchanted jewelry together. "Either you help us open the gate," the clone says as he pulls Duncan's necklace taut, "or he dies before you without the aid of his cursed magic."

"As for this one here," the other clones dig their fingers into Amanda's skin, forcing a grunt out of her, "we will imbue her with Heaven's power. Her flesh will roast, her eyes will boil, and you will bear witness to it all."

Travis grinds his teeth together.

"What say you, Travis Rail?"

"I say . . ." Travis suddenly charges. He swings and hits the clone holding Duncan, knocking him aside. But while the Rosary beads are no longer in that angel's clutches, the victory is short-lived as the clones descend on Travis, restraining him with ease.

"That was a poor choice." A clone grabs Travis's face and forces him to lock eyes with the tainted cherub.

"I'll never help you," Travis mutters.

"We'll see." To the others, the clone commands, "Start with the woman. Fill her with the energy of the sun. Bake her from the inside."

"Touch her and die!" Travis barks.

"You are not in a place to make such threats."

Travis struggles against his captors, but there are at least four angels on him.

"Look around you," the clone insists. "Your prayers remain unanswered."

Before they can start on Amanda, a bright bolt of energy flies into the house, pushing the clones back.

That bolt takes the shape of an angel.

The clones share a look of shock as they stare down their intruder. In unison, they simply hiss the word: "You!"

Chapter 26 – Too Easy?

The angels and Simon gather outside of Marcus's mansion.

"This is the place?" Simon asks.

Tizzy checks Riley's cell phone. "Disgusting."

"What?"

Tizzy makes a face. "Even his cell phone stinks."

"That's probably because his blood is on it," Simon says.

"You didn't fuck him. I did. I know what he smells—"

Simon grabs Tizzy by her collar and pulls her close. "Shut up! Now . . . is this the place?"

"Yes! Jesus! Relax, man." She shoves the phone in his face so he can see the map app. She points at the pin drop where they are located. "Right here. Unless Riley was lying, then this is the place."

"Riley wasn't lying." Balco sizes up the mansion, eyes narrowing as he stares ahead. "We have lost brothers here." To Simon: "Are you ready?"

"Are you?" Simon pulls out an automatic rifle. Checks that it is locked and loaded.

"You realize what's in there is stronger than anything else we've experienced in this journey. We may not survive. Your impatience may cost you this battle."

"I'm ok with that. There's nothing worth living for if I can't get her back."

"As long as you are prepared to die, then you are ready to proceed into that mansion."

"Oh, I've been prepared since I *freed* all of you," Simon reminds him. "If it wasn't for me, you'd still be chained up in their dungeon, getting tortured or whatever the fuck they were doing to you."

Balco's lips curve downward, forming a disapproving frown. "And this will be the last time I express to you my gratitude, Simon Lajudas."

"Then show it by getting us the manacles." Simon glances over at the mansion. "You've got wings. What can you and your boys do?"

"I suggest we split up into two groups. I'll lead a group to the roof. You, the woman and the others can circle around back."

"It's hard to tell where they will be expecting us to break in from."

"They probably already know we're here," Tizzy declares, gesturing at Riley's cell phone. "Wouldn't be surprised if that piece-of-shit bugged his phone."

"At this point, it doesn't matter if they know we are coming or not," Simon insists. "We're going to get those manacles or die trying."

The groups split up as discussed.

Balco leads several angels onto the rooftop. The sun is setting in the distance, casting an eerie orange-dark mustard haze over everything. From afar, one might enjoy the sight of seeing several agile, winged beings gracefully take flight and navigate the expansive roof of the mansion. They scale the Spanish tiled roof with ease while keeping a watchful eye for whatever might be awaiting them. They could easily burst through the walls of the mansion, but given the trap they narrowly escaped in the last safe-house, they have no desire to plow through buildings with wild abandon only to land in another bad situation. No doubt the Rift are waiting for them to come knocking.

Simon and his crew make their way into the mansion proper. He notes there are cameras watching from everywhere and motions for Zolash to move ahead and take out as many of them as he can. The lanky angel obliges, and in an instant, the cameras are wiped out, leaving behind sparking messes of electricity and exposed wires.

"Someone is watching us," Simon whispers to his crew as they make their way along the walls, keeping low and tight to the mansion edifice.

"No shit," Tizzy snaps back.

"I mean that they're going to see those cameras are offline." Simon points up at the broken cameras sizzling on their mounts. "Then they'll show, guns blazing. We won't have much time."

"Then let's just keep moving, Romeo," Tizzy quips with a brazen tongue and catches herself, making a face as if trying to suck the words back in.

Too late.

Simon shoves her towards the front of the group. "You lead."

Tizzy shrugs him off. "Whatever. I'm cool with that." She moves forward, keeping her head down low. "Follow me."

They do, not knowing any more about the scene than any other. Although they could have scoped the place out, Simon is confident that his angelic army will take down the Rift just as they had several hideouts before. They've survived two ambushes, one with the Covenant and one with the Rift, only to come out swinging. At this point, Simon and Balco's ambition to open a door to Heaven has outweighed any rational fears they may share.

As they round the corner, Simon wonders: do the angels even feel fear?

They are surreptitiously stoic and yet show fleeting moments of emotion. Are they as stone-faced as they put on?

The group moves along and stops behind a thick row of massive hibiscus bushes, mere feet away from crossing paths with two guards. They are armed with automatic weapons and standing watch in front of a massive oak door framed by a stone archway.

The radio of one of the guards crackles, and he answers. "Go ahead."

"They're here," a voice says.

"Copy that," the guard answers as his body stiffens.

"I am grateful for your loyalty, brother," the voice adds. "Both of you. Thank you."

The guards pause for a beat. Then ask, "What?"

Nothing.

The guard prods. "Sir, what was that?"

There's a glimmer of light as Zolash rips past them. The men scream as they hold up their arms. Blood spurts from their wrists as their hands, still gripping the handles of their guns, cling ineffectually to the trigger. A wild blast escapes the weapons as they unload a barrage of useless fire into the manicured foliage ahead.

"Now!" Simon shouts and Tizzy is the first to leap to her feet. She pulls out a knife and buries it into the neck of the first guard, then the second.

From above, several windows explode as guards rain down automatic fire. Tizzy grabs one of the guards, using his body as a shield; she pulls the man with her to the ground.

Simon dives as close to the building as possible, tightening the angle so that the guards up above cannot shoot down at him easily. The guards are not so easily dissuaded. Some of them lean out and take aim at him, some shoot at the angels as they dash from one end of the garden to the other. The bullets sail past the Amissa effortlessly and rip along the ground, kicking up dirt in their wake.

Simon fires, driving the agents back inside their respective rooms, but finds himself mostly ineffective from this position against the wall.

Several of the angels line up near the oak door, drawing the attention of the guards who continue to pump round after round after round in a cacophony of screaming and angst. The sound of gunfire is thundering. The air reeks of dust, earth, and shredded vegetation. Simon tightens into a ball, avoiding the hail of bullets. He and Tizzy benefit from the taunting, magnetic attention the Amissa are drawing to themselves. The guards unload a wake of wild gunfire that echoes across the countryside. Fortunately for Marcus, his home is as remote as one could wish for.

Tizzy feels the ground erupting all around her. She pulls the dead guard's body over her as the peppering of bullets draws closer. She knows it's only a matter of moments before one of those rounds penetrates the body or her skull at just the right angle and then it's lights out.

Suddenly the guard's body bursts into black dust.

Tizzy's shield is no more. She curls up, expecting to be torn apart by gunfire, but an eerie silence falls over the garden.

The hush is followed by the stifled screams of men as the gnawing sounds of flesh ripped from bone fills her ears. Tizzy slowly brings her arms away from her face and her knees away from her chest. She sits up and sees the second-floor windows have been removed of their assailants. Only blood spatters remain. Each windowsill weeps crimson, the blood trickling down the façade like grotesque tears. From the darkness of the windows, several glowing angels step forth into the diminishing dusk and stare down at Simon, Tizzy and the other Amissa.

Balco and his crew found a way in. They also took out the second floor of guards.

Simon peels himself off the ground, emerging from his safe posture to watch alongside Tizzy as the oak door opens and Balco steps out.

"They are expecting us," Balco tells them.

"Clearly," Simon says.

Zolash appears in a flash at their side. "There is little here to stop us."

"It's almost as if Marcus wants us to show," Simon muses. "This is too easy. Seems to be the theme."

"Too easy?" Tizzy exclaims. "We almost died!"

"But we didn't," Simon says. "Easy or not, we are getting those manacles. Then the pendant." He turns to Balco and adds, "And then you, my friend, will be sitting at God's side soon enough."

Balco nods.

"And I will hold my beloved's hand once more."

"And what about me?" Tizzy asks.

With a smirk, "You?" Simon chuckles. He pushes her first through the oak door. "You get to go first."

Chapter 27 – Savior

Following his violent entrance, the uninvited angel casually walks into the room, wings out, a hoodie shrouding his face – Victor.

The flock of Zolash clones speak in unison once more: *"You betrayed us."*

"Who betrayed who?" Victor asks the Zolashs.

Travis recognizes that voice. It's the same angel he spoke with at Glory's office.

"You chose to follow us here," the clones say.

"True, but where you and Balco and the others came to Earth seeking freedom and comprehension," Victor tells them, "I left Heaven because I have business to settle with the Rift." Victor points at Travis. "And I wanted to keep an eye. . . on my brother."

Travis does a double-take. Blinks twice, not sure he heard Victor correctly.

Some of the Zolashs look at Victor, some at Travis.

"Half-brother technically," Victor tells Travis. And before anyone else in the room can react, Victor whips about the room like a tornado. He leaps over the Zolashs that have Duncan and Amanda restrained, yanks those angels away, and with a final death knell, his wings spring out and he impales the clones.

The other Zolashs scatter, vaulting over furniture, and making reckless swipes at Victor. He proves too agile, too deft for them, avoiding their attacks effortlessly.

Amid the chaos, Amanda grabs one of the clones from behind and pulses her dark energy into him, sending him to a shrieking death.

As Victor is battling two clones at the same time, another one sneaks up behind him. Travis grabs that Zolash and plows him into the ground so hard that the angel's head is crushed. He backs away, surprised by his own strength and the outcome of the unfortunate angel.

Victor finishes off the two clones and spins around to face his brother. They share a moment before a scream from across the room catches their attention.

Amanda holds up the last of the Zolash clones, an unusual sight: a human lifting an angel up off the ground. But there is a reason for her strength.

Or rather, for the clone's weakness.

Blue light emanates from her hands as she is about to nuke—

"Wait!" Victor shouts.

Amanda pauses. The clone's head slumps forward.

"We need him. Or at least one of them." Victor yanks the clone from Amanda's grip and brings him to the ground with a hard thump. "You're weak," Victor tells him as the clone squirms under his grasp. "Spread yourself too thin like you always do. Your strength *is* your weakness."

The clone manages a grin. *"And yours as well, brother."*

"We're not brothers."

"We were until you abandoned us after the exodus."

Victor snarls, and asks, "Where are the others?"

With a smirk, the clone responds, "Waiting for you."

Victor shakes him. "Where are they?!"

"At the Rift mansion of Marcus Gladius. The one who worked with Torkal to trick us to coming down to this decrepit world, remember?"

"Yeah, I remember. There was no trick. We made a choice to leave. The outcome just didn't align with your plans."

"Nor with yours," the clone reminds him with a chuckle. *"The Rift still exist. But that could change. You can bring the pendant right to them and fulfill your goal of eradicating them from this Earth. I can lead you to them."*

The group exchanges looks.

"You can carry the witch," the Zolash clone nods towards Amanda. *"And I'll carry your brother."* Under his breath he mutters, *"The half-wing scum."*

Travis makes like he's going to punch the clone, but Victor pushes him back.

"*I'm not afraid of you,*" the clone taunts.

"I don't care."

"W-w-wait. What do you mean carry?" Duncan asks, with his hands up in protest.

"*Exactly what it sounds like!*" Zolash snaps.

"Like... up in the air?" Duncan points to the sky.

"*How else?*" Zolash answers.

"Yes, but aside from the altitudes and my lack of love for heights, we'll freeze to death, suffocate – perhaps both."

Zolash rolls his eyes. With a bothered snort, "*So long as Victor and I carry you, the elements will not affect you.*" He turns his attention back to Victor. "*Here's what I can offer you: I lead you to them, and in exchange you can kill all the Rift you want. But your brother must surrender the pendant. What do you say?*"

"I say I nuke your angelic brain." Amanda raises her hands and they light up like butane torches.

Travis eyes Amanda. This new side of her is catching him off guard. Whatever the Amissa have unhinged in her, seems they've awoken a permanent enemy. "I'm with her. This is a trap."

"*What other options do you have?*" the clone muses. "*The Amissa will find you. Either you bring the fight to them, or they bring the fight to you.*"

"I want nothing more than to make every agent of the Rift pay for what they did to our mother." Victor turns to Travis and adds, "Yeah... I was there. I saw what Lomak did to mom."

"But you have the pendant, Travis!" Duncan breaks in. "So, this is your call."

This proves a lot for Travis to take in:

His supposed half-brother is an angel? The angel that's been stalking him? Duncan is alive.

Amanda is a powerful witch.

Add to all of that, they're talking about taking on the Rift *and* the Amissa at the same time.

There are so many ways this could go south.

But deep inside, he knows there will be no peace until this battle is fought.

"What do you think?" Travis asks Amanda.

"Victor wants the Rift dead. I'd love to see the Amissa suffer the same fate after what they let Tizzy do to Pastor Graham," Amanda admits. "I want an end to both of their fucking stories."

The clone chuckles dismissively at this.

"Wow," Travis mutters.

"What?" Amanda asks.

"I never thought I'd hear you talk like that."

"There's a lot you don't know about me."

"Yeah, I get that."

"*Are you all ready then?*" the clone asks.

"Yes." Victor releases the clone. Then gives him a hard shove. "Lead the way."

"You're just going to give them the pendant?" Duncan asks Travis. "Are you crazy? You don't know what they will do with it."

"*I assure you,*" the clone informs him, "*our intentions are no mystery. We came here for freedom and understanding and found vacuousness and impiety. We just want to go home to be with the Father. In return, we will lead you right into a Rift stronghold, where you can exact your individual motivations for revenge.*"

"Travis, seriously," Duncan pleads. "All of you, listen, don't be led by vengeance. Vengeance is for the Lord."

Travis puts a hand on Duncan's shoulder. "Maybe the Lord is sending us just for that very reason."

Chapter 28 – Rift Plans

Simon, Tizzy and the Amissa enter the mansion without encountering additional resistance. Towering, slate-gray pillars reach into the ceiling. An expansive collection of vintage artwork adorns the walls. There are antiques and collectables everywhere: statues from every corner of the Earth, ancient sets of armor encased in glass cases, and rare weaponry mounted meticulously along the walls. The place smells of polished leather and the distinctive stuffiness of an attic space that hasn't been aired out in years.

A large fountain in the center dominates most of the room. Two stone wolves are entwined around one another spray a soft stream of water in the air. Etched along the base of the fountain are the words: *The One You Feed.*

"Smells like a thrift store in here," Tizzy complains.

Simon spies a grand staircase that coils upwards and connects with a second-floor runway that hugs the southern wall of the room. "We went from full-on assault to a veritable ghost town."

"Perhaps we have wandered into another trap after all," Balco suggests.

"Not in the least bit," a figure announces from the shadows. Marcus steps out into the light and makes his way across the second-floor loft. "This is no trap."

"That so?" Simon aims his rifle at him. "Then why did you give us such a welcome party?"

"Actually, those were *all the* men I employed. Best of the best. Loyal to the end."

"And now you have no one?"

Marcus lets out a little laugh.

"He is not alone," Balco says. He then whispers into Simon's ear, "Our brothers are here."

"You mean there are more of your kind in his house?" Simon asks.

Balco nods. "I sense them."

"Forgive my manners, as it has been a long time since I have been robbed and had the pleasure of meeting the thieves responsible. I am Marcus Gladius, though I feel you already know that. I'm sure you know plenty; otherwise you wouldn't have been so brazen about breaking into my home." Marcus approaches the top of the staircase. "And you are?"

Simon says nothing.

"That's ok. I know who you are." Marcus points at Tizzy. "That nymph is quite the big mouth. Told Riley a lot when she got drunk."

Simon shoots her a look, to which she responds, "Yeah . . . well . . . it took a lot of tequila just to power through fucking that pig."

"I find it interesting, *Simon Lajudas*," Marcus asserts, "that you are in such a rush to die."

With a scoff, Simon assures him, "I am not."

"Yet, here you are on a suicide mission," Marcus says with hands extending outward. "You could have taken your time, planned an all-out assault like you did with my other storehouses, but like a moth to a flame, you couldn't wait any longer." He pulls out an apple. As he takes a bite, he says, "You had to taste the fruit. You wanted to taste Heaven."

Tizzy feels the hairs on her entire body rise. All she needs to do is make it through this last skirmish, and she can finally get paid and leave Simon behind.

"You have come a long way to try to rob me." Marcus gestures with the apple. "Are you hungry?"

"For the pendant and the manacles?" Simon asks. "Yes."

"I share that hunger. Do you have either?"

"Don't be cute. You should be more concerned with the fact that we're going to tear this place apart until we find them, and in doing so, we're going to kill you if you don't cooperate."

Marcus lets out a laugh that resonates throughout the room. "Do you . . ." he composes himself, leaning slightly on the railing as if losing his breath amidst the amusement. "Do you really think I'm afraid to die? I couldn't give a flying fuck about my own life, but if I'm going to be walking this cursed world, you can be damn sure I am going to get what I want. Now, do you have either?"

"I'm about one cunt hair away from splitting your head open." Simon brings the rifle scope up to his good eye, takes aim. "Let's skip the bullshit. I know you have the manacles. You stole them from the Covenant. So, where are they?"

"My, my, my. Are you for hire?" Marcus puts a palm to his chest, feigns as if he just lost his breath. "Can we at least share a scotch, a cup of tea, or a healthy blunt first before we get on with it?"

The tension in the group swells as the angels size up the room, shifting their oily black eyes across every inch, every shadow.

"The manacles!" Simon shouts with a jolt of his gun. "I won't ask again. And trust me, if you don't tell me, we will trash your love shack until we find it."

"Oh, I've seen your work. The way you have bulldozed my other properties." Marcus runs a finger along the banister. "I have no doubt." He makes his way down the stairs gracefully, one step at a time.

"That's close enough!" Simon barks.

"You're afraid of an old man like *moi*?"

"You're part of the Rift."

"*Part* of the Rift? Part of the Rift?!" Marcus seethes, spit flying from his mouth as he says with a venomous tone, "*I am the fucking Rift!* I helped build it, you piece of shit!"

Simon pulls the trigger and the railing by Marcus's hand splits open as a bullet tears through it.

Marcus doesn't even flinch.

"I don't give a shit," Simon declares.

Marcus presses a finger to his lips. Smiles gingerly. "You know, something gives me the impression that you possess nothing. Not the manacles, clearly.

Not even the pendant itself."

"What makes you say that?" asks Simon.

"Because if you did, I would know."

Simon's eyes narrow. "How's that?"

"If you're going to collect God's treasures, you might want to do your research."

"I have."

Marcus chuckles. "Apparently not enough." He brings his hands together to demonstrate his point: "You see, the two halves will pulse with the light of angels and will naturally be drawn together when they are close enough. My half has not even flickered."

"You're bluffing."

"I have no reason to lie. Once I knew why you were knocking off my repositories, I wanted you to come. I needed to know if *you* had the other half," Marcus reveals. "We both want the same thing. We both want to open those pearly gates. May I ask why you want entry into His kingdom?"

Balco steps forth. "We want to go home, Marcus. That is why we are here."

Simon shoots him a look.

"You should have never left then, my dear seraphim," Marcus reprimands with a wry smile. "You took the bait; led your brothers astray following my beloved Torkal's tantalizing words and forsook paradise to dwell with the refuse. And here you are. Stuck." He blurts out the words in a spiteful hurry, "I know your tragic story because I helped write it!"

Balco moves like the wind and grabs the old man, lifting him off the ground by his neck. "Yes, you and Torkal trapped us. I will tear you apart as I did him. Then we will go home. But first," Balco takes his free hand and moves as if he is going to dig into Marcus's body like he did Riley's. "First you will experience the same pain you have caused us."

There's a loud thud as the pillars spiral, whirling in place to reveal several figures nestled inside them. The slate was a façade and hiding within them are . . . the Cleaners.

Marcus allows a choked fit of laughter to escape.

Arms crossing their chests, the blanched, bony faces of these creatures come to life. Eyes open abruptly as if exhumed from a deep, foreboding dream. Their eyeballs are black and endless, seemingly staring at both nothing and at the group at the same time.

"The heck are those things?" Tizzy asks.

Balco mutters something in his angelic language. His face expresses a sort of soft recognition. There's something familiar in those detached, bizarre creatures, but it is a distant familiarity. The scent and aura emanate an angelic signature just like his, but no longer from a lofty paradise; instead they're now warped and wrenched away into something sinister and vacant of life.

Shells of his former brethren.

"Us." Balco answers Tizzy under his breath. "They were once *us*."

"If you don't have the pendant," Marcus tells Simon, "then you are of no use."

There's the distinct sound of canvas ripping. From one of the large paintings, a curved blade pokes through, then dives downward. There is a bit of a pause, enough to cut the tension in the room with this same sword, but the sliver of metal retracts into the painting and the painting gives birth to a shaded figure, moving almost as fast as the angels themselves.

Simon turns towards the painting, towards the figure, and opens fire. Although the canvas is split apart, the figure is too fast, jumping almost impossibly off the wall, to the railing, twirling in midair like an acrobat.

That figure lands just to the side of Balco and Marcus. The figure's face is half obscured by a mask.

Quell.

With a swift upward arc, she sends the blade slicing through the arm Balco is using to hold Marcus in the air. Balco screams. Dazzling light sparks from the point of separation between his wrist and forearm. Mouth open, Balco wails in agony as his hand rolls onto the floor and evaporates in a pale dash of blue light.

Quell shields Marcus behind her. She keeps the tip of the blade squarely aimed at Balco, who is stunned, staring at the cauterized stump where his hand was moments ago.

Simon shoots again, but Quell has already shoved Marcus aside and is flying through the air. She moves at the speed of angels, and with their accuracy as well. For a fleeting second, Simon wonders if she is an angel.

A swift kick across his jaw sends him spinning backwards.

The Cleaners rise from their stone enclosures and advance on the Amissa.

Simon jumps to his feet to find Quell's blade coming down on him. He holds up his rifle to shield himself and it's sliced in half.

Quell raises the blade for a follow-up strike, but one of the Amissa zips across the room, grabs her, and the two of them collide into the far wall. She lets out a grunt; something cracks inside her body, and she slides to the ground. Her sword is still in hand, seemingly affixed in some fashion, because she does not let go of the weapon. As for the angel who pinned her against the wall, he pulls away from her, the full length of the sword exiting his torso as he does. He screams as he explodes in a storm of furious light.

Tizzy runs off and hides behind one of the statues.

The Cleaners and Amissa go toe to toe.

Brother versus former brother.

They trade blows, fists flying, and small bursts of blue light spark as they make contact. Some angels grab their twisted brothers, slamming them to the ground, into walls, against railings, and furniture turning the room to ruin.

Some angels find the opposite fate, literally feasted upon by the Cleaners as if the Amissa were food. Whole sections of their angelic frames eviscerated, vanished as if they were only made of imagination.

Balco is a wrecking ball of rage. He takes on two and three Cleaners at a time. Smashing them against one another with his good arm. Crushing their heads in the great palm of his hand. Tears in his eyes as he does so.

These were once his brothers.

He led them to this fate.

Their deaths are on his conscience.

And he will make Marcus pay, just as he did Torkal.

Simon looks on as he witnesses the most emotion he has ever seen from Balco. Meanwhile, the other angels do their best to keep him safe from the

Cleaners, fighting valiantly. He feels a hand touch his shoulder, whips out a pistol as he spins to find Zolash in front of him.

"They'll be here soon," Zolash informs him.

"Who?" Simon demands. His mind is going a thousand miles an hour.

Zolash opens his mouth to say, then screams as a blade emerges from his chest. He explodes in blue light, and behind him, Quell stands, trails of blood sliding down her lips. She wipes them aside as she aims the sword at Simon and he notices that she has secured the weapon to her hand with several rounds of duct tape.

"How are you able to kill the Amissa," Simon asks, his pistol aimed squarely at her as well, "with just a sword?"

"Wouldn't you like to know?" she answers.

"You think you can you outrun a bullet at close range?"

Quell tucks her chin, the glint of the spotlights shining on the porcelain side of her eerie mask. Her exposed eye, gleams with a look that says, *try me, bitch.*

Simon wants to pull the trigger, but also knows that at any moment, this crazy ninja chick could cartwheel into the air and slice his hand off just like she did Balco. If she can take on a tank like Balco, he has no doubt that she can take him on, too.

So, with a nod, he warns her, "Behind you."

She hesitates. "I'm not about to fall for that—"

Tizzy clocks her over the head with a chair.

Quell goes down.

Marcus scurries up the stairs.

"Follow him!" Simon commands.

"What are you going to do?" Tizzy asks.

"Help the Amissa. I'll catch up."

"Fuck 'em." Tizzy takes Simon's hand; starts to pull him up the stairs. "They'll manage. They're angels for Christ's sake! Let's go after Marcus together, grab the manacles, and get the hell out of here!"

Simon shakes her off.

Marcus sneaks quickly across the loft and slams a door shut behind him.

"Aw, come on!" Tizzy whines. "That old prune is getting away."

"Unless he's got wings, he's not going anywhere." Simon takes out a knife and cuts the tape holding the blade to Quell's wrist.

"And what if he does?"

"The Amissa can hunt him down, which is yet another reason why we need them."

"Who cares? Let's just go. Screw everyone else."

Simon feels something shift inside him. It's as if Tizzy has chipped at his tolerance one too many times. He eyes the Amissa dutifully taking on the Cleaners. Balco grabs a Cleaner, and with tears streaming from his unctuous black eyes, he crushes what trace of life remained inside the vile creature that was once a reverent soldier of God.

Simon turns his focus to his new weapon. The angel's blade seems almost translucent, as if it were forged from crystals long buried beneath the Earth.

"Ok, whatever, man. I'm going after homeboy." Tizzy turns and heads up the stairs.

Suddenly she feels a fire below.

She looks down to see the shimmering clear blade protruding from her gut and lets out a scream that her own ears have never heard before.

Simon retracts the blade and Tizzy slumps onto the stairs, clutching her stomach as it bleeds profusely.

"*Oh-my-god-oh-my-god-oh-my-god.*" Tizzy rolls onto her back and stares up at Simon. "It burns. Fucking burns!"

"I bet it does."

"Why . . ." she coughs up blood as she demands, "did you do that?"

"Because I don't like you. Never have, you obsequious little shit," Simon tells her, doing nothing to disguise the disdain in his voice. "*Fuck everyone else*, you say?"

Tizzy winces at the pain.

"No. Fuck *you*. I know you'll switch sides the moment I turn my back. Once a traitor, always a traitor." He gives the sword another look, wondering briefly why she didn't explode like Zolash had when it was wielded against him.

"I'm not gonna . . ." Tizzy grimaces as the pain steals her breath before assuring him, "not gonna . . . betray you."

"I know," he declares as he raises the sword, "because you'll be dead."

Chapter 29 – Mile-High Club

Sailing high above the clouds, the ground appears as a multi-colored quilt of green, brown and dusty beige shapes. As discussed, Zolash carries Travis. Victor carries Amanda and Duncan.

Victor's wings extend and flap in long sweeps. Duncan covers his eyes with his hands. Amanda stares at the sweeping earth below. She occasionally glances at Duncan, who squirms and frets the entire flight.

Zolash holds Travis with one hand, keeping the half-wing as far away from his body as possible. He makes a snarling sound, suddenly clutching his chest with his free hand, to which Travis asks, "You alright?"

Zolash has been hit by the singeing pain of losing his other replicas. His counterpart below had been slain by an angelic weapon, a weapon that only one has yielded against them:

Michael.

But how? Zolash thinks. *Is he here to finish his war against us? Or is someone else wielding his scythe?*

"Look," Travis interrupts. "Just let me know when you want to drop me."

With a venomous tone Zolash hisses, *"I've been wanting to drop you since I first touched you."*

"The feeling is mutual."

"Why can't you fly anyway?" the angel asks. *"Is it because you're a mistake, half-breed?"*

Travis listens to the steady swooping noise both angels' wings make as they glide closer to their destination.

"No," Victor explains, "It's because I haven't taught him yet."

"If it wasn't for Balco's fondness of you," Zolash tells Victor, "I would regard you with the same disdain as your brother."

"I don't care how you regard me."

To Victor, the Zolash clone goes on, "I don't know why you waste your time with these monkeys. In pursuit of a hollow retribution? Or are you pandering to the will of your dead mother? Seeking out your wreck of a family?" Zolash tightens his grip on Travis. "Especially this one. He is the realization of blasphemy and should be wiped off the face of the Earth and exiled from Heaven. He should be sent to the dark place."

They drift low enough that the crew can see the rooftops of houses sprawled out between great lengths of land. They're in the countryside for sure. Dirt roads crisscross through pastures dotted with the black and brown flecks of cattle herding together.

"I'll send your ass to the dark place," Travis tells the clone, who cackles in response.

"*You are funny, monkey-boy.*" Zolash points down at the rooftop of Marcus's mansion. "*There is our destination. This is where part of me has died.*" He looks to Victor. "*You could have been down there, by our sides, helping us get back home.*"

"You should have never left."

"*You're right. But now I'm going to fix that by delivering the pendant right to my true brothers.*" Zolash flings Travis down towards the mansion.

"Travis!" Amanda screams.

"No!" Victor shouts.

Duncan pulls his hands away from his eyes in time to see Travis dwindling to a tiny dot below.

Chapter 30 - Freefall

Travis has never jumped out of a plane.

Never zip-lined.

Never bungee jumped.

Though his profession of being a supernatural transporter has proven less than safe, at least he has gotten paid to do it. He's never been an adrenaline junkie doing it for kicks, but this . . .

This topped any and all risks he'd encountered while moving paranormal collectibles.

The Spanish tiles of Marcus's roof were quickly coming up to meet him.

And just before he is about to crash . . .

Time.

Slows.

Down.

Godspeed has kicked in.

He recognizes this feeling just as it had hit him when he was in Miami.

The surrounding air thickens as if the sky was now composed of jelly, not oxygen. His ascent slows to a torpid pace. The clothes on his body no longer flap violently like sails in a windstorm. The hair on his head, gently sways instead of beating blindly against his brow.

So, is this how I go out? he thinks. *A slow-motion free fall to my death thanks to that asshole?*

As gradual as the world is drawing towards him, he is still falling to his demise. He can see the distinct Spanish tiles, salmon pink, arranged in perfect vertical rows along the rooftop.

What good is being part angel if I can't fly?

Outwardly he is screaming his lungs out.

Inwardly, his thoughts shift from the chaos, to a focused, quick prayer.

Hey, God!

Travis closes his eyes, bracing for impact.

I could really use Your help right now!

He will soon punch through a rooftop like a human meteorite.

"*GOD?*" Travis shouts even though he can't hear the words.

The speed of his world goes back to normal.

Chapter 31 – Party Crashers

Inside the mansion, the battle rages on between the Amissa and the Cleaners. Both sides take losses, but the last of the Cleaners are wiped out by Balco. Now only he and four angels remain.

Simon stands above Tizzy, poised to cut her down.

The ceiling explodes.

Tile, wood, stucco and stone rain down into the fountain along with a man's body.

All of it making a tumultuous splash.

No longer interested in Tizzy, Simon storms towards the fountain.

Meanwhile Tizzy musters what fading strength she has. She drags herself up the stairs, one by one, moaning in pain with each step. One hand clutches her wound; the other grasps the next step, and the next step. She eventually makes it to the second floor then stops abruptly, her body falling limp.

Balco and the other remaining angels join Simon. He glances at the hole in the ceiling and then down at the man lying in a sloshy pile of debris. Blood obscures the man's face. His hair is matted against his skin. His left arm is twisted, almost bent completely backwards.

Simon leans close, wipes some of the blood away. "Travis?" Shakes his head and takes a second look at the newfound skylight above and sees something else falling towards him. "Oh shit!" Simon exclaims, taking a step back as Zolash drops in.

"I came as quick as I could," Zolash assures him.

"You did this?" Simon asks.

"Of course," Zolash answers. "That derivative, half-monkey deserved to die."

Simon studies Travis's broken body. Then admits, "Agreed." He grabs Travis by his blood-soaked shirt. "However, he still owes me." He aims the tip of the sword at Travis's eye.

"But he is dead," Balco states.

"Yeah, but I still want to take his eye." Simon yanks Travis's limp body towards him and the pendant spills out from his shirt. "Well, well, well. Look at that."

"Yes," Zolash says, "I was about to tell you."

Simon narrows his gaze at Zolash. "Were you?"

"I have no reason to lie, especially as I delivered him straight to you."

Simon huffs in disbelief. He lays down the sword and reaches for the necklace.

"Wait!" Zolash protests.

Simon freezes. "What?"

"If you are not worthy, you will perish upon touching the pendant."

"Hmmm," Simon muses, "just like the Eyes of God."

"And why have you not taken the pendant from this abomination yourself?" Balco asks Zolash.

"Part of me attempted to do so," Zolash admits as he nods his head submissively. "And died."

"But these are holy relics. We are superior to these simians and should be able to possess the things of God."

Zolash pauses. Then suggests, "Perhaps the impurities of this Earth have detracted from our worthiness."

Balco seethes, gestures to Travis and spits, "And yet this abomination wears a nail of Jesus around his neck like costume jewelry!"

"I don't know what to make of it myself, Balco. That's why I delivered him unto you, so that we can sort this out."

"Let's sort it out later." Simon undoes the chain – careful not to touch the pendant itself – and holds the necklace up, admiring the silver cross. "Such a simple design."

"God is simple," Balco explains. "It is humans who make things difficult."

Simon scoffs. "Says the angel who spearheaded a mass exodus out of Heaven."

"An action I will regret forever."

"Don't waste your time regretting. Soon you'll be back at cloud city." Simon removes a satchel from his side and carefully slides the necklace inside. "I mean if you want to talk about a godsend, literally one of the keys to Heaven just dropped into our laps."

Balco glowers at Simon's jubilance. "There is still a matter of us being worthy enough to open the gates."

"Let's go grab the manacles from Marcus first," Simon suggests.

"Before we handle Marcus," Zolash interjects, "we should take out Travis's friends."

"What?" Simon asks with a scowl.

"I had to lead them here, to trick them."

A streak of blazing light crashes into Zolash, sending him slamming through a wall and leaving a gaping flaming hole behind.

"What the fuck was that?" Simon exclaims as he and the Amissa turn in the direction of the flash's origin.

Amanda stands at the doorway, arms outstretched, palms swirling with bluish-white currents of energy.

"It is the witch who murdered our brothers," Balco announces.

Amanda's gaze shifts towards Travis's body. She lowers her head, eyes fixed on the angels before her now.

They took Pastor Graham from me, she thinks. *And now Travis!*

Her arms burst into furious waves of azure-blue fire. Her skin tone goes black. The room booms with the sound of a thunderstorm. "I want you all to taste the darkness you've brought forth from me."

Simon points at Amanda. "You guys deal with super-bitch. I'm going after Marcus."

Balco nods.

Simon runs up the stairs, sees Tizzy lying face down, and shoots past her. He enters Marcus's office to find the old man on the balcony quietly gazing out at his garden.

"Marcus."

Marcus doesn't turn around.

Simon approaches warily. Sword in hand. "Tell me, what's the story behind this sword? I mean . . . it kills angels."

"I'm surprised a collector such as yourself does not know all the treasures of God."

"It's not like there's a website I can go to add these things to my cart."

Marcus turns to face Simon. A pipe in the shape of a dragon is stuffed in his mouth. "That is the Angel's Blade. It's a broken piece of a scythe that belonged to none other than Michael the Archangel himself. I had it repurposed, forged into the very sword you hold."

Simon gives the sword an affirming shake. "It's gorgeous. Thank you for the gift." He points the blade at Marcus as he closes the distance between them. "Now where are the manacles?"

Casually, Marcus raises an eyebrow to the glass case where they rest.

Simone chuckles. "That was easy enough."

"You still need the pendant to open the manacles."

"I know."

"And even if you find them," Marcus grins as he takes a relaxed puff and inquires, "are you worthy to combine the two?"

"I'll figure that out later." Simon walks over the case. Sizes it up. His first instinct is to smash it, but he hesitates. "You open it. No telling if that thing is booby trapped."

"Fine." Marcus waddles over to a large desk, rests his pipe, and plops down on a plush, rose red office chair that seems to swallow him up. "I'll get you the manacles."

"Wonderful. And just in case you've called for backup, we won't be here much longer."

"I would hope not." With a laugh. "I mean, if you are successful, you should be up in Heaven."

"Who says I'm *going* to Heaven?" Simon asks with a hint of annoyance. "Perhaps I want to take something *from* Heaven."

"Interesting." Marcus secures a large brass key. With a nod, he proposes,

"We both share the same goals. Control over the gateways to the afterlife. Why not let me partake?"

"Because you haven't done the work."

"*Haven't done the work?*" Marcus's expression sours, his jowls drooping as he frowns. "Do you think that the manacles just showed up at my doorstep? Do you know how many agents I've lost? How many transporters of the Covenant I had to kill just to find them?"

Simon lets out an exasperated sigh. "Just shut up and open the case."

Marcus rocks himself out of his chair with a grunt. "You're going to have to open the gate first." He unlocks the case, and as he does so, the manacles flash bright blue. He wavers. "I thought you didn't have the other half?"

"I never said that. You assumed," Simon says. "Now hurry up."

Marcus obliges, sliding his hands under the pillow and then presenting the manacles to Simon. "Where exactly did you get the pendant?"

"You hear that loud boom?"

"Of course. I'm old, not deaf."

"That was God delivering the pendant right to me."

Frustration builds in Marcus's face. "But . . . how?"

"Lay the manacles on your desk."

Marcus does as instructed.

"How?" Simon removes a handkerchief and uses it to carefully place the manacles into another red satchel, keeping his sword aimed at Marcus the entire time. "Travis, the one transporter you haven't killed . . . well he landed right smack in the middle of that ugly-ass fountain of yours. That's how."

"What?"

"Yep. The Lord brought the deliveryman to the Rift's doorstep, only to give the package right to me."

Marcus makes a noise, like the hiss of a balloon, deflating.

"Ironic, right?" Simon asks. Just as he is about to cut Marcus in half, a hand grabs his shoulder and whips him around to face—Quell.

She kicks him in the groin, and he keels over, dropping the sword in the process.

"What is more ironic," Marcus explains, "is that you knew this was a trap; yet you still walked into it."

Quell glares at Simon, half of her face is a rippled pink mess from torturous burns that have long since scarred over. A thin swath of blood seeps down her neck from the blow he delivered earlier. She snatches the sword and, with it, traces the scar on Simon's face, studying it with a morbid curiosity before commanding, "Give him the pendant and the manacles."

Simon snarls at her as he fishes out the satchels and tosses them at Marcus's feet.

"Once I figured out what you were up to," Marcus informs him as he grabs the satchels, "I gradually pulled back my efforts to stop you."

Quell forces Simon to look up at her, and she has a clear view of his fake eye. "That's pretty."

Simon spits on her. She wipes it away before delivering a slap that knocks his head to one side.

Followed by another slap.

Then a solid kick to the ribs.

Then another.

"Quell!"

She freezes.

"Save your energy," Marcus advises.

Quell withdraws with a sneer.

Simon wipes blood from his lip. Asks Marcus, "What good are the pendant and manacles going to do you? I'm sure your fat ass is unworthy."

"I can wait an eternity to find someone who is." Marcus reveals his rosary necklace. "Can you?"

"You think you can stop the Amissa?" Simon asks as he rubs his side.

"Yes," Marcus nods towards the opposite end of the room before revealing, "and they're going to help."

Several bookcases slide open revealing darkened corridors that lead into the bowels of the mansion. From those depths a group of Shaker witches emerge, arms raised, heads jerking erratically.

"Kill him," Marcus tells Quell. "He served his purpose."

She plants her boot squarely on Simon's back, forcing him down onto his stomach. "I'd like to pluck out that fancy eye of his, sir, if that's ok with you?"

"Be my guest. We're heading downstairs," Marcus informs her as the Shaker witches surround him. "We'll see if we can clean up the mess and create more Cleaners from our angelic miscreants."

"Are you sure you want to give my eye to your subordinate?" Simon asks.

Quell digs her heel into Simon's spine, earning a grunt from him. "I'm going to drive this blade slowly into—"

"Quell!" Marcus barks. "What are you talking about, Simon?"

"Get this ugly bitch off my back, and I'll tell you."

Marcus ponders this, then motions for her to back off. To Simon, he instructs, "Go on."

"Seems you don't know about all of God's treasures either." Simon taps his eye. "This is the Divine Eye. It contains the essence, the blood of angels. Seraphic energy trapped in a bottle, if you will."

Marcus strokes the wispy, greasy strands of hair that frame his head. "I'll admit I have not heard of this treasure."

"With it, you can sense when an angel is close by, which is what helped me track down all the Amissa you kidnapped." Simon pulls it out, exposing the gaping pink hole of his eye socket. He holds up the eyeball between his index finger and thumb. The bluish fluid glints. "Its core liquifies when angels are near."

"Fascinating!" Marcus says with glee.

"That's what I said."

"I'll take it." Marcus reaches for it, but Simon pulls away.

"Let me show you what else it can do." Simon shuts his eye and smashes the Divine Eye into the ground.

Everything goes white. It's as if the cosmos itself has rebooted right there within the four walls of Marcus's study. Accompanied by the concussive symphony of several cannons firing at once.

Screams follow.

Simon feels his body free fall, even though he is still flat on the ground.

The blinding light fades.

The screams dwindle and are replaced by sounds of exasperation.

Simon opens his eyes to see the witches writhing on the ground, curled up in fetal positions, crying tears of blood. Quell rocks back and forth, fists pressed into her eye sockets. Marcus is slumped against the wall, hands covering his face. Streams of blood slip between his fingers.

The Angel Blade lays close to Quell. Simon grabs it and, looming above her, he takes off her head and hands in one clean motion. Blood sprays everywhere as she slumps lifelessly to the ground.

"Not recovering this time, huh?" Simon asks as he proceeds to cut down each of the witches where they lay.

"Please . . ." Marcus keeps one hand covering both eyes, uses the other to push himself unsteadily to his feet. "Please!"

"Please what?" Simon walks over to him.

"Please, don't kill me." Marcus spins on his heels, keeping one trembling hand out as a guide for his newfound blindness. His other hand is still glued to his face as streaks of crimson stain his cheeks. Seems the magic of his beads cannot overpower the divinity of the blade. "I   I —I can help you."

"Help me what?"

The grandiloquence of Marcus's speech is now supplanted with a quivering frailty that Simon finds musical to his ears. "I can help you find one worthy enough to open the gates."

"I'm working with a team of ambitious angels that you screwed over. They're itching to get back home, so between us, I'm sure we'll find a way without you."

"But I can save you all time . . . if you'll spare me."

"What do you mean?"

"There is one worthy. He is the same one who was able to use the Eyes of God. Vanessa knew this and was going to use him." Marcus grimaces as pain threatens to overwhelm him.

"Go on."

"Promise you will spare me," Marcus begs as he holds up two bloody, quivering hands. His eyes are nothing more than puckered black holes, seeping brownish-red blood.

Simon upturns his lip in disgust. "Fine. I'll spare you."

"Travis Rail," Marcus reveals. "Only he was worthy."

"Yeah, well I figured as much seeing as he was wearing it, but since I didn't make myself clear when I mentioned that he crash-landed into your fountain," Simon informs him with a laugh, "he's very dead right now."

"That—that doesn't matter." Marcus shakes his hands furiously as he campaigns, "We are practiced in the schools of Necromancy! We've mastered a diablerie powerful enough to resurrect him for our purposes."

Simon ponders this. "Bullshit."

"Wha—wha—what?" Marcus stammers, eye sockets glaring in Simon's direction like two bullet holes. "I am telling you the truth. We can revive—"

"You think I'm stupid?" Simon insists. "If we use black magic on anything, that shit is tainted. And while I may not be the most religious guy in the room, I will bet that would negate any sort of worthiness."

"You don't know that, you pompous prick!" Marcus bristles at Simon's arrogance.

"I know that you're just buying time until either backup gets here, or you figure out something else." Simon uses the sword to lift the rosary beads necklace on Marcus's neck.

"What are you doing?"

"Getting rid of dead weight."

Marcus feels the beads move, instinctively reaches for them, but Simon has already flicked the blade upwards. The necklace splits in half; a hail of beads peppers the floor, rolling out in every direction.

"No!" Marcus's skin quickly blackens as if burning from the inside out. "*Nonononononono,*" he screeches as he grabs at his neck; his face and fingers ignite with the angry red and yellow shades of charcoals flaming to life at a BBQ. "Ahh!" He rolls onto his stomach, steaming and screaming. He reaches for a rosary bead, *any* rosary bead, but without the benefit of sight, he claws desperately at empty air.

Within moments, Marcus is a heaping pile of cinder. The centuries of belated infirmity now reclaim his body with a smoldering vengeance.

Simon kneels, shoves his hands into the ashy mess and retrieves the two satchels.

"Guess you're not so eternal after all." He shoves the satchels into his pockets and heads back into the main room.

Chapter 32 – Heaven Sent

The world is a fog, a beautiful fog, with clouds surrounding him. Travis is lying on his back in a lush, green field that stretches for miles.

He blinks several times, then sits up, surprised he can even move.

The last thing he remembers, he was free falling toward a Chateau.

Now he's in the middle of an unending countryside dotted with flowers of every color of the rainbow.

"Hey, Travie."

Travis clumsily gets to his feet.

His grandmother is standing there. A radiating aura around her. She leans forward and plucks a handful of flowers. Sniffs them. The grayish curls of her hair turn pale blonde, then fiery blonde. Her skin follows suit, changing, transforming, the years melting away.

Her features soften. Wrinkles giving way to a fresh, vibrant face.

His grandmother appears forty years younger.

Beaming with a generous smile, she hands the flowers to Travis. "Here," she offers with a gentle shake. "Take them. Give them a smell."

Travis reaches for his Beretta, but it is nowhere to be found.

"You don't need that here."

"Where's Amanda?" Travis asks. "Duncan? Victor? The Amissa?"

"Not here."

Travis eyes his surroundings. "Where's *here*?"

Words reverberate within his mind:

Everything is ok.

Everything is, was, and will always be ok.

The words are accompanied by a subtle, tranquil feeling. An undeniable warmth, almost an invisible blanket of peace fills him, both unnerving and calming him simultaneously.

It's as if his body has fallen under the spell of the most potent sedative in the world. Only he doesn't feel like sleeping, but instead like . . . doing nothing but sitting on the verdant meadow and staring up at the soaring clouds that reach interminably into a tawny sky.

"If this is Rift magic . . ."

"If this was Rift magic, you wouldn't be experiencing the peace you feel now." With a smile, she adds, "They cannot manufacture such a sensation."

"Yeah, they could." With a laugh, he quips, "With drugs."

"Just smell the flowers, Travie."

"Are they drugged?"

His grandma folds her arms.

Carefully he brings the flowers to his nose. Inhales deeply and is hit with a cacophony of scents: fresh cut grass, feathers of a bird, the air before it rains, the saltwater mist by the ocean, the core of a rose, Amanda's sweet but almost imperceptible perfume—

"You smell that?" Grandma asks.

Travis examines the flowers as though they've come from some other world, because they have.

"That is the essence of all things. The simplest of things are the most important of things."

"Where am I?" He tries to return the flowers but they evaporate into a delicate vapor that trails off into the distance.

"Where do you think you are?"

"No clue."

"Then why are you at peace with it?" she asks as she takes a seat, folding her legs neatly as if about to meditate, pray or tell a story. "Sit."

Reluctantly he does, mimicking her posture.

Why does everyone answer my question with a question? he thinks.

"Because you have an insatiable *need* to understand everything," she answers his thought.

Travis stiffens.

"And what you will often find is that the answer will only lead to more questions," she tells him. "It's the reason a young child always asks *why* followed by *why*, followed by another *why*. There is no need to understand everything because that will not lead to happiness, nor completion, nor satisfaction. Accepting that things are the way they are is the only way. Things just . . . *are*. There is no necessity to unravel the secrets of the universe as man is always seeking to do. The secret of the universe is in appreciating the essence of life itself."

"Grandma, I love you, but you're making my head hurt."

She gets a chuckle out of this. "Let me explain it this way: think of your favorite food. Now, if I listed everything in it, every spice, every ingredient, would you enjoy it anymore?"

Travis stares at her, studying her face. "Zach . . . is that you?"

His grandma suddenly morphs into Zach.

"I knew it," Travis says under his breath.

"Your grandmother wanted me to talk to you."

"Well, first of all, that was creepy," he tells the prophetic angel as he stands up. "Where is she? And where am I?"

Zach floats up to his feet. "You're both in the same place."

"So . . . I'm dreaming?"

Zach says nothing.

"Ok, so, I'm dead?"

"We do not use that term here."

"I'm *dead*!"

"Travis, please stop saying that."

"That freak angel killed me. That scrawny little *mothefslusgmg!*" The last word falls apart in his mouth, as if his teeth and tongue were suddenly made of jelly. A sharp pain makes him woozy. It takes him a moment to recover.

"Travis, you cannot sin here. Not with thought or with tongue."

Thankfully, the pain abates just as abruptly as it came. Travis asks, "Alright, so am I in Heaven?"

Zach nods.

Travis's gaze falls to the ground. "And again . . . where is my grandmother? And why did you pretend to be her?"

"I wanted you to be comfortable."

"By pretending to be my grandmother?" Travis puts a hand to his forehead. "I must be dreaming. Just another one of those strange dreams."

"This is no dream."

"What's even more strange is that I feel," Travis paces while thinking aloud, the wheels turning in his brain, "oddly comfortable with the notion that I'm . . . well . . . dead."

"I asked you to please stop saying that."

"And I asked you, where is my grandmother? And my mom, for that matter?"

"They can't see you."

"Why not?"

"Because then you won't leave."

"Won't leave?" Travis scoffs. "I just got here."

"But their presence would sway you to stay."

Travis's eyes narrow. "What are you talking about?"

"It is not your time yet."

"But I die—I mean, I am . . . here now."

"Yes. One of our fallen has thrown you to your death. But that was not your intended end and it was not God's will. He still wants your help, so you still have a choice to make."

"What do you mean?"

Zach kneels, digs his hands into the ground, and pulls apart the foundation as if it were nothing more than papier-mâché. Instead of an infinite supply of dirt, they look down onto the rooftop of Marcus's chateau.

The rooftop seems to vanish, and now they see inside the mansion where Amanda is taking on the Amissa by herself. Victor has crawled out from the hole in the wall where he shoved the Zolash clone. Duncan swings a chair at an angel. Travis's body lies rumpled in the fountain.

The Amissa surround Amanda and charge in.

"Amanda!" Travis leans into the hole. "Amanda!"

The hole closes.

"You can save them," Zach informs him as he rises. "You can preserve the sanctity of Heaven, or you can choose to stay here. The decision is yours, as you have free will."

Travis swallows hard at what he's just seen. "If they die, will they come here too?"

"If they do, understand that they will know that you abandoned them when given the opportunity to return to Earth and help them."

Wonderful, Travis thinks. *A permanent guilt trip.*

"We prefer the word *eternal*."

"I don't need to be convinced," Travis assures him. "Open that hole back up and let me go!"

"Fine, but please know that there is a cost to return to Earth," Zach warns. "A cost that may make things harder for you to stop the Amissa. But if you can persevere, you may find the changes to your advantage. Regardless, you won't be the same once you go back."

"What are you talking about?" Travis feels his sense of peace falter.

"You're a half-wing. A rare breed. Therefore, I cannot foretell what you will experience if you return to Earth, for only the angels may travel back and forth. However, you are something else and only God knows fully what that is."

"Can you give God a call? Maybe ask Him what the—hell*sdfadpouisdfs*—" A bolt of pain strikes Travis square in his brain. He winces; then as pain passes, he treads lightly as to not curse or think of cursing, "Can you . . . ask Him . . . what that cost is?"

"Ask Him yourself." Zach gestures for him to kneel and pray.

"Right now?"

"If you are serious about returning to Earth to help your friends."

"Isn't that what you want?" Travis asks.

"Is that what you want?"

"Yes! Alright! Yes!" Travis begins to worry, wondering if time moves the same on Earth as it does in Heaven.

Have the Amissa killed Amanda by now?

What about Duncan?

And Victor? But he's an angel . . . so how does that work exactly?

Travis shakes off the thoughts, drops to his knees, and begins to pray for direction. Asks for protection and help to persist through the pain at all costs.

There's a ripping sound.

Travis's eyes open just in time to see Zach splitting apart the ground again before shoving Travis below as if being tossed out of a plane into the wild unknown beneath the false green floor of Heaven.

Chapter 33 – The Chateau Fight

A pair of Amissa pin Amanda's arms behind her back. She tries to ignite her hands, power up her magic, but can't focus, distracted by the pain of her arms being jammed up against her.

Another angel clutches her face. "I'm going to make you sing the way you forced our brothers."

A chair sails over the angel's head. He spins around and sees Duncan, who proceeds to sign the cross and mouth a quick prayer.

The angel studies him. "What did you just ask for?"

"I—uh." He can barely say the words. Sweat trickles down his forehead and runs along the bridge of his nose. His glasses start to slide downward, but he adjusts them. "I—I—I . . ."

The angel advances.

Duncan walks backwards until he's against the wall.

"Leave him alone!" Amanda shrieks.

The angel ignores her. He prompts Duncan again, "*What* did you just ask for?"

"A—a miracle."

The angel catches sight of Duncan's rosary beads. "God doesn't bless the blasphemous with miracles." He tears them from Duncan's neck.

Duncan screams and clutches his stomach. The old wound from Lomak's kukri reopens.

"No!" Amanda shouts as she struggles to break free from the angels.

Blood flowers across Duncan's shirt, pours from his lips. He shivers, stumbles sideways and collapses.

Déjà vu.

Only this time, the necklace is broken and the beads are everywhere. He slumps to the ground, blood bubbling from his mouth as his cheek lies pressed onto the cold tile floor. The glasses hang crookedly from the bridge of his nose, as his gaze locks on Amanda, who becomes a shrieking, volatile mess.

"Sorry . . ." Duncan gurgles out the side of his mouth, " . . . I lied . . ."

Amanda wrestles against her captors, shouting her brother's name as if her lungs are on fire.

But Duncan moves no more. He stares blankly as a semicircle of blood expands from him.

The wall tears open, and Victor emerges from the gaping hole. He holds Zolash's head in his hand—its jaw hangs open, eyes wide in shock.

The head evaporates into a white pulse of energy.

Victor catches sight of Duncan lying on his side in a pool of blood, Amanda fighting against the angels, and Travis's blood-soaked body slumped and half-floating in the fountain.

Victor starts towards the duo holding Amanda—

Something catches his feet.

He's swung in a circle and released, sending him sailing right into a pillar. The stone gives behind his back, but the pillar holds. He slides down the length of the column, dazed, but coherent enough to catch site of Balco thundering towards him.

The monstrous angel pulls back, and takes a swing—

Victor ducks.

Balco's fist smashes through the pillar. Shards of stone fly everywhere.

Victor is already on his feet, about to put some distance between them, but Balco unfurls his massive wings. He whirls around, whipping Victor across the face, knocking the angel sideways.

Amanda stares in shock at her dead brother.

There is no coming back this time. No tricks. No beads. He's gone and there's not a thing she can do about it, unless what the Amissa and Simon are after really works. Perhaps she can bring her brother back from Heaven—

No.

She is tainted. Even if she were to waltz into Heaven with the keys, she is marred by black magic and the terrible things she has done. She would have to pray. Ask forgiveness from God before setting foot in Heaven, but even before all that were to happen . . .

She would have to forgive herself.

With Duncan and Travis gone, what does it matter?, she thinks. *I might as well embrace who I am instead of keeping it buried inside me.*

Amanda trades glances with the two angels holding her. Their vapid, obsidian eyes stare back at her, detecting her intent to do something horrible.

Amanda cries out in a way that even surprises herself.

The color of her skin darkens and she is suddenly engulfed in blue flames—flames that spread to the two angels, consuming them.

The three scream in unison.

From the second floor, Simon, with his Angel Blade in hand and satchels tucked tightly at his side, is greeted by the sight of the dead Covenant agent, three bodies aflame in blue, and Balco and the rogue angel going toe to toe.

Victor flies into the air, makes a sharp turn, and dives for Balco, hoping to take the beastly seraph down like he did Zolash.

Unfortunately, slamming into Balco proves to be like crashing into an oak tree.

Balco absorbs the blow and even with only one arm, he still manages to grab Victor in a half-bear hug and pile drive him face-first into the ground. Using his leg, Balco pins Victor down, grabs ahold of the rogue angel's wings with his good hand and then proceeds to rip them from Victor's body as if they were nothing more than vestigial organs.

Victor wails.

Balco tosses the wings aside, grabs Victor by his throat, and flings him into the hole where he had killed Zolash.

Meanwhile, the two angels holding Amanda are turning as bright as the sun.

They explode.

Amanda, breathing heavily, shaking yet still aflame, focuses her attention on Balco. She charges at him, fully intent on destroying the great angel—

Simon jumps between the two.

Blade first.

Amanda plows right into Simon's weapon, and it pierces her stomach. She lets out a choked, whimpering noise.

Simon runs the sword deeper, until the hilt is against her skin. She slumps against him for a moment, blue flame waning, and then tries haphazardly to grab at his face, his shoulders, anything—but he pushes her off of the sword. She stumbles, twirls backwards and lands face first on the ground.

As he watches the flames on her body dwindle, Simon lets out a satisfied *humpf*. Then tells Balco, "Let's do this. We now have the keys to Heaven."

Chapter 34 – Resurrection of the Fallen

Travis is pretty sure that a jackhammer to his skull would only cause a fraction of the agony that he is suffering now. His skin, his brain, his bones feel like they are on fire. His vision is jarred as if strapped to a roller coaster going a hundred and fifty miles an hour. A kaleidoscope of colors and shapes rotate around him, psychedelically animated in a way that pyrotechnics geniuses could only dream of. He's speeding towards something, somewhere, but it is all just a colorful blur.

If there were an optimal time for Godspeed to kick in, this would be it.

Where is this horrific tube leading? What is a dream? What is reality? What is Heaven? Where is the beginning? The end?

A light ahead is drawing close, swelling in size like a fireball headed right for him.

The burning intensifies and is accompanied by the booming of a thousand rockets taking off into nowhere.

It's enough to make any man or woman break—

There's a splash, followed by a gentle trickle of water.

Travis awakens, body creaking to life. Something digs at his spine, feels as if he fell asleep on a staircase. He sits up, pain radiating through his body. He rubs his eyes to find that the world is about as crystal clear as the south end of a Coke bottle. His face feels damp. He touches it, examines his bloody fingers.

The fuckkkdfddfdfdfdf?

The word melts in his brain like a snowflake exposed to the Florida sunshine.

Travis leans forward, cracking and popping as searing jabs of bright pain greet him. He grits his teeth.

Where am I?

Voices echo into the room like airwaves transmitted from another planet:

"Weeeee-eeeeeee-eeeeeee-vvvvvvvvvvvv got-t-t-t-t-t-t-t the-the-the-the-the-the pend-ant-pend-ant-pend-ant-pend-ant."

Travis peels himself off his broken throne. His backside is soaked. Everything is soaked. He sees stars. His mind is whirling like a toilet that just won't flush.

What the hellsdsfdfsdaoiewruwe . . .

The words dissolve, replaced by an ache in the brain.

He looks around, vision muddled. He might as well be under water staring up at a poorly lit world. If God or Zach slipped him some holy tequila, he's definitely feeling it.

It's a monstrous hangover.

There's a body in front of him. Given his poor eyesight, he's unable to discern who it is.

"Come-come-come-come-come-come-come on-on-on-on-on," a voice bellows. "Time-time-time-time-time-to-to-to-to-to-to-open-open-open-open-open . . ."

The dizziness makes him want to throw up. His stomach is doing cartwheels.

The voices trail off. Travis staggers as he climbs out of the fountain. He slumps to the floor, nearly landing on his chin. He pulls his way towards the body.

As he inches closer, the pain and nausea finally subside. His eyes focus at the prone man lying in front of him. He sees that that the man's cheek is pressed to the floor, mouth slight ajar. A pair of glasses, marred with bloodied fingerprint smudges and a tiny crack along the left lens, sit crooked on his nose. A kidney-shaped pond of blood expands from his torso.

At first, the word is trapped in his throat, but then bursts from his lungs, "Duncan!"

As Travis's vision improves, he sees that Duncan is lying with his arm draped across his stomach, intestines spilled out in almost the same manner as they had been back at the unfinished suburb in Florida. The same brutal end that Lomak had granted him has repeated itself.

"Duncan!"

Duncan stares up at Travis with eyes absent of life and spark.

"Duncan, come on!" He smacks at his face, but Duncan's gaze is empty. "Duncan . . . I'm sorry, man!" he shouts as he is overcome with a vacuous sense of finality.

Duncan is gone.

"I'm sorry I got *pissedddlhsdfd.*" The word "pissed" seems to melt in Travis's mouth. "I'm sorry . . . for getting . . . upset." He grits his teeth, groans and tries to shout *Fuck!* but the word never materializes. The more he attempts to express his anger by cursing, the more apparent it is that he cannot do it, and the angrier he gets.

Then he catches sight of Victor, whose body is slumped on the floor. Two gaping wounds stare back at him from his brother's shoulders.

"Travis!" a woman's voice calls out.

Travis looks over his shoulder to see Amanda reaching toward him.

Travis feels his stomach drop.

Not her too!

"You're . . . alive," Amanda whispers and then closes her eyes. Her head softly falls to one side.

Chapter 35 – We're Opening that Gate

Simon and Balco casually walk through the garden as if the battle inside the mansion had never happened.

"I'm sure the Rift has seen us. We can't have possibly taken out every camera. But by the time their reinforcements get here," Simon assures him, "we should be long gone."

Balco nods.

Simon eyes Balco's stump. "Don't you guys regenerate?"

"Not when it was the Angel's Blade that dealt the damage."

"Right." He turns to Balco and adds, "So now we must find someone worthy. I hope you can still help me with that."

Balco nods again, then makes a sweeping gesture with his good hand towards the chateau, suggesting that someone inside is a likely candidate.

"Why are you pointing back there?" Simon asks. "Everyone's dead."

Balco says nothing.

Simon demands. "Who then?"

"You know who."

"The super bitch?"

Balco stays quiet.

"Travis?"

Balco nods.

"You're kidding?" A scoff. "He's gone, and I'm not using any sort of Rift magic to resurrect him. Marcus tried to sell me on that, but I wasn't buying."

Balco remains still, unmoved by Simon's protests.

"What? Speak! You suggesting he's alive? He fucking *fell* from the sky.

And even if he survived—how is it that *he's* the one worthy enough to put the halves together?"

"I cannot answer all of these questions, for God decides who is righteous. Since it appears we are no longer venerable in His eyes, then I'll guide you to those who I can sense are worthy. And I am sensing something." Balco then adds, "Unless you would like to find someone else? Which could take several years. Perhaps a lifetime."

"Fuck that." Simon clutches the sword tightly in his hand and heads back toward the chateau. "I don't care if I have to hold Travis's dead hands together; we're opening that gate . . . *today.*"

Chapter 36 – Too Little, Too Late

Travis races over, scoops up Amanda in his arms. Her face is sweaty, her damp hair obscuring her face. Cradling her, he caresses her face as he rocks back and forth.

"You're . . . here . . ." she murmurs.

"Of course."

"Am I . . . dead then?"

Travis shakes his head furiously. "No. You're not dead." Tears well in his eyes. He forces out the words, attempting to reassure himself more than her, "You're a little beat up, but you'll be fine. Who did this to you?"

Blood seeps from her stomach. "Simon."

Travis feels a bomb go off inside him. "I'm getting you out of here."

She smiles softly. Eyes drift as if she's going to sleep—

"Hey, hey, hey." He taps her chin lightly, telling her, "Stay with me."

Amanda responds with a faint nod. Then, "Travis?"

"Yeah?"

She grimaces suddenly, tensing up as the searing pain of her injury stiffens her body. Then she relaxes. "You need a bath."

Travis laughs. "I thought I just took one."

"Well . . . you . . . you still stink . . ." she manages a weak chuckle, "like . . . death."

"I'll bathe in Old Spice as soon as we leave." He brushes his thumb along her cheek. Her skin feels like cotton. "Just stay with me."

"No."

"No what?"

"No Old Spice." Another weak laugh as she adds, "I'm a . . . Dolce Gabbana girl at heart."

"Ok. I can do that." Travis fights back the tears. Clears his throat of emotion.

This can't be happening, can it? he thinks.

Where's Zach when I need him? Where is Zach ever?

Where's the miracle?

I've been brought back from Heaven only to miss her on the way down.

This can't be happening!

She brings a hand to his face. "Thanks."

"For?"

"For never leaving me."

"But . . . I did leave you."

"Well . . . you're here now." She coughs violently, blood gushing from her mouth.

"Ok, we're going." He starts to rise.

"No. I'm . . . staying."

"What?"

"I want to be . . . next to my brother."

Travis struggles to suppress the tears. She can't see him cry. He *has* to be strong. "No! We're leaving." But she doesn't respond. Only stares up at him. The delicate blue of her eyes darkens, appears a slight shade grayer.

"Amanda?"

Travis shakes her.

Nothing.

"Amanda!"

Travis holds her close. Mumbles, "*Nononononononnono.*"

Her body goes limp. He's covered in a mix of his blood and her blood.

Clenching his teeth and his fists, he tells himself, "This. Isn't. Happening."

She can't be gone.

He smooths her hair away from her forehead, tucking it gently behind her ear, and stares at her for what feels like an eternity. He shakes his head again in disbelief, unable to accept her passing. The surrealness of this proves to be too much—

Amanda bursts into black dust.

Travis freezes.

The dust of her body goes everywhere. All over him, the floor and some of it wafting upward.

Did that just happen?

Travis stares down at his empty, shaking hands. There's black dust on them, too.

Amanda's dust.

He feels his body go cold.

Feels his mind sink into an endless pit of shock and despair.

That just happened.

He brings his soot-covered hands to his face, glaring at them as if they belonged to someone else.

I'm covered in Amanda's dust.

She's fuckingggggggnssdfserete gone!

The curse word falls apart in his brain, becoming nonsensical mush.

His mind reels.

He thinks about Heaven.

About Zach's teachings.

About the recklessness of man.

About the Rift.

About how the Covenant, as he knows it, is practically gone.

Duncan is gone.

Amanda is gone.

All because of . . . Simon.

Simon.

Simon!

I'm going to make him pay.

Vision no longer hazy from his rebirth, he instead goes blind with rage. A mushroom cloud erupts inside his head. His eyes gloss over. He squeezes his fists tightly into shaking balls of fury.

"Simon!" He shouts and the man's name echoes throughout the chateau.

"Right behind you."

Travis spins to find Simon standing in the doorway.

Chapter 37 – Rage of the Fallen

"Not sure how you survived that fall," Simon announces as Balco files in behind him, "but you're one lucky son of a bitch."

As Travis glances off to the side, still absorbed in the trauma of having Amanda not only die but physically blow up in his face.

Luck is the furthest thing from my mind.

"Here's the deal," Simon goes on, "help us open the gate, or join your friends."

Travis remains silent, fixated on the bodies of Duncan and Victor.

"Hey, dickhead!" Simon yells. "I'm talking to you."

The muscles of Travis's jaw bulge as he stares at Simon. "I'd rather join them." He takes deep, fervent breaths, and lowers his gaze locking eyes with the murderer before him. "But you won't kill me, because you need me."

"I get it." Simon surveys the room for Amanda's body but it's gone. He continues anyway, "You want to be with her. *Wherever* she may be." He points at himself. "I understand that more than you know. The one you love . . . no longer here. Everything about this world offers you a shallow copy of what used to bring you joy. There is no excitement, no delight in anything. Only a hollowness that no material thing, no great success, no amount of money can fill. Nothing matters once they are gone."

Simon rattles on, but Travis isn't listening. There's an obvious snarl on his face as he's focused only on the fact that this man has taken away the few individuals who truly mattered to him.

Balco warily observes the uncomfortable exchange between the two, ready to move if Travis attacks.

"I understand what you are feeling right now," Simon assures him. "I live it every day."

"You don't know what I'm feeling!"

"Like absolute shit. But we can change that if we work together," Simon promises as he brings up a fist, shaking it as he speaks. "We can get back the ones we love. You see, I've spent my life on things that never mattered. Money. Prestige. A lucrative business."

Travis's focus wanders. He can't take his mind off Amanda, the waning glow of her skin, the fact that she died fighting—all while he was in Heaven, or stasis, or purgatory.

She died.

She detonated in front of him, going the way of every Rift scumbag he ever ended.

And now this monster wants to try to relate with me, he thinks. *He caused all of this!*

"Then Cynthia was diagnosed with cancer. I prayed. God didn't answer. She died." Simon takes a deep breath. "Originally, I was collecting God's treasures for fun; then I found myself collecting for a purpose. The purpose is to bring her back, and the way I see it, God owes me this."

"God doesn't owe you anything."

Simon pauses. "Point is, you want to see your friends again. I want Cynthia. The big guy here," he hikes a thumb at Balco before continuing, "he just wants to go home. It's a win-win all around. So, you're right, I need you. We need each other. I have your pendant and the manacles. We both want our loved ones. Let's just get this over with."

Travis closes his eyes, takes a deep breath. Nostrils flaring, teeth grinding, he feels several acrimonious quakes ripple through his body.

"Well," Simon asks, "what do you say about helping us?"

Chapter 38 – Showdown at the Garden

Travis glowers at Simon and Balco. He feels the heat of rage and vehemence smoldering within him.

"Hey! I need an answer!" Simon snaps his finger several times at Travis. "Help us open the gate, or we'll find someone who will."

Travis says nothing. Stands there and fumes.

The sound of engines roaring in the distance steadily grows. Simon glances outside, notes several black cars racing through the sandy Florida backroads, kicking up dust clouds in their wake as they beeline for the chateau.

"Fuck," Simon mutters.

"The Rift," Balco says.

Travis remains unmoved by the news. Gaze transfixed on Simon.

"Lift your hands," Simon commands.

The prominent white hate in Travis's eyes is clearly visible as he replies, "No."

Simon nods at Balco, "Take him outside."

Balco flies behind Travis. Even with only one good hand, Balco secures him with godlike strength and tosses him outside onto the dusty ground.

Simon retrieves his satchels and follows. He looks to the horizon. The cars draw closer—four of them total. All SUVs with black tint.

"Look . . . if you don't open the gates, then I'll negotiate a deal with the Rift. Have them help expedite things so that it's not on Balco and me to find a worthy replacement." Simon kneels close to Travis. "We'll get what we want, and the Rift can keep the keys. I could care less what they do once I've got Cynthia back. So, either you'll open the doors, or they will."

Balco hoists Travis up from the dirt.

"And what makes you think that they'll help you?" Travis asks.

"I'll take my chances. But I promise you this—if you force me to work with them, I will resurrect your precious blonde bitch-witch, and I'll give her back to the Rift, so that they can have at her. I'm sure they wouldn't mind the reunion. I'm not an idiot, Travis. I know she didn't learn magic at Sunday school. Now," Simon tosses the satchels at Travis's feet and insists, "your move."

Balco releases Travis and takes a step back.

Travis glares at the satchels, then scoops them up. Without hesitating, he pulls the pendant and manacles out, examining both closely.

There's a gleam of excitement in Simon's eyes. Even Balco stares on with interest.

Travis finds a relief on one of the manacles in the shape of a cross. It is exactly where he needs to lay his pendant.

The cars are almost upon them.

Travis hesitates.

"Do it already!" Simon barks.

Travis takes a deep breath.

The cars pull up to the chateau, tires screeching against the asphalt.

"Hurry!" Beads of sweat multiply on Simon's forehead.

Travis slowly brings the halves of the keys together. There's a distinct click as the pendant locks snuggly inside the relief.

There is a taut moment of silence.

Nothing happens.

The next sounds that follow are those of car doors slamming, hurried footsteps, and mumbled commands between the agents.

Simon snarls. He turns to Balco. "What's the deal? Does it not work after all?"

Travis stares intently at the combined treasures.

Not a spark, not a flicker of light seeps from between them. He might as well have put two stones together.

"Well, well, well! Caught you shits in the act!" A breathless man proclaims as he and several Rift thugs, guns drawn, aim their automatic rifles at the trio. The man looks much like Riley, and for a second, Simon thinks that Riley has been resurrected by Rift magic. Even Balco pauses, staring at the man with a hint of confusion. The man informs them, "You maggots killed my dear brother, Riley."

Simon shrugs.

"I watched that shit on camera," the brother says. "Watched the feed several times. Ol' boy put up a good fight." He snorts and spits a wad of goo in their direction. "And now in honor of him, I'm going to level the lot of ya. Then we'll be taking back what you got there, Mr. Rail."

The Rift troops raise their weapons.

"That's Rift property you're holding," the brother tells Travis.

Travis never takes his eyes off the treasures.

"Too bad they don't work," Simon complains as he weighs his options. The sword is still in his hand. He might not be able to take out all these agents, but he and Balco can sure try.

At this point, if there is no getting Cynthia, then nothing matters now.

"We don't care," Riley's brother says. "That's for us to figure out and you blokes to sod off."

"If you want them so bad, why don't you come get them yourself?" Simon taunts. "Shoot us and take them. What are you waiting for?"

"Right then!" the brother says.

Simon gestures to Balco that they are going to have to strike these thugs down. He grips his sword tightly. Balco signals his understanding, just as he always does.

The treasures begin to shake in Travis's hand. *He* hasn't given up hope that they will work. Teeth gritting. Black lines of dirt mixed with sweat cascade down his forehead. Body quaking.

No, he hasn't given up hope that the keys will work because he doesn't care at this point.

He has given up hope on humanity.

On his life having meaning.

All of this was for nothing.

Why did Zach send me back here? What was the point? So that I could find Duncan and Victor dead and have Amanda die in my arms?!

Travis shuts his eyes tightly as Riley's brother raises his voice, ordering Simon to back down and for him to drop the keys, but Travis doesn't move.

The world is background noise now . . .

The background noise to his prayer:

God, tell me there's a reason behind this. Tell me that there's a purpose. That I have a purpose. Why'd you bring me back only to see that my loved ones are gone?

"I'm going to give you three seconds before we flatten you blockheads," the brother yells. "Three."

Travis takes a deep breath.

"Two."

If Travis has lost everything, then what is the point?

"One!"

When Travis opens his eyes, nothing has changed.

There is no crack from the sky.

Only the blasts from the muzzles of every gun surrounding them . . .

And the blinding light that blasts from the keys in his hands.

Chapter 39 – Vortex

The keys let out an explosion that carries for miles.

All but Balco are thrown backwards.

The treasures float midair, emanating a turbulent display of whites and yellows that pulse outwards in vast waves.

Balco watches in awe as the keys are swallowed up by the source light—a circle that brightens and widens to a hole that hangs perpendicular to the ground. The circle expands and elongates, now large enough to fit a car through. The air around it is hot. Sparks flicker from off its edges. It smells of ozone and scorched electronics. Within the circle is a whirlpool of light raging like the stormy skin of Jupiter.

Some of that light is reflected in Balco's impenitent black eyes.

The Rift men stagger to their feet, rocked by the explosion.

Shaking off the concussive blow, Simon and Travis follow suit—

Balco reaches into the portal, scoops up a handful of the light as if pulling mud from the Earth. He flings the coruscant energy at each agent, one-by-one. It cuts through their torsos with an unapologetic, laser-like efficiency, and they are turned to dust.

Riley's brother is hit as well. He barely gets out a word. His slack-jawed expression is frozen in shock as the piercing beam bores through him, rendering him an ashen swirl of cinder that dissipates.

Simon beams. The portal to Heaven is open. He tells Travis, "We no longer need your services. You're fired." To Balco: "Kill him."

For a moment, Balco and Travis exchange looks. Balco senses the angelic change in Travis but is loyal to Simon to a fault. He tells Travis, "Perhaps we shall meet in Heaven."

"Doubt it," Travis replies as he readies himself. There's not much cover here in the garden and considering the speed at which Balco can fling that energy from the portal, he might not be able to close the space between them.

Balco scoops up more light and hurls it at Travis—

Godspeed kicks in.

The world . . .

Slows . . .

Down.

The light still clocks Travis like a heat-seeking missile. He tries to dodge it, but even with the aid of Godspeed, he's hit. The light cuts through him, taking him down.

Godspeed fades just as quickly as it came.

The speed of the world resumes.

"Balco, come on! Let's do this, already," Simon urges.

Balco pauses. Stares at the smoke trail rising from Travis's chest as he lies flat on his back, unmoving. He turns back to Simon. "You have to make a choice. Enter the gate and reside with Cynthia in Heaven. Or have me enter and bring her out to you."

"If I wait here, how do I know you'll come back?"

"I will not betray you, Simon Lajudas. You have helped me find my way back home," Balco answers. "Now you must choose quickly for the gate will need to shut soon, lest one of two outcomes occurs."

"Those being?"

"The gate will close and we will have to find a way to reopen it." Balco pauses. "Or Michael comes to meet us from Heaven. He knows when a gate has opened, and he will end us on the spot. He will send us to the dark place."

"The dark place?" Simon laughs. "Isn't Michael going to kill you the moment you step into Heaven anyway?"

"I am hoping I can make my case to God before that happens. Now . . . what is your decision?"

Simon thinks this over. Can he trust Balco in this final hour to bring his beloved back to him? Or should he step forth and follow him into Heaven?

Why not leave this world behind? What does he need here, anyway? Cynthia is his everything.

His world.

His Heaven.

But her life was cut short by cancer. Why can't he give her a second life? Then they could live a full life. Pass away together, on their time.

Should Balco flake on him, he still has the keys. He can still reopen the gates.

"Simon!" Balco blurts out. "I can feel Michael's presence. He knows the gate is open!"

"Well that didn't take long," Simon says with a laugh.

"Earth time is not Heaven's time."

"Fine," Simon concedes. "Find her. Bring her back. But don't screw me over."

Balco stares him down.

"If you do, I promise I'll give the keys to the Rift and let them have a field day with cloud city."

"The only reason I won't make it back, is if Michael has struck me down."

"If you don't come back, I'm jumping in after you." More cars rumble in the distance. Simon catches sight of them. "You gotta be fucking kidding me!"

"I will find her faster than you can." Balco reaches into the portal. "Now, come to me."

Simon hesitates.

Balco spreads open his palm and reaches for Simon's forehead. "I need to see her, pull her vision and essence from your mind so that I can find her. Heaven is vast, but souls are as unique as fingerprints, and I need to sense her signature."

Simon takes a deep breath. Steps forth.

Balco's palm is cold, electric, and a spark throws Simon's head back.

Balco pulls away. "I've seen her now." He turns towards the gate. "Wait here."

"How long will this take?"

"In your time," Balco says, "not long at all."

"How long?"

"Minutes . . . perhaps."

"Ok. Go!" Simon eyes the cars that are fast approaching. This time there are twice as many, and they are moving twice as fast. "Just get back before the Rift gets here. In hindsight, we should have picked a better spot to open the door."

"At least it is open," he says as he dives into the portal.

Simon stands there, clutching the sword, staring into the churning, cloudy abyss. A mixture of excitement, nerves, hope and dread fills him. The chance to touch Cynthia again, to smell her, to kiss her rosy red lips, has been more than enough inspiration, more than ample reason for this journey.

"Come on, Balco." Simon taps his foot as the thrum of the engines draws closer. Perhaps Balco can destroy the next wave of the Rift again using the gate? It is not a risk he wants to take. They need to get Cynthia, shut the gate and leave. Otherwise, things could get a lot more complicated.

The minutes seem like hours—

Suddenly Balco emerges, climbing out of the soup of clouds. The unearthly colors of the gate reflect off his angelic wings, making him appear evermore ethereal. Simon is grateful to see the big ape.

Then his heart sinks as he notices that Balco is empty-handed.

The words stammer out of him, "Where's . . . where's Cynthia?"

Balco lowers his head.

"Tell me!" Simon barks. "*Where. Is. My. Wife?!*"

"I'm afraid she is *not* in Heaven."

Simon swallows hard. " . . . what?"

"Her spirit is not there."

"No." Simon shakes his head in disbelief. "Bull . . . shit!"

"I did not risk returning here to tell you a lie." Balco looks back at the gate, then at Simon. "She is not there."

"Then where is she, *Balco?*"

Balco stiffens. Steps back towards the gate.

"Where is she?" Simon yells.

"She is," he answers, "in the dark place."

Chapter 40 – Dark Places, Familiar Faces

S imon is at a loss for words. Like a wrecking ball dropped from the sky and landed on his soul. He's crushed.

"The dark place?" He mutters the words to himself, trying to make sense of it. He assumed that she would be in Heaven. His beloved Cynthia, such a caring, loving, devoted wife. The woman who inspired his philanthropic efforts. Someone who spent her free time – what little she had – volunteering at the local homeless shelter. Heaven was made specifically for people like her.

A woman who put their relationship first.

Who loved her parents and family more than God himself loved them.

His Cynthia wouldn't hurt a fly.

She reveled in putting others first.

She.

Was.

Perfect!

She may have well been a saint in his eyes. In pain, hairless, emaciated and depressed, yet she endured.

Was all that for nothing? Simon asks himself. *I don't understand. Why would she not be on the other side of that gate?*

Simon grabs the angel, though Balco barely moves. He might as well be grabbing a tree.

"What do you mean, *she's in the dark place?*" Simon points at the chateau. "Everyone in that house should be there, not Cynthia!"

Balco snaps to attention like a cat hearing a noise. Sensing something near them, he surveys the garden.

There's a glimmer of light as Travis moves at breakneck speed towards Balco and Simon. Dashing between the two, he snatches the Angel's Blade from Simon and runs it through Balco's chest. The great angel reacts wildly and throws a punch meant for Travis, but misses, instead hitting Simon squarely in the chest, knocking him off his feet.

"Abomination!" Balco roars as he stares at Travis, eyes narrowing as he watches the gash in Travis's stomach close shut. "The echoes of Zolash were right," he says with a hiss, "you are a blasphemous creature!" He throws another fist, and although Travis tries to avoid the blow, this punch connects with the side of his face, sending Travis tumbling aside.

Electricity sparks out from the entry point where the Angel's Blade has pierced Balco's chest. He cries out as he unsheathes the sword from his ribcage. Then he holds it over his head as Simon watches on.

"Cut off his fucking head!" Simon commands as he rises, body unsteady from Balco's punch. "Then we'll know he's dead for sure."

Balco unfurls his wings and leaps toward Travis, but Travis rolls aside, hops to his feet, grabs Balco by his wings and swings the angel as if he were a ball on a string. Travis releases him, sending him sailing towards the whirling mouth of the gate. With a quick snap of the wings, Balco puts the brakes on and stops midair.

Simon charges from behind and sinks a knife into Travis's side.

Travis grunts, backhands Simon, yanks out the knife and looks up in time to see Balco flying straight towards him. He moves so fast; Travis is barely able to get out of the way.

There's another blur of light.

That blur slams into Balco, driving him sideways into the ground with the impact of a crashing meteorite.

The Angel's Blade skids away.

The searing pain from the knife jars Travis. How his healing factor works is still a mystery to him. And right now, he's not healing fast enough to deal with Simon striking him with kick after kick, punches, elbows, and what feels like a thousand cuts. Simon wields another knife, and even with only one eye, the man has killer aim and accuracy.

"I hate you!" Simon shouts as he violently stabs at Travis, who attempts to block as many blows as possible. "You're a cancer in my life!" He lands a kick in Travis's groin.

Travis goes down.

"Time to collect what you took from me." Simon straddles him and brings the knife to Travis's eye. "An eye for an eye, right?"

Behind them, the commotion and dust of screeching tires comes to a halt. Simon looks over his shoulder. More Rift agents have arrived.

A lot more.

"Where do these roaches keep coming from?" Simon mutters to himself.

And this is all the distraction Travis needs. He wraps his hands around Simon's knife, and with a hard jerk, cranks the blade into Simon's torso.

Simon lets out a choked gasp. Travis bucks Simon off him like a wild bronco, who does a little hop in the air and slumps onto his side.

Travis gets to his feet. Sees Balco holding up Victor by his throat.

"Victor!"

The Rift file out from their vehicles. Guns drawn.

As if his stump were a ladle, Balco scoops energy from the gate. "You abandoned us, Victor. You are a traitor."

One of the Rift agents, wearing mirror-tint glasses, holds up a hand. "Wait!"

Balco pauses.

"We know what you're capable of," the agent insists. "Let's make a deal."

"There is nothing to negotiate," Balco replies.

Travis wonders if he can get to Balco and his brother before the Rift let the bullets rip.

"Hear us out!" the agent pleads. "We know Marcus locked you up, but we don't work for him. We work for another."

Balco pauses.

"We can get all of your brothers back," the agent promises. "The one we work for . . . she is the most powerful of all the Rift. She has been shunned, but we want to bring her back to power. And we could use your help to do that. You . . . and the angels that Marcus and the Cleaners sent to Hell."

Simon crawls towards the gate, blood seeping from his wound. He pulls himself closer to the gate.

"I will find my brothers in my own time. Not with the aid of those who tortured us." Balco unfurls energy from Heaven and whips it at the Rift agents, who immediately scramble.

Those caught in its wake are wiped out. Others shield themselves behind cars.

Travis guns for Balco but isn't fast enough to stop him from disposing of Victor. The angel drives his stump arm into Victor's torso.

"*Victor! No!*" Travis shouts.

Victor kicks frantically. The shredded nubs on his shoulders – where his magnificent wings once stood – now flick in vain as he instinctively tries to fly away.

Balco tosses him aside.

Travis slams into Balco, colliding with the brick wall of an angel. Unmoved, Balco cracks Travis across the head and kicks him away like an unwanted stray. With his good hand, Balco reaches for the gate.

"Let us try this again," Balco tells Travis as he attempts to scoop more energy from the foaming swirling mouth of the gate.

But something is not right.

Balco glances down at his forearm.

It is stuck in the gate.

He tries to pull it out but can't.

Before he can question what is happening, he winces, then lets out another roar. He leans his massive body back and, using all his might in this tug-of-war against an invisible opponent, he gradually pulls himself free of the gate.

Dislodging himself reveals his other hand has been sliced off.

Bewildered, he stares at his missing appendage.

Travis wobbles back to his feet. The pain of his injuries distorts his vision. Dark shapes are the only hints he has of the few surviving Rift agents who cower behind their cars.

As his vision comes into focus, Travis witnesses a towering shape *emerge* from the gate.

That shape spreads its wings.

A name pops into Travis's head: *Michael.*

Chapter 41 – The Great, Winged Wrath

I f Balco were a monster truck, Michael would be a freight train.

Michael stands before Balco, shoulders adorned with overlapping, golden plates of armor. He brandishes a halberd with a four-foot blade, mounted atop a gold staff embellished with the same resplendent magnificence as the rest of the angel's armor. He moves with an authoritative gait, his chain mail clinking, boots thumping against the ground as he closes the gap between himself and Balco.

The Rift agents stiffen, frozen by a mixture of admiration and fear as they look on.

Simon pulls himself along the ground, finding a hiding spot behind a shrub.

Travis watches as Balco falls to his knees before Michael and confesses, "I have failed you and God."

Michael comes to a halt before Balco and plants his staff in the ground.

"I only wanted to understand why he loved these creatures so," Balco admits as he lowers his head. "And yet, for all we have lost, I still do not understand."

Michael eyes Balco. Although he is older than time, the imposing angel's face is perfect, flawless, and youthful. He has flowing mane of brown hair that is in a constant state of drift, as if he were floating underwater. When he speaks, his voice resonates throughout the garden. "You do not need to understand."

"But we are perfect," Balco argues as he looks up at Michael, "And they are not."

"Only God is perfect. And you took Heaven for granted."

Balco lowers his head once more. "For that, I am eternally sorry."

"As am I, brother." Michael takes the halberd and slices off Balco's head. A torrent of blinding light tears across the garden, forcing everyone to turn their heads.

Michael turns towards the gate, sticks his hand inside the soup of energy, cranks a hard right as if turning some unseen lever on the other side. The gate darkens briefly, but then flickers back to life.

This time the flames are a fiery lava-rich tone of red. The vortical clouds now swirl in the opposite direction.

"For those who revel in darkness," Michael tells the Rift agents, "I grant you access to that which you covet." He races between their cars, scooping the wriggling agents up into his colossal arms. He stops in front of the gate and with one deliberate heave, sends them screaming into the fiery, red vortex of the gate, vanishing forever.

Michael turns to Simon, who cowers in pain behind a bush that provides little cover. Michael grabs him, then brings him to the gate.

At first, Travis thinks Michael is going to throw Simon into it like he did the others, but instead the angel tosses Simon onto the ground and asks, "You seek your loved one?"

"Yes" Simon shakes his head as he clutches his wound. "I want to see my Cynthia again."

Michael glares at the man for a moment. Then he darts in and out of the gate. It's so quick that Travis nearly misses it with a blink.

"Then I will grant you what you want." Michael sticks his hand into the gate and pulls out . . .

A skeletal figure—a sickly, haggard woman with skin as gray as asphalt. She is slick with some sort of shiny, putrid yellow substance. Her goo-covered hair is matted to her face, obscuring her features.

Simon feels his stomach drop as he watches Michael pull her out from the gate. It's as if the angel is retrieving the woman from the depths of a lake. But Michael stops short, only bringing her out to her waist.

She floats parallel to the ground.

Her hands dangle limply at her sides.

Her hair hangs downward, dripping with that unearthly ooze.

Simon grimaces, not sure what he is looking at.

The woman comes to, head snapping upward. Eyes ablaze with hellfire. Cracks of red splinter her skin as if she is being baked from the inside out. She slowly opens her mouth, as if for the first time, and lets out an agonized shriek.

"What the fuck!" Simon shouts. Looks to Michael and demands, "What the fuck is that?"

"*That* is your Cynthia."

Jaw slung open and dripping with black muck, Cynthia lifts her arms toward Simon the way a toddler reaches for its parent.

Simon recoils, stutters, his mind reeling. "W-what? That isn't her!"

"Indeed it is," Michael insists.

"H-how? How's this possible? Why is she not in Heaven where she belongs?"

The black muck drips from Cynthia's lips as she says, "Upon my death bed, I was approached by an angel with dark wings and coal-colored eyes as bottomless as the blackest depths of the sea. He promised me an eternity with you . . . in exchange for my soul."

Simon shakes his head. "No!" *This can't be happening*, he thinks.

"Of course, not wanting to lose you, I accepted." Cynthia continues, "But upon my death, God reached out to me. Conveyed his sadness for my decision to condemn my own soul to Hell. In His mercy, He allowed me to reach out to you – just once – to warn you *not* to seek me. But your pride would not heed my warning."

"No!" Simon protests. "This isn't real!"

A thick clump of black goo is pushed out of Cynthia's mouth, as if the words she's about to speak, nearly choke her, "This is real. My love for you is real, and it reaches beyond the cold, vapid shadow of death to touch you once more."

Simon gawks at this foul, horror-show version of his wife and finds that words escape him.

"I am now grateful that you didn't heed my warning." Cynthia smiles, exposing a mouth of putrid, pitted teeth. "We can be together forever."

Simon shrinks away. "*No-no-no-no-no!*"

"You have condemned both man and angel to death for your selfish desires, Simon Lajudas. Committed many a sin to find your way to her." Michael lifts Simon up by his shirt and flings him into her awaiting arms. "Now go be with her."

Simon screams, but his cries fade as she tightens her embrace and pulls him back into the whirling abyss.

Michael sticks his hand into the gate and cranks to the left.

The lightshow fades.

The gate closes.

Only the pendant and manacles float in midair now. Michael seizes them in his great hand. He picks up Victor's body and steps towards Travis, hovering over the transporter like a thundercloud.

"What are you doing with my brother?" Travis asks.

Michael studies him for a beat. Then answers, "I am taking him home."

"Taking him home? Even though he escaped Heaven with the Amissa?"

"He came here for revenge but gave that up to watch over you."

"I don't understand." Then shakes his head as he adds, "And I really don't understand why God has chosen *me* in all this?"

"Because He has." Michael gives him one final glance before he leaves. "You have much to learn, Amalgamātus. Half-wing."

And much like Zach, with Victor in his arms, Michael shoots off into the sky.

Chapter 42 – One of Us

The world has lost all meaning and flavor.

Travis looks off into the distance, face devoid of emotion.

For a moment, he considers running back into the mansion and scrounging up any stray rosary beads and seeing if he could perhaps revive Duncan, though he knows that's not how they work. He has seen the results first-hand with Vanessa's undoing.

Instead, he stands there, numb and still in a state of shock, ruminating over the deaths of his friends and the half-brother he had only hours to get to know.

Surely the commotion will soon send either the cops or more Rift or both on their way. One of Marcus's neighbors had to have heard something. And although the mansion is very remote, judging by the number of empty vehicles surrounding the place, the Rift is likely already sending more reinforcements. Part of him relishes the thought of exacting some revenge on the source of all this pain, and part of him feels detached and dead inside.

I should go get Duncan's body and leave this place, he thinks.

His cell phone buzzes in his pocket. He's amazed that it still works given the fall, the fountain and the fighting. He takes it out of his pocket and eyes the case. It is still intact. Weathered and beaten up, but still very much protecting the phone. It vibrates again in his hand.

On the screen, the caller ID shows a +972 country code, followed by an eight digit phone number.

Travis answers, "Yeah . . ."

A man with a gruff voice responds, "Travis?"

Travis says nothing, staring ahead with a vacant gaze.

"Yeah . . ."

"Travis, it's me. It's Jakob."

"Ok . . ."

"My brother Noam and I work for the Covenant. You got the Eyes of God to us."

Travis continues staring at nothing, eyes unblinking. Offers a frail, "I remember."

"Where are you?"

"In a place of death," Travis says, followed by a long pause.

"Amanda had texted me that you were on your way to a Rift stronghold. Did you find it?"

"Yep."

"And? What's going on?"

Travis chews on his lip. Talking, especially about what just went down, is the last thing he wants to do.

"Travis?"

"I'm here . . ."

Jakob sighs in exasperation at Travis's brevity. "Can I just talk to Amanda please? I have been trying to call her."

"Amanda's dead." Just saying the words snaps Travis out of his stupor.

"What?" Jakob asks, voice cracking. "She's . . . dead?"

Yes! Travis thinks. *Dead!*

As in d-e-a-d!

Dead.

Worse than that, she exploded.

On Me!

Dusted.

I held her in my arms, and she turned to dust!

Just like the Rift.

But she didn't deserve to go out like that!

She deserved more!

Travis takes a deep breath, the way a dragon does before it's about to exhale fire.

Jakob stammers, "I—I—I can't believe this—"

"Duncan's gone too," Travis adds. "Died a *second* time. But this time," he shakes his head as he quietly reports, "he's not coming back."

"No." There's a long moment of silence. Follow by a tepid declaration of, "No . . . no way. That can't be. They . . . they . . . they can't be dead. They were doing God's work!"

"In case you forgot, many have died doing God's work." Travis closes his eyes for a moment. Clenches his fist. Feels everything inside him boil. "As much as I wish they were, seems they weren't exempt."

Off in the horizon, a caravan of SUVs speed toward the chateau.

Unbelievable. This world's like an anthill, and it seems that no matter how many of these pricks die, more just keep coming, Travis thinks. *Whatever. Maybe I should wait for them. Put a bullet in each one of their heads.*

Something inside him, something faint yet distinct, urges Travis to go.

"I have to go," Travis tells Jakob.

"But-but there is much to discuss—"

"Oh, there is. I have your number. I'll be in touch."

* * *

Travis is on his porch, back at his cabin. He stares at the sun as it sets, watching the trees sway and birds sail overhead. He's envious of them. The foliage. The fauna. The fact that every non-human living thing in this world doesn't have to carry the burden of rational thought.

Of trying to make sense of this life and the people in it.

Of trying to understand what the point of it all is.

He feels different. Haunted by the loss of Amanda, Duncan, the revelation of having a brother, as well as his dream or visit or whatever from Heaven. There's also a prevalent sinking feeling of despair that plagues him, having lost the few things he even remotely cared about. Ignorance is bliss, but that is a gift he was never offered by man or angel.

It would have been one thing moving here, not knowing what was going on with the Covenant and simply writing off that pervasive unrest in his stomach as mere latent anxiety. But once he knew that they needed him – that she needed him – everything changed.

Now, sitting here at the house he so desperately longed to escape to, sipping coffee that tastes like dirt, the world feels like a shallow copy of what it once was to him. Not that he held things in the highest regard before, but even less so now.

What was the point of all that?

To lose more people that I cared about?

To stop bad people from doing bad things?

They'll go on to do those things with or without me. If the Rift has already survived four hundred years, who's to say that they won't go on doing evil deeds after I'm six feet under?

I mean . . . I'm not immortal.

I'm going to die at some point.

The Rift will go on doing their thing, so what is the point?

Travis contemplates putting his beloved Beretta to his temple and ending it all.

"Two things to note about that," an all too familiar voice announces as Zach appears next to him, seated comfortably, peering out at the same setting sun. It's as if he'd been sitting there all along.

Travis gives him a cursory glance, then turns away.

"First," Zach explains, "it will take more than your gun to kill you."

Travis sips his coffee and stares off at a flock of birds taking flight.

"Second, if you did manage to kill yourself, you would join Simon and his inamorata, Cynthia, in an eternity of nothingness."

Travis takes another sip, then sets the mug aside, all without looking at Zach once.

"Hell is not fire and brimstone as is popularized," Zach explains. "It is the grand abyss. The place barren and void of God."

"Everyone I cared for is officially gone." Travis turns to Zach. "Feels pretty barren here."

"The bitterness in your heart grows like a weed. Don't fertilize it. You have much good left to do."

"What if I don't want to do any more good?" Travis asks with a haphazard shrug. "What if I don't want to do anything?"

"Perhaps you'll reconsider . . . given your promotion."

"My what?"

Zach hops to his feet. Motioning with his hand, he tells Travis, "Please rise."

"What?" Travis huffs. "I'm really not in the mood—"

Zach's voice thunders in a way that scares every bird perched in every tree within a mile of them, sending them shooting off into the sky. *"I said rise!"*

With a long face, Travis clenches his fist and reluctantly stands up.

"This will hurt at first," Zach warns, "but eventually you will do this on your own."

"What's going to hurt?"

Zach lays a palm on Travis's left shoulder and then steps back as if waiting for some magic trick to manifest itself.

"What did you—" and before Travis can finish his sentence, he feels a vicious pain in his shoulders that steals the wind in his lungs and the words from his mouth. He grunts as his bones splinter and reorganize themselves, popping and cracking.

The pain drops him to his knees.

A single protrusion erupts from his scapula. This protrusion unfolds, extends and unveils an angel wing.

Breathlessly, Travis pushes himself off the ground. As the pain subsides, he looks to his left. "What is that?"

"You do not know what that is?"

Travis has a single, cloud-white, feathered wing that glistens under the twilight glow of the setting sun.

Zach nods. "You are one of us now, Travis."

Travis is in a state of panic, awe, and grief. Too many emotions. It is a lot to handle all at once.

What's happened to me? What's going on? What—

Zach taps Travis's left shoulder and the wing retracts with one agonizing snap. Travis winces.

"I know you have much to process, but for now you should rest," Zach says. "You need time to search your heart and pray. See if you are truly ready to quit. Your brother never gave up on you. Neither did your friends. Are you willing to forsake them?"

Travis is so overwhelmed he can barely form a sentence. Before he can respond, Zach takes to the skies just as he always does, leaving him to figure out if he is ready to give up.

Or ready to take the fight to them.

To take on the Rift himself.

Chapter 43 – The Awakening

The sweat-imbued gym reeks of pain and harsh words. An instructor in her late forties paces the room, eyeing each of her students. She shouts declarations of callous encouragement to her all-female kickboxing class.

"Come on, ladies!" The instructor's throaty voice is unnervingly rugged. "Put your core into it." She weaves between punching bags that hang like slabs of meat from the rafters, secured to the joists with knotted chains.

The women kick and punch the bags as if their egos depended on it. Chains jangle as the bags shudder under the unyielding impact. Speakers along the back wall pump out industrial techno music, providing the soundtrack for today's workout.

"Dig your heels in," the instructor barks. "The energy comes from the *ground* up. You guys are lightning. Strike the bags like you're electrified. Like you're smashing in your ex-boyfriend's face. Or that douchebag who took that parking spot from you even though you had your blinker on!"

A blonde, pigtailed student chuckles.

The teacher shoots her a cross look. The student clears her throat, shrugs off the laugh as if it were an accident.

"Think of that brown-nosing jerk," the instructor continues, "the one who got the promotion when you clearly earned it and wreck these bags like you would their careers."

The instructor observes the students, watching dutifully as they strike their respective bags. One of them catches her attention, a woman in her thirties with ebony hair that's tightly braided back from her scalp. Arms covered in tattoos, tribal ink coiled around her biceps, they appear to swim across her flesh as she bashes the bag. She sends it careening with each blow, clouting it with an uncanny power and perfection that brings a proud smile to the instructor's face.

"Dammit, girlfriend," the instructor tells her. "Now *that's* how you do it!" The instructor aims a remote at a stereo up front. Cranks up the blaring techno. "Come on, ladies." Waves her arms in the air. "You got this!" She nods her head to the music. "One more minute!"

As the black-haired student picks up her pace and quickens her jabs, a jarring set of words comes unbidden into her mind and thunders in her brain to the beat of the music—words that overshadow the sounds of those around her and the encouragement of her instructor:

It's . . .

a . . .

lie!

The room becomes an engine of flesh and fury. Awash with the stench of sweat and rubber. The individual, quiet, focused intent of each student driving their strikes into the bags results in a symphony of successive smacks against the punching bags. The instructor closes her eyes, savoring the pent-up rage now channeled into flawless, deliberate, useful strikes.

"Thirty more seconds, ladies," the instructor bellows, "and we're done!"

Where does all this pent-up rage come from?

The answer comes to the black-haired student as sparks of light explode inside her mind, followed by flashing images of unbelievable madness and horror:

A bonfire.

Women and men tied to stakes.

Faces blackened, charcoal over flesh.

Skin blistering.

Mouths open.

Pain.

There's so much pain.

"You guys might hate me now," the instructor's voice sounds like a distant phone call from the 80s as she declares, "but after this class, you're gonna feel like you can take on the world . . . because you can!"

The rapid staccato thumping continues around the room.

"Keep it up!" The instructor's voice snaps the black-haired student out of the nightmare. "Don't stop!"

The black-haired student catches herself. She did stop.

"Keep it up, girlfriend," the instructor tells her, "you got this!"

The black-haired student resumes. Strikes her bag with renewed vigor and intent.

There are grumbles and groans from the women as they toil away, pummeling the bags.

"And trust me when I tell you tonight's glass of wine will taste like Heaven. Like God herself poured it for you."

Some of the women tire, their punches lagging, but they press on, not allowing themselves to falter under the weight of their own fatigue.

The music swells toward its drumbeat crescendo, bass rattling the mirrors lining the room. The neighbors next door who run a fly-by-night real estate company could easily mistake this for a club and not a fitness center. But the instructor had made it clear more than once that she could give a shit.

Let those paper-pushers complain! she'd often joke to the class. *Better yet, let them survive a class, and maybe I'll consider turning the stereo down a notch from eleven.*

"Just a few more seconds!" the instructor shouts. "Keep it going."

The bassline thrums in perfect time with the pounding that the bags are enduring from these tough women.

"Five."

It's a dance-club of focus and ferocity.

"Four."

The black-haired student steps back.

"Three."

Then she advances, delivering a volley of kicks and a few solid elbow strikes.

"Two."

The black-haired student closes in on the bag.

"One."

Unloads a barrage of rapid punches, striking the bag as if it wronged her in a past life.

"Yes!" The instruction shouts in the black-haired student's direction. She claps her hands together. "Now *that's* what I'm talking about!" She addresses the rest of the class, "Oh my god! You guys need to give yourselves a pat on the back. That was awesome!"

Almost everyone in the room is struggling to catch their breath. Some keel over, propping themselves on their knees. Some slump to the ground, gasping for air. Some, like the black-haired student, seem like they could go a few more rounds.

"Ladies, give yourselves a round of applause."

A few students clap. Others barely muster the strength to move their arms.

"Pardon my French," the instructor declares as she surveys the room, "but man, that was fucking epic!"

"And that's," the black-haired student adds, "why we come."

It's a lie!

The words ring in her head.

It takes the black-haired student everything she has to ignore them.

Those cursed words follow her everywhere. No matter where she is, whether it's at her reception job, the grocery store, or even here at the gym.

The words follow her.

It's a lie!

Thankfully, to some degree, the gym helps.

Keeping active helps.

But sometimes . . . thoughts of violence satiate her mind. These thoughts serve as a sort of Xanax for shutting up that screaming, horrible croaking voice insider her head: *It's a lie!*

What's a lie?

This infernal noise in her brain has been going on for what feels like years. She can't recall when it started. What she can recall is this odd recurring nightmare:

There's a roomful of strange people, all dressed in black, gothic-style clothing. They surround her, hang over her like monoliths. She's grabbed from every direction, yelled at, and told repeatedly that she will not inherit the throne. That she's not welcome.

It's a weird dream.

And she rues every night she's plagued by it.

Which is *every* night.

She has considered seeing someone, a shrink for this issue. Maybe getting drugs. But the mere thought of either of those alternatives gives her a world-ending migraine.

So being active helps.

She takes Krav Maga a couple of times a week. Then boxing. CrossFit. Fencing. Hell, if it involves sweating, fighting, or being physical, she is all about it. Especially if it shuts up that incessant mantra: *It's a lie!*

She heads for the locker room and catches sight of herself in the mirror. Her youthful appearance. The vibrant, healthy skin of a college student. *Not bad for a thirty-year-old*, she thinks and gives herself a reassuring wink.

Then a surge of pain nearly knocks her over. She clutches her stomach. Dread wriggles inside her like a parasite nibbling away at her sanity.

Her cell phone rings. She fumbles for it, then puts it on speaker without even checking the caller ID. She rests her phone on the counter as she composes herself. "Yeah?"

"This Viola?" a young woman's voice asks.

Viola hesitates. Stares at herself in the mirror.

Yes, I'm Viola and I'm going insane and I don't know why.

The young woman at the other end of the call breaks Viola's thought by saying, "Hello?"

"Yes, this is Viola." Viola yanks several paper towels from the dispenser and wipes the sweat from her face. "Are you selling something? I've been on the no-call list."

"I'm not selling anything."

Viola pauses. Balls up the paper towels and slams them into a garbage can. "Who is this?"

"My name's Tizzy." A beat. "You don't know me, but I work for the Rift."

269

"You work for the what?"

"I work for the Rift."

"I'm hanging up now."

"There is no light without the darkness," Tizzy mutters.

Viola freezes.

A million lightning bolts strike her mind all at once. She clutches her head as if it's about to tear apart and explode.

A montage horror-show floods her brain:

People tied to a stake.

All of them on fire.

Mouths open, screaming desperately.

Skin crackling.

A woman reaches out to her.

Momma?

"Momma," Viola says with a gasp.

Another wrench of pain.

Images of the boardroom.

The Council.

"Vanessa is dead."

The words echo throughout the room.

Tenebrous shapes rise.

Viola is pushed to the ground.

Shadows stretch above her.

Her mind feels like it's being stabbed.

It's a lie!

The visions subside.

A violent ardor infects her soul.

Viola stares into the mirror. Stares down the black-haired woman glaring back at her.

Her eyes light up, turning a vicious shade of red. Burning like two distant fireballs, aflame with the fires of Hell.

One of the other students walks in and catches Viola staring at her reflection.

"Oh, hey Viola."

Viola leans her head closer to the mirror and ogles herself.

"Are you ok?" the student asks.

Viola's head snaps in the student's direction. Breathing heavy, eyes alit, she hisses. "It's . . . a . . . lie!" Then she punches the mirror. It shatters, forming a spiderweb of cracks around her knuckles.

The classmate throws her hands up in the air in surrender. Stepping backwards, she says, "My bad. I'll leave you alone." As she scurries out, Viola slides a trashcan in front of the door, blocking anyone else from coming in.

She grabs her phone. Steadies her breathing. Then asks, "You still there?"

"Yes," Tizzy answers.

"What do you want?"

"To wake you up."

Viola plants both of her hands on the counter, steadying herself. Shoulders heaving. Eyes pulsing with untamed, sanguine hues.

"The Rift put you under a spell," Tizzy explains. "They wanted to stop you from going crazy and taking over under the guise of vengeance."

Viola fumes. This all seems distantly familiar, but her brain is mush. The spell the Council put on her has nearly lobotomized all her knowledge of the Rift.

She has been lied to!

The Rift has lied to her!

But they can't stop her.

It was she and Vanessa who started the Rift.

And now it is just her.

"Viola, listen, I need you as much as you need me."

"I don't need anybody!" Viola shouts at the phone.

"Trust me, you do. The Rift has become broken in the absence of you and your sister. Fractured. Each councilman has their own plan, their own fucked-up motives. But now's the best time for you to come back. The Covenant are all but wiped out."

"They are?" Viola asks, her tone softening.

"Yes, and I have more good news for you, if you will agree to meet with me. If you'll agree to protect me."

"Alright. I'll protect you," Viola agrees as she takes this in. "And I'll meet with you."

"Great. I'm glad to hear that," Tizzy says with a relived sigh. "Now, as far as your sister, I know who killed her."

Viola feels her chest swell with wrath as she utters, "Tell me."

"His name is Travis Rail."

Other Books by Jonathan Chateau

The Travis Rail Series
Faith Against the Wolves (Book 1)
Faith Against the Angels (Book 2)

Other works by Jonathan Chateau
Nightmares in Analog
The Death Wish Game
The Sprawling
Energy Drink
The Saltwater Marathon
Video is Dead

About the Author

Jonathan Chateau grew up reading books by Stephen King, Dean Koontz, and Michael Crichton. However, it was Fight Club—both the 1996 novel by Chuck Palahniuk and the 1999 film by David Fincher—that inspired him to pursue writing. He has also had a love of movies since he was five and was even named after James Caan's character, Jonathan E, from the 1975 cult classic, Rollerball.

He has completed five novels, Nightmares in Analog, The Death Wish Game, Faith Against the Wolves, Faith Against the Angels, and The Sprawling.

When Jonathan's not writing, he's working out, painting table-top miniatures like those from Warhammer or the Walking Dead, playing way-too-many video games, eating spicy food, jamming out to Emo & EDM, or spending time with his family, friends and his spoiled cats.

He resides in Tampa, Florida.

To find out more about him and to check out more of his books, visit https://jchateau.com/.